A CHAMPION FALLS

THE CHAIN BREAKER BOOK 8

D.K. HOLMBERG

ASH
PUBLISHING

CHAPTER ONE

The El'aras ring constricted on his finger slightly, and Gavin twisted it to try to get the ring into a comfortable position. He could feel a surge of power coming through the object, but it was faint. He didn't have any idea what he felt, only that there was something to it.

"What's wrong?" Wrenlow asked. He had his hand up against the wall, tracing his fingers against the writing on it. The book that Tristan had left Gavin was flopped open in front of him. Wrenlow compared the two, working from one to the other, as if searching for answers to a puzzle that only he could figure out.

And it was likely that only he could. Wrenlow was the person who had solved some of the issues that had plagued Tristan's ability to find the third temple. It was because of Wrenlow that he had succeeded.

Gavin looked at the walls along the length of the

El'aras hall. They glowed with faint blue light, the result of him pouring power out of himself and into them. He turned his attention back to Wrenlow. "It's just the ring."

"Is it still bothering you?"

Gavin nodded. "Still."

Wrenlow paused, lowered his hands from the wall, and glanced down at the book. The writing in the hall made it so that enough light illuminated everything, giving him plenty to see by, though it was possible that he didn't even need the light. Gavin didn't know for sure, but he suspected that Wrenlow had an enchantment on him that would allow him to see even without any light in the tunnel.

"The book doesn't really say anything about what happened," Wrenlow said.

"I doubted it would."

"I thought that maybe…" Wrenlow shook his head and scrubbed a hand through his shaggy brown hair, then shrugged at Gavin. "Well, I thought that maybe I would figure something out. I had hoped I'd find an answer here."

"I still think you will."

"I know it's likely." There was no evidence of arrogance in the way Wrenlow said it, especially given that what was written on the walls wasn't in his natural language, and that he had to piece together details from what he claimed were three different languages used in the book.

Gavin might be good at patterns, but this was on

another level beyond what he could manage. And it required a level of patience that he simply didn't have.

"It's just that I was hoping I would find something to help you understand the ring and what happened with the nihilar," Wrenlow said.

Gavin twisted the ring again. He could still feel the strange influence it had taken on when he had drawn the power of the nihilar into the ring. From what he'd been able to tell, it hadn't destroyed the ring, though it had altered it, along with the power Gavin could call upon. He was just beginning to try to understand that kind of power, but it had changed and was now so different than what he had hoped to use and understand before.

"You don't need to be down here with me," Wrenlow said. He turned his attention back to the wall, tracing his finger along its surface again. "I am perfectly content to stay down here myself."

"I know you are. I'm just—"

"You're bored. That's what you are." Wrenlow smirked at him. "I've seen that side of you before, Gavin. And when you get bored, you tend to cause trouble."

"Are you saying it's time for me to leave?"

"I don't *want* you to leave," Wrenlow said.

Gavin smiled to himself, realizing that Wrenlow made a point of not actually answering the question. When Gavin had left Yoran the last time, he had done so thinking that he was going to be gone for quite a bit longer and that he would try to learn about his El'aras abilities, mostly so he wouldn't be a detriment if something were to happen. He had known that there was more to his ability than he had mastered so far. Gavin thought he would have time to come to terms with what those abilities meant, but it seemed as if events continued to conspire against him, preventing him from doing all that he thought he needed to.

For his part, Wrenlow continued working.

"I'm going to look at the inside of the temple again," Gavin said.

"Are we sure that it's a temple? I know you and the others think it has to be, given the way it was situated, but the markings aren't the same as other temples I visited over the years. It's unusual."

"Which is why I think it probably is a temple," Gavin said.

Wrenlow shrugged. He glanced from the book up to the writing on the walls from time to time.

Gavin took a deep breath, and the stale air filled his lungs. He worked his way down to the larger chamber that was situated somewhat beneath Yoran but also outside of it. It was connected through a series of tunnels that he believed were all tied to the El'aras, though he increasingly started to question whether that was the case.

The walls were irregular, and they weren't etched with the same markings that were in the other halls leading up to it. There were remnants of sculptures that once had been here, though time had caused them to crumble. Some paint lingered on the walls, though even that wasn't easy for him to decipher. Wrenlow had attempted to piece together whether there was anything useful written on the walls but had not found anything.

A white light glowed in the distance, and Gavin immediately focused on his core reserves to call on the power within himself. He anticipated that there would be a greater danger, but he released it when he realized who was inside the chamber.

"Tristan," Gavin said, shaking his head as he stopped in the doorway leading into the chamber.

Tristan turned back and looked at him, his fingers working in a pattern at his side. "Am I not permitted here?"

"I haven't decided."

Tristan snorted, then turned his attention back to a section of the wall that had more writing on it than others. "I'm convinced there's something here," he said, as if that was an explanation.

"Wrenlow has been through here, and he hasn't found anything," Gavin said, approaching him and looking at the wall.

Tristan turned to Gavin, a faint smile curling his lips. His eyes were a flat blue, somewhat paler than Gavin's own eyes. "And I should trust him?"

Gavin shrugged. "Well, seeing as how he was able to analyze something that you weren't able to, I would think you'd rely on Wrenlow's interpretation."

Tristan said nothing for a bit as he continued to stare at the wall. "I have spent far more time studying this than you," he finally said.

"I'm certain of it."

Gavin remained on edge and called on his core reserves again, feeling the power that existed within him.

It was buried deeply, a part of him that had been locked inside until he'd learned the key to how to release it. It had taken Gavin a long time to understand how to do that, and even now he didn't use his abilities to their fullest potential. The other El'aras he had interacted with always used their core reserves—or their magic—in a continuous fashion, something that Gavin had tried but found far too exhausting. There were benefits to the way the El'aras used their magic, though. Benefits that Gavin did not have. If he were able to use his in a similar manner, he would be able to keep himself augmented at all times, enhancing his eyesight, hearing, speed, and strength—all improvements that Gavin had to intentionally focus on.

But there were other advantages for him in the way he used them.

He could avoid drawing on his core reserves and suppress that power, something that had been critical when he'd faced the nihilar. Without that ability, Gavin might have been overwhelmed.

"Are you just going to stand there," Tristan said, "or are you going to have the conversation with me you've been aching to have?" He didn't turn back to Gavin and instead simply stared at the wall.

Gavin took a step toward him. He wasn't going to stand behind Tristan any longer.

"I haven't been aching to ask you anything."

Tristan snorted. "We both know that's not true."

"What we know is that you have continued to try to manipulate me. And to be honest, I've allowed it."

"Is this your way of telling me that you don't plan on

letting me manipulate you any longer?" Tristan chuckled again. "Because I'm not trying to coerce you into taking action you don't want."

"Not openly," Gavin said.

"Not at all." Tristan finally looked over to him. His eyes narrowed for a moment, taking on some of the hardness that Gavin remembered from when he'd worked with Tristan as a child.

It was a look that Gavin had feared until he'd gained enough skill to understand that it was Tristan's way of encouraging Gavin to find strength within himself. Even now, Gavin tried to do that, but he didn't know how he could, and he didn't know whether he had what he needed.

From time to time, he still felt as if he were that child all those years ago, a child who had been taught to fight, when he could have learned how to control the power within himself. Or maybe he couldn't have. He just didn't know.

"What are you looking for here?" Gavin asked. He knew he wasn't going to get anywhere trying to argue with Tristan.

"This is ancient," Tristan said, ignoring the question as if moving on was the very thing that he had wanted all along. "Old enough that it predates the El'aras."

Gavin had started to suspect that, but then Wrenlow's comment about it had confirmed it. "How much earlier than the El'aras?"

Tristan frowned. "I had archives that I once had access to, but unfortunately, I've been separated from them."

Gavin laughed. "You had archives?"

"Do you think that all I know how to do is fight?"

"You made sure that was all I knew how to do."

"How long do you think I trained?"

The sudden change in topic jarred Gavin a little bit, though he knew that it shouldn't. "Considering what I've heard about you, I would imagine hundreds of years."

Tristan glowered at him. "Exactly. You will live equally long, or at least you have the opportunity to. Once you have mastery of one aspect of yourself, then you can begin to work on others."

"So you were wanting to make sure that I had mastery of the physical aspect of myself," Gavin said, shaking his head. "I see."

"You don't, but that's just because you don't have the opportunity to truly understand. Maybe in time you will, but even if you don't, it doesn't matter. Those of us who have lived longer, seen more—we understand the dangers that exist, and we understand everything that needs to be done."

"Is that right?"

Tristan shrugged. "Right as rain."

Gavin decided not to push. "Did you know the nihilar would be here?"

Tristan shook his head. "I told you. I knew of two of the temples, and even those two were challenging. Really, I only knew of one, and the second I only came up with recently."

"So you knew about Hester, and you learned about

Arashil recently, but you didn't understand that Yoran was somehow tied to all of it?"

That seemed far-fetched, especially given everything that Gavin had seen within Yoran while he'd been working here.

"I knew it was important," Tristan said. "There are enough records that reference this place. Maybe not Yoran in particular, but what it was before."

"And what was it before?"

"The El'aras called it Val'athan."

Gavin had talked to Anna about many things during her time in the city, but she'd never mentioned that. "And before that?" he asked.

Tristan turned his attention back to the wall in front of him, and he frowned for a long moment. "That, I've been trying to work out."

"You don't know."

"And neither do you. Or your friend, for that matter. He's using the archives I've found to come up with answers, and he won't be any more likely to do that than I will be."

"Only that it's Wrenlow," Gavin said.

"There you go again, thinking that somebody who's barely into their twenties can understand things that have taken me centuries to learn."

"And there you go again with the arrogance that your age somehow matters when it comes to this."

Tristan glanced over to him, but he said nothing.

Gavin left him and made a small circuit of the inside of the temple.

This was where he had fought Chauvan and barely survived, and also where he had started to have a greater understanding of the nihilar. The silver metal staff that Chauvan had brought here to summon the nihilar remained propped up against one of the stone walls, looking almost as if it were left behind. Gavin had studied it, but he hadn't found anything from the staff that would help him better understand Chauvan or what he had been after. Wrenlow hadn't understood anything either.

Gavin was left either trusting Tristan or reaching out to others who might be able to help. When he'd tried to contact Anna using his enchantment designed to communicate with her, there had been nothing but silence on the other end. This was despite the fact that he had somehow connected to the enchantment in a way that should have allowed him to communicate more effectively to her, but there was nothing. Just emptiness.

"Take a look at this," Tristan called.

Gavin grabbed the metal staff and made his way over.

Tristan regarded the staff for a moment before turning his attention back to the wall. He pointed to a section that Gavin couldn't quite make out. "Do you see these markings here?"

Gavin wouldn't call that writing, though there were grooves in the stone. He focused on his core reserves, drawing on his awareness of them to try to augment his eyesight. The technique was one that Anna had taught him how to use and master, and though he was not nearly as skilled at doing so as many of the El'aras were, Gavin could improve his eyesight well enough to be useful for something like this.

"I see *something* here," he said.

"Something," Tristan replied, shaking his head. "There's something all right, but it is the pattern that matters." He looked up at Gavin expectantly. "I suppose you can't see anything from that?"

Gavin shrugged. "I can see the pattern, but I can't really make out anything within it otherwise."

"That's too bad."

Gavin stared. "And you think I should?"

"I think there should be something there that you, of all people, should be able to come up with, but maybe that was my mistake."

"Maybe it was."

"You know, I did train you better than this," Tristan said.

"Oh, I know that you want me to believe you were responsible for all things," Gavin muttered. Irritation flared within him, as it often did these days around Tristan. It wasn't anger, which he had felt for a long time, so much as it was frustration.

"Now you are acting like a spoiled child."

"Is that right?"

"It is," Tristan said, but he laughed slightly as he did. "And you act as if I have somehow wronged you."

"I'm not so sure you haven't in some way," Gavin said.

"You're not sure, which means that you were not wronged. Otherwise, you would know."

Gavin snorted. "You can tell yourself whatever you

need to keep yourself content." He leaned forward, tracing his finger over the markings, and he hated that he did start to see a regularity to the pattern. As much as he wanted to deny that Tristan had taught him well, he had.

Gavin had become the fighter he had because of Tristan's instructions. He'd become the assassin he had because of what Tristan had demanded of him. And he'd come to understand the patterns that existed around him because of Tristan's training.

As he studied them, he started to piece together a pattern in the scratches in the stone. At first, it was subtle, but the more he stared, the more certain he was of that pattern.

"You see something," Tristan said.

Gavin smiled. "I would've expected you to pick up on something as well."

"I trained you to do that," Tristan said.

"No. You trained me to fight on your behalf. You trained me so you didn't have to fight."

"I trained you to be the Champion."

Gavin wasn't going to keep arguing with him. There was no point in it.

"I'm not sure what it is," Gavin said instead. "There's a pattern here. It repeats itself up the wall, but..." He looked over to the other wall near him and realized that the pattern didn't exist on it. There was a different one. "It probably means nothing."

Tristan shook his head. "The ancients had reasons for everything they did. Especially in this place."

"We don't know exactly what they did or what this place was."

"It was a way of touching the gods," Tristan said.

Gavin expected him to smile, to admit that he was making a joke, but Tristan looked completely sincere. "The gods?"

Tristan nodded. "What do you think this power is? It's the power of one of the gods. That's what Chauvan and the others were trying to reach for."

"Like Sarenoth?"

"There you go again, speaking of things you don't really understand."

Gavin shrugged. "Then explain them to me."

Tristan frowned at him. "I've explained enough to you over the years."

"Actually, you taught me how to fight, to kill, and to identify patterns that you can't, but you never taught me about the gods."

"Because there wasn't time. Not with everything else you needed to do and master in order to become what you needed to be."

"I still have the feeling that you aren't exactly sure what I needed to be," Gavin said. "Other than you wanting to turn me into something that *you* couldn't be."

Tristan shot him a look. "If you want to make comments like that, then you can figure this out on your own."

"Now you're going to refuse?" Gavin said with an incredulous laugh.

"I'm not doing anything. I'm just telling you what I'm willing to do."

"And what is that?"

"Help you find the truth," Tristan said.

"If you wanted me to find the truth, then you would have shown me all of this from the very beginning."

"You wouldn't have been able to do what you needed to if you knew what you were expected to be."

Gavin shook his head again and decided to change the subject. "What gods?"

Tristan started to answer, but a voice interrupted through Gavin's enchantment.

"You need to get up here, boy," Gaspar said.

"Where?"

"Ruins. Now."

Gavin glanced over to Tristan. "We're going to finish this conversation later."

Tristan smirked as if to tell him that they wouldn't, but Gavin was determined to get him to talk.

He raced through the hallway until he reached the stairs leading up into the ruins. There had been a time when this had been little more than a maze for Gavin, but he had navigated it enough that it was easy for him now, and he knew exactly where he needed to go. The urgency with which Gaspar had spoken meant that something was going on, so he called on his core reserves as he went. He bounded up the stairs and popped up into the open.

The stone enchantments he had placed for protections were battling something. Gavin hurriedly surveyed everything around him. Shadows looked as though they had come alive, and they swirled around the enchantments. He had never seen anything quite like that before.

"By the rocks," Gaspar said through the enchantment. "Can't do much of anything. They're too powerful."

"Nihilar?"

"It's different than last time. My enchantments worked, but…"

Gavin unsheathed his blade.

The nihilar was a destructive force he thought he could use. Maybe not as well as the others could, but he had some experience with it now. It filled his ring, and he had learned that he could push it into his blade, drawing some of that power from it.

Gavin focused on what he felt around him now. The power didn't restrict him from reaching for his core reserves the way it had before, and it didn't suppress the connection that he shared to the El'aras ring, but there was something to it that was difficult for him to master. It was control.

He needed experience. He needed practice. More than that, he needed somebody who could explain how to use that power, but it was something that Gavin did not have. Tristan didn't fully understand how to use it either, so he wouldn't be able to offer what Gavin needed. Even if he could, Gavin wasn't sure that he would agree to his help.

Instead, he had to battle blindly, and sometimes foolishly. Which was exactly what he did now.

He stepped forward, and he focused on what he could detect around him, but there wasn't all that much. Just a hint of the darkness, and an awareness that there had to be some sort of power here.

Magic constricted around him, trying to confuse him. Gavin thought he could fight through it, but in order to do that, he had to push past what he felt.

He focused on the El'aras ring and drew power from that.

He wasn't going to let this battle last too long.

Gavin heard a crash and the sound of stone cracking. One of the massive enchantments protecting the ruins stumbled and fell. The golem was shaped like a man, but one that was nearly four times any normal person's height and with blunted features. The thing was made entirely out of stone, with hands that were gigantic and legs that were stiff and unbending.

He couldn't even tell what had happened, but he managed to catch sight of something like a lightning bolt shooting and causing the stone to crumble down to the ground. He had to jump out of the way before one section struck him.

Gavin pushed power out from himself, through the ring, into the sword. He stormed forward, readying for the attack, and swept his blade around as quickly as he could, intending to carve through the nihilar here. But as the power filled his weapon, he felt something strange. It was almost as if there was a trembling sense against the blade, and energy seemed to reverberate off it.

Shadows continued to sweep toward him. He carved through them, and they separated around his blade. When they did, he saw nothing.

Gavin brought the sword around in a series of patterns he fashioned after the Leier style. The shadows began to ease, the resistance around him fading completely, and the darkness lifted.

There was nothing left, only the enchantments that had been placed as protection. He looked around, searching for more of the nihilar, but there was no sign of them. He turned to Gaspar, who was still crouched behind one of the stones with a pair of knives in hand and enchantments encircling his wrists and fingers.

"What was that?" Gaspar asked.

"I don't know. I thought it was the nihilar, but there was something new too."

"I wonder why they returned."

"I'm not sure."

Unless Chauvan had been involved, there wasn't any reason. Gavin had claimed the power they wanted and had secured it.

He found a small metallic item resting on the ground near the remains of the golem that had been destroyed. It was made from the same strange silver as the staff, and when Gavin reached for it, he felt an echoing sense from within the El'aras ring he wore. Nihilar energy was in there.

He frowned and hesitated, holding his hand above the device.

"What is it?" Gaspar asked.

"As far as I can tell, that's an enchantment."

"A nihilar enchantment?"

Gavin reached for it again, feeling an echo of power

press against him. "I don't think so. I don't know what it is, but we have to figure out who placed it."

As he took it in hand, it crumbled into nothing.

Gavin rushed and searched around the clearing, where he found five others. Each was made out of the same silver metal, and each disintegrated when he tried to pick it up to study it.

They had been designed to fail.

But for what reason?

CHAPTER TWO

Gavin took a few moments to examine the space around the boulders, searching for signs of additional enchantments. He found nothing other than the ones that had crumbled when he'd tried to pick them up. This was a different kind of attack than what Chauvan had used before, but Gavin wasn't exactly sure why, or what it meant.

Gaspar searched with him. "Do you think they were looking for the temple, or was it something else?"

"They knew how to find the temple. When Chauvan was here before, he knew where it was. Which suggests to me that it wasn't about finding so much as it was testing me. But it's more than that. There's something on those enchantments that has me worried." He looked at Gaspar. "I've seen those markings before."

"Where?"

"Another place of power. El'aras." He crouched down, but the markings—and the enchantments—were gone, having collapsed. "The problem is that I'm not sure I even remember them correctly, but if I do, then it *could* have been Chauvan."

"Would he want you to go back there?" Gaspar asked.

"They know I have the ring and the sword, and that I've connected to the power of the nihilar. It just seems unlikely that they would risk coming here unless they're after something, but I can't think of what that might be." They hadn't found anything in the temples. Just more writing, and nothing that he thought Chauvan would care about.

"Unlikely don't mean it's not possible," Gaspar said.

Gavin nodded. He was right, but that didn't make it any easier to know what he needed to do.

"I'm not sure we're going to find answers out here," he said.

Gavin looked around. A few rocks created an illusion that masked the entrance to the temple, but it wasn't so effective that it had prevented the nihilar from finding it. That was how he referred to them. *Nihilar.* It was also what he called the power.

Because the nihilar knew where the temple was, they would have no difficulty with uncovering it. The protections placed by those within Yoran could do only so much. The golems prevented access, but how long would that work? Eventually, even the stone creatures wouldn't be enough to defend this place.

Gavin looked over to Gaspar and found him looking back at the city, a distracted look in his eyes.

"Maybe you'll have to look for answers, though that might be what they want," Gaspar finally said. "You'll need to be prepared for *that* possibility."

"A trap?"

Gaspar shrugged. "To pull you away. Put you somewhere you can't prepare. Sounds like something I'd do. You're protected in Yoran. He's got to know that."

"That's another concern," Gavin said. "I've stayed here while I healed"—Gavin healed quickly, but his arm had been broken and his leg injured, which took time to recuperate from—"but maybe it's really time for me and this ring to depart."

Gaspar frowned and shook his head. "Or it could still be just about Yoran and whatever might be here. We just don't know. You know, none of this is really easy, is it?"

"Not a bit," Gavin agreed.

"We go about thinking that the city has faced the last attack it can, and then you run off and we deal with another one."

"I'm also not convinced that whatever tied them to the city in the first place is over," Gavin said.

"Me neither. I suppose there's something we could do." He turned to Gavin. "At least, to test whether it's you or the city."

"Test?"

"You need to know, don't you?"

Gaspar wasn't wrong.

"What do you propose?" Gavin asked.

"Well, I haven't given it much thought, but…" The way he said it suggested that he had, in fact, given it quite a bit of thought. "We could go someplace where we don't have to worry about anyone else getting hurt, but close enough that we can return if something were to happen. We have to make sure that we stay in communication with others in Yoran." He tapped on the enchantment in his ear and motioned to the one in Gavin's. "And give it some time. If they're after the city, we wait and see if the city is attacked again. If it's about you, well…"

"You want us—me—to be bait."

"Better than me, and surely better than the city."

"Great," Gavin said.

"I will take any other suggestions you might have."

The problem was that Gavin didn't have any suggestions. Not ones he thought would be effective, at least. In this case, it seemed to make sense that he get digging.

"Tristan has to come with us," Gavin said. "Mostly because I don't want to leave him in Yoran if there might be a danger to others here."

Gaspar nodded. "Agreed."

"And we need to make sure that we have plenty of defenses. If we're attacked, we want to be able to defend ourselves as well as possible."

Already Gavin started to think through the various possibilities of what he might need. Zella had given him dozens of different enchantments before, but this time, he had specific ones he thought might be beneficial. The golems were particularly useful, but he needed something that would be more than just useful—he needed something destructive. But he thought he also might want something that could contain the nihilar. Gavin wasn't exactly sure what that would take, or whether there would even be anything that could contain that power.

"I have a feeling you would have better luck with Zella than I would," Gaspar said, reading his mind.

"I'm not so sure about that," Gavin said.

Gaspar arched a brow, then gestured toward the city. "Come on. We should start making preparations."

Gavin hesitated, glancing toward the opening leading down to the temple.

Gaspar shook his head. "It's not going to change anything for you to go down after him."

Gavin appreciated that Gaspar understood his hesitance and what he was considering.

"He might learn something."

"That's what you want, isn't it?" Gaspar asked.

"I'm not exactly sure what I want."

He stared at the opening, considering what he wanted to do, but maybe Gaspar was right. Let Tristan have time to study the temple. If there was something there, then maybe Tristan would come up with it. If there wasn't, it wouldn't harm anything. Besides, Gavin needed to prepare.

As he started back toward Yoran, he realized that maybe he had lingered too long anyway. He'd been here long enough to make a full recovery, and he should have already started traveling back to the El'aras to continue his training, but he had remained.

It wasn't that he didn't have a desire to better understand the nihilar power, though that was part of it, especially as he knew the El'aras viewed it as dangerous. A great darkness, in fact.

This was more about his own hesitation to leave Yoran again.

By the time they reached the outskirts, he found one of the constables investigating the barrier enchantments around the city. The man was dressed in the dark blue uniform of the constables and swept an enchantment out in front of him. It glowed softly, and Gavin could see the symbols etched on it. The device was likely nothing more than a way to probe at the barrier to ensure it remained stout. Davel would likely have the constables doing that regularly.

Gavin nodded to him. He didn't know the man very well, but he recognized him. In addition to him being a constable, the way he was testing the enchantment also suggested that he had enchanter abilities. He might not have used them during the time when enchantments had been forbidden in Yoran, but he certainly had some predilection toward them and seemed far more comfortable with them than most.

As they passed through the barrier, Gavin was aware of the energy coming off the enchantments, and power flooded through him.

"I presume we're on the other side," Gaspar said.

"Right. We walked through it. You know where the enchantments are, don't you?"

"I have a general sense of where they are, but knowing is a different thing," Gaspar said. He glanced back, nodding to the constable. "But then, they aren't doing a whole lot to hide what they have done."

"Why would they need to hide it? Those who know what the enchantments do understand the need for them, and those who don't just think the constables are patrolling."

"It's more than that," Gaspar said. "But maybe it doesn't matter."

They reached one of the outer markets, and Gaspar paused. The market was little more than a wide-open square, not nearly as busy as it could be during certain times of the day. Merchant carts lined the area, and a small crowd meandered from cart to cart.

"Listen," Gaspar said. "I'm going to talk with a few of my sources, and then we need to think about our departure."

"I'm going to Zella first. Then I'll have to go back to the Dragon and eventually have words with Wrenlow."

"The kid has to stay here."

"I know," Gavin said.

"You think he's going to be upset about it?"

Knowing Wrenlow as Gavin did, he didn't think so. Wrenlow had learned to fight, and certainly had learned to defend himself. But what they were about to do—serving as bait—might be more than Wrenlow could handle.

"I doubt he's going to be too upset," Gavin said.

"Good. Like I said, for the plan to work, we need somebody on this side to alert us if something happens."

"He's going to be more than happy to be our ears."

Gaspar frowned. "I'm not sure about that. When you left the last time, he was a little restless. I think we all were, to be honest. Any time there was even a hint of magic in the city, he looked into it. I think he kept searching for you."

"I wasn't gone all that long," Gavin said.

"Not too long, but long enough that... Well, you get into a bit of a pattern, and you start to look for comfort."

Gavin snickered. "You can say that you missed me."

"Don't go putting words into my mouth."

"I would not put anything into your mouth."

Gaspar glowered at him. "I'll just find you at the Dragon."

It didn't take long for Gaspar to disappear into the crowd.

Gavin made his way through the rows of wagons at the market. He slowed, enjoying the chaos around him. It felt so familiar. Then again, he had spent quite a bit of time in Yoran, far more than he had in many places over the years. The city had become home to him.

And now he was talking about leaving once again. Of course, he needed to leave.

He passed stalls where people were bargaining and ignored a few merchants who tried to call him in to buy their wares. He reached the far side of the market, then paused.

The enchanters' fortress was not far. Gavin gradually made his way toward it, weaving through the streets and watching for signs of anything unusual, though he didn't really expect to find much. Not out here, and not given the current situation with the city.

By the time he neared his destination, he had figured out what he wanted to talk to Zella about and how to approach her for what he needed. It was more than just enchantments. It was the help that she could offer him.

"I saw you coming," a voice said from an alley near the wall surrounding the fortress.

Gavin turned. A dark-haired girl stepped forward out of the shadows. He hadn't seen her in several months, which, now that he thought about it, was probably too long.

"It's good to see you, Alana."

"I felt what you were doing to my enchantments."

"I wasn't hurting them," Gavin said.

Alana chuckled. "I didn't think you would. I don't know that you could."

"I was just trying to link to them so that I could use them better."

"Did it work?" she asked.

"I think so."

She stepped closer. Alana was probably no more than twelve years old, but she was one of the most powerful enchanters he'd ever been around.

"I have others," she offered.

Knowing what he did now about the enchantments, and how the power was linked, Gavin didn't know if he felt comfortable taking enchantments from her. He had the paper dragon, which could fold down small enough to fit into his pocket, or it could expand to an enormous size.

"Don't know if I should," Gavin said.

"You don't have to worry about me. It doesn't hurt, if that's what you're concerned about."

"It doesn't hurt when I use the enchantment, but what about if it gets damaged?"

Alana frowned. "Do you think it could be?"

"Any enchantment can be destroyed," he said.

"Even ones that you work with?"

Gavin almost said that they could, but he didn't really know. The kinds of enchantments he influenced were different now. He had some familiarity with them, but it was more than just that. His experience with them was tied to how he added his own connection to them.

"I still think that any enchantment can be destroyed."

"Anything can be destroyed, Gavin, but that's not what you want to do. I know what your nickname is," she said, smiling at him. "But you aren't the Enchantment Breaker, are you?"

Gavin shook his head. "I'm not. I wouldn't do anything to hurt you."

She laughed and glanced toward the fortress. "You must be getting ready to go again."

"Why do you say that?"

"It's the only time you come visit her. She doesn't mind. She knows you mean well."

"Has Zella said something about that?" he asked.

"Oh, she says things about a lot of things. Most of the

time, she complains, but I think she means well." Alana let out a small laugh. "Sort of like you. You complain, but you mean well."

"I didn't realize I complain so much," Gavin said.

"Oh."

"What is that about?"

"Well, if you didn't know, that just means you *are* like that," Alana said.

He chuckled. "I suppose I can be cranky."

"More than some, not as much as others. But given the things you've been doing, I suppose that can be forgiven."

He smiled at her. "Thanks."

"Do you want to see what I've been working on?"

Gavin did, but he also felt a sense of urgency to what he needed to be doing, and staying here with Alana wasn't necessarily the right use of his time. Now that he had decided to try to draw the nihilar away from the city, Gavin felt as if he needed to get moving on that and then prepare for what else he might have to do.

But Alana looked at him with an earnestness that reminded him of how much she had helped him. Not only with the paper dragon, but with the ravens she had made as well. What if she had a new enchantment that might also be useful?

"I would love that," Gavin said.

"You can visit with her when she gets back, anyway. She isn't here."

Gavin laughed as Alana strode past him and up to the gate. She tapped on the stone, and it slid open. Nobody stood guard the way they had the last time he'd been here, and he realized that it wasn't stone that slid away. It looked to be paper.

"Yours?" he asked.

"It helps," Alana said. "It's more useful than you realize."

"Oh, I have no doubt about that."

He followed her into the garden outside the fortress. The smells of the flowers around him assaulted his nose. The dozens of different flowers and animal-shaped shrubs left him wondering if they were enchantments or just plants that had been groomed. Gavin was quite certain that the sculptures he saw were enchantments. Given their size, he had little doubt that they would be dangerous creatures. Was there an element of sorcery here as well? The enchanters had denied having any ability with that kind of magic.

The most recent time he'd come here had been in the darkness, and he had seen none of it. He didn't even remember the flowers.

"How much of this is enchanted?" Gavin asked as they approached the front door.

"Everything is."

"So these are all defensive measures?"

"For the most part. Zella doesn't want to be surprised," Alana explained.

"What does she think might happen?"

"Oh, I don't know. I think she's been through a few things that are hard for her to overlook. She wants to be ready."

Which meant that she was ready for either sorcery or

the constables. Not that Gavin was terribly surprised by that. Zella had seen the enchanters through a difficult time, and she needed to be ready to defend them.

They entered through the front door. The inside of the fortress was quiet, and the place was decorated differently than it had been when the Captain lived here. The plush carpets, the paintings on the walls, and the sculptures decorating the halls gave the interior a sense of warmth. Though Gavin suspected most of the sculptures were enchantments of one sort or another. The entire fortress was well lit with enchanted lights, pushing back shadows and giving a comfortable atmosphere to the whole building.

The air was cool, and it seemed drier than it had been before. Alana hurried forward, and Gavin was forced to chase after her to keep up, but she paused every so often to glance back at him. By the time she reached the massive staircase leading up to the second level, she had scarcely slowed. She looked back, motioning for him to hurry along.

While Gavin followed, he scanned for signs of anybody else within the fortress. As far as he could tell, it was empty.

"No one is coming."

He reached the top of the stairs. It had been a while since Gavin had been this deep inside the building. The last time was when he had chased Tristan, though he hadn't known it was him at the time. The upper level was decorated quite a bit differently now than it had been before. When the Captain had occupied the fortress, it had been sparse, with only plain stone walls. Similar to the entrance, this part now had paintings, which Gavin suspected were enchantments, as well as sculptures, which he *knew* were enchantments. Several flower-filled vases were set into alcoves along the wall, though he didn't know if those were also enchanted. The air had a floral fragrance that was more potent than he expected it to be.

"The flowers," Gavin said.

Alana looked back. "Aren't they wonderful? They don't do much except smell pretty."

"Somebody enchanted flowers to be… more fragrant?"

"Not all enchantments have to be violent, silly."

"I realize that," he said, though he usually spent time thinking otherwise. "It's just that they happen to be the kinds of enchantments I have the most experience with."

"You have the wrong kinds of experience, then," she said, her tone serious.

Alana stopped at a door, and she tapped on it. Much like with the gate, it seemed to slide away, though he realized that it rolled more than slid. She stepped inside, and Gavin paused at the doorway to run his fingers along the door that had opened.

It was paper too.

"My enchantments are a little different than others," Alana said. "Zella doesn't really understand it. She tries to explain it to me, but when she does, I sort of get lost." She waved a hand as if to dismiss the idea. "And I don't always care. She does, and she wants to try to help me understand, but…" Alana shrugged. "It doesn't really matter.

Don't tell her I said that. All I know is that things work for me. I focus on what I want, I push it out, and it takes hold."

It was the closest Gavin had gotten to understanding how an enchantment worked. Nobody really spoke about it, and he didn't know that it even mattered. His type of magic would be different than that of the enchanters, who created something that was different than what the sorcerers did. Anna had demonstrated that the El'aras could create enchantments similar to those made from sorcery, but even in that, Gavin didn't know if the method was so distinct that it made a difference.

He stood in the doorway and looked into the room. Alana's bedroom, he realized. A large four-poster bed had what looked to be a massive piece of paper draped over it. Symbols decorated the paper, which he suspected were enchantments. Pale butterflies circled in the air. With a start, he realized that they were all enchantments as well.

A stack of paper rested in the corner of her room, and Alana plopped down next to it.

"How do you command it to take hold?" he asked.

"You have magic, Gavin. You should be able to do this too."

"I don't have *your* kind of magic," he said as he continued to study the butterflies. They were lovely, and they likely served no function other than to look nice. That wasn't to say they didn't have other purposes, though. He wouldn't put it past Alana to add a hint of danger to those butterflies if it came down to it.

"You just have to think about what you want," she said. "It's about as basic as that."

"I don't think mine works that way."

"Why not?"

She grabbed a piece of paper and set it on her lap. She quickly began to fold it, turning it into a familiar shape—a raven. Those were incredibly useful enchantments. Once she finished folding it, she cupped it in her hands.

"You just have to think about what you want," Alana said again. "I want this to be a raven that can talk to you."

As she said it, she closed her eyes, pressed her mouth into a tight line, and squeezed. Gavin could practically imagine the magic coming out of her. She looked as if she were trying to focus on the power within the enchantment, then pouring it out of herself and into the paper.

"See?" she said.

The folded paper had shrunk down into a smaller form, but it wasn't just that. Gavin could feel something from it that he hadn't been able to feel before.

"What else did you do to it?" he asked.

"I told you, silly. I was just talking to it. I told it what I wanted, and it listened. That's what you have to do."

"I don't think I can use enchantments the same way you do."

Alana grabbed another piece of paper and started folding. "You could, but you just have to find what you want and how it fits with you."

"What do you mean, how it fits with me?" Gavin said.

"I suppose I wasn't telling you all you needed to know to make them. It's not just telling it what you want, but you have to feel it. It has to be felt deep within you."

That fit with something he'd heard, though he couldn't

remember where he'd heard it. Emotion had something to do with the enchantments, and the more emotion that was poured into the enchantment, the easier it was for them to carry out what was asked of them.

"Maybe the way you do things is different," she said as she pulled out another raven. She closed her eyes and set her jaw, and Gavin watched as she placed power into it. When she was done, she held it out to him.

"I thought you said you had something new."

Alana grinned. "I do."

She hurried to her feet and slipped the two paper ravens into his hand, before going to a trunk at the end of her bed. When she pulled it open and reached down, she did so carefully, almost as if whatever she was reaching for was dangerous. She stood up, and Gavin saw what looked to be a book, though it was oddly shaped.

"I used seven pieces with this one," she said, her eyes glittering with excitement. "I've been trying more. It's tricky, though. When you use more than one piece, you have to keep it held together. Two was hard, three was even harder, but Zella told me to stick with it. She thinks I can get as many as I want to. I just have to learn how to keep them sticky."

"And what did you do to make this sticky?"

"It's all in how you talk to it," she said. "Well, that and how you fold it. If you fold it just the right way, paper doesn't come apart. It's sort of like what carpenters do. At least, that's what Mekel tells me."

"Is that right?"

Gavin hadn't seen Mekel much since they had

returned to the city. He needed him, as well, especially his enchantments. If Mekel was willing to come with him, then Gavin would feel better prepared for facing more of the nihilar.

"I don't know how he knows that, though," Alana said, taking a seat on the ground and motioning for Gavin to sit in front of her. "It's not like he's a carpenter. Maybe a sculptor, but his sculptures start off as rocks, and he just pushes his magic into the rocks to get them to take their shape."

Gavin blinked. "Wait. Mekel doesn't carve those himself?"

She looked up, and she smiled at him as if he were ridiculous. "Of course he doesn't. You didn't think he had time to make all of them that way, did you?"

He frowned, not entirely sure what he'd thought. "So his enchantments are carved with magic."

"Mostly," she said. "It's all in how he talks to the stone. He tells it what he wants, and then it does it."

She opened the book, and Gavin realized that it took on a three-dimensional shape as she began to separate what looked to be pages. But they were something else. As she unfolded the paper, it separated outward into wings, an enormous beak, and even a tail.

"I haven't tried this one myself," she said, "but there's no reason it won't work."

"What is it?"

"I don't know. I saw a picture in a book, and I wondered if I could make it. I talked to the paper, and it agreed. So we made it."

She finished unfolding, and the creature looked like no bird Gavin had ever seen. It was blocky, and somehow the tail had taken on spikes. The wings were much larger than the dragon's and seemed thicker than they needed to be.

"I've never seen something like this before," he said.

"Me neither." She folded up the bird, turning it back into a book again, and then handed it to him.

Gavin shook his head. "I can't take this."

"Why not? I made it for you."

"You made it for me?"

Alana shrugged. "Well, this one seems like it might be able to help you in ways the dragon can't. At least, that's what I was telling it when I was making it."

"You were telling it to help me?" he asked.

"I told the dragon to help you, so why wouldn't I tell this to help you?"

"I guess I don't know."

She chuckled. "You can be kind of silly, you know that?"

Gavin smiled at her. "I guess I do."

"There you go again. Guessing. Anyway, take it. You've got the two ravens. You can go ahead and link to them if you want. I can still feel them, but I can tell they don't mind."

Gavin realized that she had been aware of it when he'd linked to the dragon, though why wouldn't she be?

"Gavin Lorren."

He turned. Zella stood in the doorway, dressed in a deep blue cloak. Her black hair was pinned up, and she had a stern expression on her youthful face.

"Did you come to visit with Alana, or did you have another reason for your visit?" Zella asked.

Gavin flashed a grin at Alana, who had turned back to her paper and begun to fold more. He couldn't imagine how many enchantments she could make at one time. Dozens? Hundreds? If it was limited to her folding ability and how she convinced the paper to take on the shape she wanted, it seemed like there would be no limit. But none of her enchantments had any real defensive technique to them. They were all useful for various reasons, but as far as he had seen, none of them could be used to attack.

"I came to see if you might have some enchantments you'd be willing to part with."

"Another attack?" Zella asked.

"More like the possibility of another one," he said. "We're going to be leaving the city for a while. I'm hoping I won't need them, but I also kind of hope I do."

She frowned at him, flicking her gaze briefly to Alana before turning her attention back to him. "You don't make much sense, Gavin Lorren."

"I realize that," he said. "But I'm needing enchantments so I can serve as bait, I suppose."

"You?"

"We're trying to make sure that I'm what these attackers are after, and not the city."

She glanced over to Alana one more time, and Gavin realized that Alana had paused and locked gazes with Zella before turning her attention back to her paper. What had passed between them? Maybe it was only the fact that Zella wanted Alana to make different enchantments. Maybe there was something else.

"If that is the case, then I might be able to help," Zella said.

"Good," he said. "We're thinking of leaving as soon as possible."

CHAPTER THREE

Three stone golems marched alongside Gavin. All were shaped like wolves, though they had a different aura than any wolf he had ever seen. They radiated a sense of energy and moved with a fluid grace that was not quite lupine. One of them even acted playful. Gavin rested his hand on its back as they moved deeper into the forest. Eventually, he would take a position up on the back of the wolf, but not yet. He was moving slowly and intentionally.

They were a small group, made up of Gaspar, Tristan, Brandon, and Rayena. Mekel had offered his services, but Gavin had been reluctant to have him come with them until he knew whether the city was going to be in any danger or not. They might need his particular type of enchantments and the protections they could offer. Besides, with where they were going, Gavin thought it was appropriate to have a smaller group.

"We could take that flying enchantment you have," Tristan said.

He'd grumbled about leaving, but he had joined them anyway. Gavin thought that he secretly wanted to come, and as they weaved through the forest, he found himself watching Tristan for any sign of his true intentions. It had been difficult to see anything from him, though. If Tristan wanted anything different than what he revealed, he was keeping it to himself.

"I told you my plan," Gavin said.

"And I'm telling you it's a terrible one," Tristan said. "If they're after you, then putting space between you and them is the best way to determine it."

"And if they're after Yoran, then if I leave too quickly, I put the city in danger. I don't intend to do that."

Tristan shook his head. "You won't be able to protect them forever."

Gaspar frowned as he watched Tristan. Suspicion seemed to fill his eyes every time he did. Gavin kept waiting for Gaspar to say something, but he didn't. He supposed he should be thankful for that.

"This is my plan," Gavin said.

Tristan flicked his gaze to Gaspar. "Is it really yours?"

Gavin held his hand up. "Stop. If you intend to be divisive like this, you'll be carried with one of these other enchantments," he said, reaching toward his pouch and pulling out one of the larger stone golems that Mekel had offered. It was meant to be more of a true attack golem, but he wouldn't refuse using it against Tristan if it came down to it. "I can have him hold onto you, if you'd like. I'm sure the golem would be more than capable of that."

And it was more than just that, though Gavin wasn't about to tell that to Tristan. He wanted to see what Tristan was capable of. Would he be able to break free from the stone golem? Did Tristan have the same abilities as Gavin and have any control over his El'aras abilities? Gavin had not seen it. Not yet. Either Tristan had held it in reserve, or he simply didn't have that skill. Either possibility posed its own challenges, and Gavin increasingly felt as if he needed to know.

Tristan shrugged, and he turned to talk to Rayena, his voice quiet and hushed.

"The two of you bicker like children," Brandon said.

"More like *a* child," Gavin said.

Gaspar continued to frown and stare at Tristan, and Gavin had a sense that he was bothered but was not willing to acknowledge it.

He tapped on the enchantment in his ear and lowered his voice. "What's bothering you?"

Gaspar didn't show any sign that he had heard.

They weaved around the massive trees rising in the midst of the forest, though they were not quite as large as the bralinath trees found closer to Arashil.

"He's not wrong," Gaspar finally whispered back. "Maybe we should have taken a ride on the paper dragon."

"We might need to return in a hurry. I'm not leaving Yoran defenseless."

"But they're not defenseless, are they? There are plenty

of people who can defend it if needed. You would just be leaving it—"

"I'm not leaving it defenseless," Gavin repeated.

He had no intention of moving any faster than they were going already. Partly, it was because he wanted to see if the nihilar would be drawn to them, but there was another reason—one that he had not shared with Gaspar or any of the others.

He needed to watch Tristan.

He was looking for signs of betrayal. More than that, he was looking for anything that Tristan might be trying to accomplish by planning a slower attack. So far, he had been relatively quiet, but Gavin didn't expect that to remain the case indefinitely.

Which meant that he had to monitor Tristan as much as he could.

They fell into a comfortable silence as they went. All of them were enchanted, so even though it felt as if they were moving at a brisk clip, they were practically racing through the forest, far faster than Gavin had done when he had traveled to Arashil the first time. It wouldn't take long for them to reach the settlement. Though they were going by ground, they were still not going slowly. Just slower than Tristan had suggested.

Later in the day, the forest started to change. Gavin had spent quite a long time in Arashil, so the sudden appearance of the bralinath trees, with the oak and elm looking up to their gigantic forms, was familiar. Not comforting, though. Gavin had never felt quite at home within Arashil like he did in Yoran.

"We're getting closer," he said, looking over to Gaspar.

"You were all the way out here?"

"Not so far, is it?"

"Well, considering how fast we've been moving, it's still farther than I thought," Gaspar said, "but I guess it's also closer than I expected."

He paused and reached for a bralinath tree, but Brandon grabbed his wrist. Gaspar pulled one of his knives from his pocket, flourishing it quickly while glaring at him. Brandon yanked Gaspar back.

"You don't touch them," Brandon said.

"I don't *what?*"

"They are sacred," Tristan explained, stepping up to Gaspar. "And you have to be careful with them. The El'aras don't take kindly if you disrupt the trees. They believe that the trees themselves have thoughts and personalities and—"

"And you don't touch them," Brandon said.

Gavin found it surprising that Brandon was so emphatic about all of it, especially given that he had come from the plains far to the north and not from the forest. But perhaps the bralinath trees were celebrated even there.

"Do you know anything about this?" Gaspar asked, looking over to him.

"I know the trees are important," Gavin said. "But I don't really know why."

Gaspar grunted. "So I don't touch the tree."

Gavin shook his head. "Don't touch the tree."

"Do you know what would happen if I did?"

"Not exactly. I've heard that the trees themselves might have some conscience or sentience, though I'm not exactly sure whether I believe that. And there's a very real possibility that nothing will happen."

"The trees will make sure you know," Brandon said.

Gaspar frowned, but he stayed silent.

They continued onward, and it wasn't much longer before they reached Arashil.

The ancient settlement was situated in a clearing within the forest, with bralinath trees surrounding its entirety. Now that Gavin knew more about the place and how there was a temple here, he understood that this place was impossibly old. He knew the bralinath trees were old as well, and it was likely that they had been here for centuries.

"We're here," Gavin said.

Rayena let out a soft sigh, and Gavin glanced over to her. The last time she had been here, she'd lost all of her Order—everyone she had worked with and known. She stared straight ahead, a sad look in her eyes as she surveyed the ancient El'aras settlement. Some of the buildings had been overgrown by moss, and others had crumbled. Much of that change had happened in the time since Gavin had left, as if the El'aras presence here had kept these structures stouter than they would have been otherwise.

She and Tristan split off and headed deeper into the settlement.

"Where are they going?" Gaspar asked.

"If I'm not mistaken, I suspect they intend to go see where the others of the Order died," Gavin said.

There was no sign that there had been a battle here not long ago. The El'aras bodies were gone, and there was no evidence of blood or rot. Nothing but the emptiness of the forest. The settlement itself didn't have the same life and vibrancy that it had when he had been here before, though he wasn't surprised by that.

"It looks like a ghost city," Gaspar said.

"It is now," Gavin said. "Even though it had been a small contingent of El'aras, they'd kept people here."

"Until recently."

Gavin nodded. He made his way through the narrow streets and reached the building he had saved Anna from. He drew on his core reserves, activating the door, which slid quickly aside. The last time he'd been here was when he had seen Anna.

At the time, he had thought that all he had to worry about was trying to understand the side of him that was El'aras. Now there was so much more for him to try to understand, so much more for him to master. Would Anna and the other El'aras be the right way for him to learn about that?

Gavin didn't even know. It was possible that she couldn't help him. It was possible that going to the El'aras was a mistake, especially given their view on the nihilar. Now that he had that power trapped inside of the ring, he didn't know if it would somehow pit him against the other El'aras, or if they would simply come to him with other questions.

He stepped inside, and with his core reserves, he powered the lettering on the walls. He couldn't read it clearly, though he knew there was something here.

Gaspar stood in the doorway, looking into the old temple. "What is this place? The writing looks like what's beneath Yoran, but the shape of it is different."

"I think they're a similar kind of place," Gavin said. "I'm not entirely sure. The hall beneath Yoran is old, but this..."

This was even older. If he was right, then it was as old as anything. He stepped back outside, and he looked toward the temple in the distance. When he had been here before, Gavin hadn't known that it was a temple, but having seen the others and having seen the destruction, Gavin understood what it was.

He made his way through the empty streets of Arashil, glancing at some of the smaller stone structures and marveling at the El'aras construction. There was a sense of power here, though it was subtle. If Gavin had better control over his core reserves, he suspected he would feel that power more directly. Perhaps the El'aras always were aware of that.

He motioned to Gaspar and glanced back at Brandon, who remained behind him. Neither of them spoke much, though there probably wasn't much for them to say.

Gavin stood motionless for a long while, watching the temple. He had a feeling that Tristan was inside, checking what Chauvan had taken, if anything. Gavin had no idea what Chauvan might have been after, only that something here had been important for him. Something that the El'aras still protected.

Had Anna known?

Gavin made his way back into the temple before hesitating.

Like in the other two places, a set of stairs led down. Gavin descended into the depths of the earth, feeling as if the structure itself was swallowing him. The darkness engulfed him, and the power that was all around him started to press downward. It took a moment to realize that he felt an enchantment, one that squeezed him ever so subtly.

He waited for a moment, half expecting that his connection to his El'aras ability, or perhaps the nihilar, would be stripped from him, but it never happened. He still had control over those.

Whatever happened was different.

When he had faced the nihilar before, he had been focused solely on trying to stop them, and not on anything else. But it was more than that. He released his core reserves. As soon as he did, that strange pressure faded. When he'd come through here before, he had intentionally tamped his power down, knowing the danger of holding onto it.

He looked back at Brandon. "Can you feel anything here?"

"This is one of our people's most sacred tombs," he said. "What you feel is the weight of the ancestors."

"It's a tomb?" Gaspar asked.

"More than that. A temple," Gavin corrected.

"Perhaps it once was," Brandon said, though the frown on his face suggested that he wasn't convinced about that. "We have always known it as a tomb. This is not the only one. There are others in many other places."

Gavin remained motionless on the stairs, and then he began to call on his core reserves again, letting that power fill him. As soon as he did, the weight pressed down. It didn't separate him, though. If this was intended to make it so that he couldn't use his El'aras abilities, it did not work. But the heaviness made him far more aware of it.

"Why do you call it a tomb?" Gaspar asked, as if knowing that Gavin had that question as well.

"As I said, you feel the weight of our ancestors here," Brandon explained. "You can talk to them, or so some believe." He had a solemn expression that he didn't often wear, and he stood rigid, though his shoulders were slightly slumped. It was almost as if he truly could feel the weight of the tomb pressing down on him. "Any who come here must do so with the appropriate heavy heart. You mourn those you've lost. It is said that the more you've lost, the more you will feel the weight."

Gavin could definitely feel it, but he could also feel how to release that weight. Did that mean he had somehow lost more than others? Or was it just tied to his El'aras abilities?

He continued down the stairs and found Tristan on the lower level. Tristan worked his way around, moving from place to place and tracing his fingers along the dark stone walls. Gavin recognized the markings on the walls as El'aras writing. This area reminded him of the space beneath Yoran, though not entirely. The writing here was different and didn't glow.

"It's just like the one in Yoran," Gaspar whispered.

Gavin shook his head. "Not exactly like it, but near enough. The intention has to be the same, but I'm not exactly sure why."

"They're both related to the El'aras," Brandon said. "That place, this place, and even Perisaln. Though he didn't have much time to explore there. I suspect it was a tomb, though I didn't know it at the time."

Would that mean that what was in Hester was also a tomb? Brandon had been there.

"Did you feel the same weight in Hester?" Gavin asked.

Brandon frowned. "I don't know. I wasn't paying much attention at the time. I think, given everything else we've been dealing with, I was more focused on not having the nihilar destroy me."

"And you were calling it a temple," Gavin said.

But perhaps a tomb was a more fitting description.

Gavin nodded to Tristan. "Well?"

"Well, what?"

"You came here looking for something. Have you found it?"

"I have never been to this place before," Tristan said.

Gavin arched a brow at him. "You left the book in the stone outside this city."

"That was outside. I was hoping that I might find something here. The Gateway was opened. Whatever they did here—"

"Whatever?" Gavin frowned. "You didn't know?"

"I did not learn of the key."

That surprised Gavin, though perhaps it shouldn't.

"Are you trying to see what they did here?" Gavin chuckled. "And that's what you were doing in Yoran as well. You wanted to know what they had done, and how they were able to open the Gateway."

"We need to understand it so that we can control it," Tristan said. "We need to make sure that no others can do the same."

"They just wanted to open it so that they could put power into the ring," Gavin said.

"Do you think they'll be the last ones who think to open the Gateway to nihilar and to draw upon that power?" Tristan held his gaze. "If you have failed to think through the possibilities, then you are more of a fool than I realize."

"They aren't going to be able to succeed. They destroyed Perisaln. Hester is closed to them. And Arashil…"

Gavin realized that they were going to have to do something here to ensure that Chauvan and the others couldn't do anything in these places again.

"They will just find others," Tristan said.

"But we can follow them. We can learn what it takes to stop them."

Tristan shook his head. "I'm still not convinced there is going to be a way to stop them."

He looked over to Rayena, who remained silent. He strode past her, marched up the stairs, and disappeared.

Gavin worked his way through the tomb. Thinking of

it as a temple had felt better. Every time he started to call on his core reserves, he was aware of the weight pressing down on him. It was different in Yoran, though. He hadn't felt the weight there.

That had to be significant somehow. Why had he not noticed that before?

He paused, and he unsheathed his sword. Brandon did the same, as did Gaspar, his knives coming out with a flourish. They both looked at him expectantly. The only person who didn't react was Rayena. She had been quiet, almost broken ever since the assault in Perisaln.

"We aren't under attack," Gavin said softly, looking at both of them. "I was just testing whether I could feel something."

"You should give me a little warning, boy," Gaspar said. "What with everything we have felt lately."

Brandon nodded, but he kept his sword unsheathed.

Gavin continued looking around. He didn't see any other markings on the walls, which was what he suspected Tristan had been looking for. A yellow light glowed, though it seemed to come up from the stone and glimmer along the walls like metallic sparkles. It was enough for him to make out some definition in the walls, but not so much to illuminate everything.

Gavin drew on his core reserves and pushed the energy out through the sword. In the past, when he had used his core reserves like that, the El'aras sword would glow with a pale blue light. Ever since he had connected to nihilar, it had been gray and not blue, which left him feeling as if there was something within nihilar that muted his own connection to his El'aras abilities. When he did, the weight of the tomb pressed down on him again with a sense of heaviness. It felt almost as if it were trying to suffocate him.

He continued to try to push power out from himself, through the blade, wanting to use that so he could pick up on the energy within him, and so that he might be able to find any writings on the wall. But he saw nothing.

Finally, he released the power, and the blade flickered for a moment before falling dark once again. As soon as he let the magic go, that heaviness faded. He breathed out a sigh of relief.

"Did you find anything?" Gaspar asked. "I was looking while you had the sword glowing with that strange light, but I can't see anything. I've tried using enchantments, but they aren't doing much for me."

"I didn't see anything," Gavin said. "I feel like I'm missing something here. I don't know what it is, but it's tied to my power." He looked to Brandon, who had taken a position near the stairs. Rayena had started up them. "The heaviness is only there when I reach for my El'aras abilities. It's sort of like the nihilar is trying to suppress it, but not quite. With the nihilar, I could feel it cutting me off from my abilities, but this is just a weight."

"What if it's connected to it?" Gaspar said.

"It doesn't feel like that. I would think that if it were related, I would feel that when I reached for the connection."

Gaspar shrugged. "Can't say that I know. All of it is a bit beyond me."

"I'm just trying to understand it too."

"Then you need to talk to Tristan, I suspect."

"That's what I was afraid of," Gavin said. He started back toward the doorway, closing his eyes as he tried to feel for the energy that was here, though it remained too vague for him to detect much of anything. When he reached the stairs, he motioned to Brandon. "Come with me."

"I thought you wanted to investigate more."

"There isn't much here."

Brandon looked around, then followed Gavin back up the stairs, out of the temple, and into the fading daylight. The weight lifted from him as he stepped away.

He found Tristan standing in front of the temple, or at least what he now believed was truly the temple. He started forward to intervene, not wanting Tristan to have access to parts of Arashil that he wasn't supposed to.

A crackling sound came through his enchantment.

He paused.

"Did you hear that?" Gavin asked, looking back to Gaspar.

Gaspar shook his head. "I didn't hear anything."

"In the enchantment. Did you hear something? A voice?"

"Do you think the kid is trying to get a hold of you?"

Gavin hadn't, but... "Wrenlow?"

"I'm here," Wrenlow said after a brief pause. "The sound of this enchantment is quite a bit better since you did whatever you did to it, Gavin. Is everything going okay? You haven't reached out, so I thought that—"

"Were you trying to reach me?"

"It wasn't me."

Gavin peered around the settlement. "Okay."

"If you need me to—"

"I need you to be quiet for just a moment," Gavin said.

Everything fell still and silent again.

And then he heard it. His name, though faint.

"Anna," he whispered.

"Gavin? Are you there?" Her voice was quiet, and it seemed to come from a great distance.

"I'm here. I'm—"

"Gavin? Watch out for the—"

The enchantment fell silent, and Gavin couldn't hear what she said next. He tried to call to her again and attempted to activate the enchantment, but he heard nothing more.

Only a thumping sound.

"I don't suppose that was here when you were in this place before?" Gaspar said.

Gavin frowned. The thumps came from someplace nearby, but deeper in the forest. "It did not."

His unsheathed blade started to glow. And a glow like that suggested only one thing.

Magic.

He whistled. Gaspar looked at him, and Gavin sighed.

"Well, at least we know that the attackers were after me and not the city. And it seems like something is coming now."

Gavin turned to the forest and prepared himself for what was heading their way.

CHAPTER FOUR

Gavin focused on the thumping sound around him, trying to figure out where the source of the power was coming from. As he listened, there was nothing distinct enough that allowed him to determine the source of it. He held his blade out, wishing that there was some way it could guide him, but so far, all he detected was the flickering light within the sword. There wasn't even anything from his ring to warn him.

The thudding persisted with a steadiness, but he couldn't tell where it was coming from or what it was, only that it was heading in their direction. It was a deep rumbling sound that echoed from beneath the ground.

Brandon jogged alongside him and glanced over to Gavin's sword. "Is that some sign of sorcery?"

Gavin nodded. "Sorcery, or perhaps El'aras, or—"

El'aras?

Gavin had just heard from Anna, and there was some sort of warning.

What if this is her?

He wouldn't have expected her to come, though. Not so soon, and not with what she had planned to do when she'd left Arashil. There was no reason for her to come in this direction. She would be back in the El'aras lands, and there would be nothing more for her to do.

"It's not El'aras," Brandon said.

Gavin glanced over to him and found him staring off into the trees. "If it were, the bralinath trees would've spoken."

"Wait, now they speak?" Gaspar asked, coming up behind him.

"You think I'm making things up, don't you?" Brandon said.

"I'm just trying to understand your kind."

Tristan strode toward them. "It is not the El'aras," he said to Gavin, then flicked his gaze toward the trees. "Listen to the signature."

Gavin didn't notice any signature, though he felt the power that was coming toward them, and he was distinctly aware that something was making its way here.

"If you listen, you can hear it," Tristan said. "There is a frequency to the power."

"What power are you going on about?" Gaspar asked. He had a pair of his knives unsheathed, but if there was something dangerous, Gavin questioned whether Gaspar was going to be much use against it.

"Your kind can't hear it," Tristan said.

"My kind?"

Tristan ignored Gaspar and focused on Gavin. "You can hear it. I know you can. You were trained for this."

"How was I trained..."

But he knew.

It was one of his early lessons, and one that Tristan had kept reminding him about. All those years, Tristan had worked with Gavin, wanting him to understand the depths of what they were going to have to face, teaching Gavin how to deal with magic. At the time, Gavin hadn't wanted any experience with magic. It was too dangerous, and he was unequipped for it, though Tristan had warned him that even if he didn't want to deal with it, he didn't always get to choose whether he faced that kind of power. Sometimes magic would come upon you when you didn't have any choice in it. For Gavin, he had found himself facing magic continually ever since coming to Yoran. And he had learned how to detect it.

He had also learned that there was a certain power to it. Now all he had to do was focus on that, and then he could come up with an understanding of that power and even try to trap some of that energy within himself.

He focused.

The thudding had a rhythm, but it was more than that. There was a pattern.

"I feel it," he said.

"If you can feel it, you can follow it," Tristan said.

Gaspar had a look of frustration on his face, but when Gavin started forward, the thief was the first to come with him.

"Make sure you're not trusting someone you shouldn't," Gaspar whispered through the enchantment.

"I know," Gavin said.

And he did. He understood that he had to be careful here. Tristan might be leading them into a trap, especially if he was still working on behalf of the nihilar. Tristan had trained Chauvan. He had tried to turn him into the Champion, just as Tristan had turned Gavin into that same thing. That had to be some part of a plan.

Gavin followed the pattern of the steady thumping, letting that guide him. He weaved through the trees, heading toward the sound. He recognized the pattern and thought he might be able to understand something about it, but it was complicated and strange.

The thudding came as a deep, strange groan all around him. He had no idea what it was.

Brandon stopped and held his hand up. "It's the bralinath trees," he whispered.

"What are you going on about?" Gaspar said.

Brandon looked over to him, his eyes slightly wide. "The bralinath trees. That's what we're hearing. They're speaking to us."

"What are they saying?" Tristan said.

"I don't know. Perhaps if one of the elders were here, or somebody who grew up around the trees…"

"They aren't saying anything," Rayena said.

"Can you hear them?" Gavin asked.

"It's a warning. I've never heard it. I've heard *of* it, though, and it was once a cry for help."

"For what?"

"For those about to fail," she said softly.

Gavin reached the nearest bralinath tree at the edge of the forest and studied it. He didn't see anything unusual about it that would suggest it was trying to speak to them. But the ground was trembling, and the steady groaning sound was coming from someplace deep, almost beneath him. He could imagine the tree stretching its roots down below them and twining with the roots of another tree, the two of them connecting and then speaking to each other.

But how would it be sending the steady drumming?

Tension rose within him, though Gavin didn't know if that came from someplace external or his own concern about what caused that thumping.

He suppressed that unease, ignoring it as he moved forward.

The drumming started to intensify.

He looked up at the tree, but it didn't move. The air around him was still. Quiet. Just the drumming. It seemed to come from within his body, echoing with his heart, and it raced in time with him.

Thump, thump, thump.

Gavin started forward again.

He looked around him, anticipating sorcerers, nihilar attackers, anything that might ambush them.

Thump, thump, thump.

His heart pounded in time with that sound, and he tried to understand the rhythm, to know what the trees were warning him about. Brandon's comment that the sound was coming from the bralinath trees felt right, even though Gavin didn't fully comprehend how such a thing would be possible. He felt as if the trees were trying to speak to him, but he didn't have any way of understanding what they were saying. Had he been a true El'aras, had he been raised with the people, maybe he would understand those things. But as it was, Gavin had only a warning.

Maybe it was important enough that the bralinath trees were trying to warn him at all.

Thump, thump, thump.

He could tell that something was coming. He could tell it would be happening soon. The pressure built, and he could feel a sense of the energy around him.

Thump, thump, thump.

And then there was a shaking that came from deeper in the forest.

The others with him started to spread out. Gavin reached into his pocket, grabbing several of the enchantments Zella had given him. At this point, he didn't know if they were going to need them, but if this was the nihilar and they had some way of separating him from his abilities, he wanted to be prepared for that possibility.

Speed. Strength. Stone skin. The usual enchantments.

And then he thought about something else. He pulled out one of the paper ravens Alana had just made for him, touched it on the side, and watched as it quickly unfolded.

Gavin connected to it, then whispered a command: "Search."

By drawing on his own power, he linked to it so he could see as the raven saw. The colors from this one were far brighter than some of the others Alana had made. She really had grown in her skill, and her connection to the ravens was far more than it had been when he had first taken some of her enchantments. The raven hovered in the air and started to sweep between the trees.

"I'm not so sure that an enchantment like that is going to be of much use here," Gaspar said.

"It can hunt for us," Gavin said.

The trees were still shaking, though it was still far enough away that he wasn't sure what it was, except that it was coming toward them.

Thump, thump, thump.

The bralinath were sending their warning, though Gavin couldn't tell what it was or why the trees were warning them.

The raven flew ahead, staying above the ground but below the treetops as it wove through them. The enchantment moved with speed and grace, flitting like an insect. No, more like one of the butterflies he had seen inside Alana's room, he realized.

Maybe he had taken the wrong enchantment. The butterflies might've been just as useful as the ravens, and certainly smaller, making it easier for them to navigate in places like this.

Thump, thump, thump.

The raven started to slow and circle, and an image began to take shape.

It seemed as if the forest itself was moving toward them.

"Oh," Gavin muttered.

"What is it?" Gaspar asked.

It was times like these when Gavin wished that he could somehow connect others to his enchantments. The raven could be incredibly useful for him to pass on to others so that they could see what he could.

"There's something out there moving toward us," Gavin said, "and it looks like—"

"The trees," Tristan said.

"That's right. How did you know?"

"Because I can see them," Tristan said.

He pointed to the forest, and Gavin shifted his focus. When using the raven's eyesight, he had to concentrate on what the raven showed him and watch through its eyes, but there was a distinct transition that he had to make to look otherwise.

Part of the forest appeared to be changing. The trees moved toward them, but not the bralinath.

Whatever was coming stayed away from them.

"Would other powers be afraid of bralinath trees?" Gavin asked.

"They are powerful," Brandon said.

Gaspar frowned. "Why would enchantments be afraid of trees?"

"What if they aren't enchantments?" Gavin said, though he didn't have any explanation about how actual trees could be moving.

A branch came swinging toward him, keeping him from considering it more.

Gavin had faced other large enchantments that were strangely lifelike, but never anything like this. The stone wolves, so painstakingly made by Mekel, had an aspect to them that was obviously not real. They looked real-istic enough when they took on their enchanted form, but they were not truly real. And the enchantments he had seen from sorcerers were never this exquisitely detailed.

This was something else.

Thump, thump, thump.

The bralinath trees continued to send their warning. Gavin turned to them, knowing he had to somehow figure out what it would take for him to get past this.

The trees were the defenders of Arashil, and they would help. That had to be their warning. But they hadn't helped when the nihilar had attacked.

What made him think they would help now?

This was their forest, though. This was their home. If the trees were as powerful as Brandon said, then they had to help. Didn't they?

He had his sword, plus his speed and strength and stone skin. The idea that he would count on trees to protect them seemed laughable. But Gavin watched as these other enchantments—also trees?—made their way toward them, moving around the bralinath trees.

He ducked under a swaying branch that moved almost lazily fast. A massive branch swept at him, which he could see easily and knew he could duck away from. But it also whipped at him with a speed and grace he would not expect from something so large.

With a spin, he tried to stab his sword toward the trunk of the tree, but he was swatted away by another flying branch and tossed off his feet. He tried to twist in the air, but another branch struck him while he was tumbling. Gavin spun again, pain shooting through him.

How was he supposed to fight a tree?

He slipped his blade around, slashing at the branches swinging toward him. He cut through a pair of branches, but another one struck him, sending him tumbling.

At least he landed this time.

He got to his feet and looked around. The others weren't faring much better. Brandon backed away, and Rayena joined him. Tristan danced between the trees, moving with the familiar fighting style of Grotha, though he wasn't truly attacking. Any time he tried to lunge at the branches, he couldn't get close. The only one having some success was Gaspar, and that was because he had moved close to the trunk and was jabbing at it with his knives, though Gavin had no idea whether that would even be effective.

Another branch swung toward him, and this time Gavin rolled into the trunk. Because of how close he was to it, the branches couldn't strike him.

That had to be the key.

"Stay close to the trunk!" he hollered.

Two of the strange trees turned toward him. They swept their branches at him, whipping at him at the same time. Gavin drew on his stone skin enchantment, adding power through the El'aras ring and letting that fill him.

There was a flicker of something that hadn't been present before. He could feel nihilar blooming within him, and he borrowed that energy, tracing that sense as it came through him. That was what he needed to focus on.

It was a difficult power to call on, though he could use that as well. He prepared to strike. Instead, the branch struck him, sending him staggering off to the side.

Gavin stumbled and landed near Tristan.

Tristan glanced down at him. "You need a better style than that."

"I don't see you faring any better."

Tristan chuckled, and he spun out of the way of two branches before landing almost in a split in front of Gavin. "Just have to avoid them."

"It's not so much a matter of avoiding them as it is stopping them," Gavin said.

"I thought your plan was to force them toward the bralinath trees."

"Has that been working for you?"

Tristan frowned, and he danced out of the way of another branch, which swung toward Gavin's head. Gavin brought his sword up, powering the El'aras ring and mixing it with some of the nihilar, and the blade blazed with a gray light.

As the branch swung at him, he hacked at it. There was no form, no technique, no grace in the style, but as the blade struck the branch, the tree whipped back, withdrawing as if it were in pain.

Gavin smirked. "See?"

"All I saw was you hitting a branch," Tristan said before twisting away.

Gavin needed to use the sword, and he needed to use the nihilar power within it somehow. But what was that going to involve? The only thing he could think of was that he had to find some way to dart toward these trees, and he had to figure out what it was that he could summon.

The power of nihilar flowed within the blade, which he could use against the trees. They withdrew from that power, not his El'aras abilities.

Gavin ducked underneath another blow, and he got close to the trunk of one of the strange trees. Branches sprouted out from the ground, and he realized they were roots meant for it to walk on. The tree pulled its roots free and lumbered forward.

Somehow, Gavin needed to immobilize the tree. Then it couldn't attack. Better yet, if he could cut through the roots, it might kill the thing.

He laughed to himself.

Gaspar grunted. "I hear you, boy. What's so funny?"

"Oh, just the idea of trying to kill a tree. Can you imagine what Wrenlow would say if he were here?"

"I can hear you," Wrenlow piped in, coming through the enchantment as clear as if he were standing right next to them. "I can't believe you're fighting trees. What kind of enchantments are those?"

Gavin ducked below a sweeping branch, and he landed near the trunk again. He hacked at a root, but he missed. It pulled free and swung toward him, like a foot trying to kick him. He rolled away.

"I'm not even sure they're enchantments," Gavin said, jumping to his feet near another tree.

"If they aren't enchantments, then what kind of trees can walk?" Wrenlow asked.

"The dangerous kind."

Gavin stabbed his blade into the trunk. He pushed the power of both the El'aras ring and the nihilar into the blade, and it exploded into the tree.

The sword hummed and trembled for a moment, as if it were trying to figure out what it was going to do. Gavin pulled his blade free, and the tree swung its branch toward him, but it was slower this time. He stabbed again, barely avoiding the blow. His sword struck the tree, and he forced as much power out of himself as he could, sending the El'aras energy, along with that of the nihilar, into the tree.

The blade vibrated again.

Another branch came toward Gavin, but this one was slower still.

It's working.

He ducked out of the way of the branch, and he jabbed his blade into the tree again and again. Each time he did, it felt as if the tree fought against him. How many were here?

And what of the others?

He ignored those thoughts.

He stabbed the tree again. Now the branch swinging toward him slowed further. A few more blows, and more pressure built from him, both El'aras and nihilar. Each time it did, Gavin could feel the tree slow even more.

And then it stopped.

The tree trembled and shook as if it were trying to move, but it could not. One of the roots that popped out of the ground caught Gavin's attention, and he brought his sword up, then down in a sharp arc. He hacked at it as if he were taking an axe to a log.

When he cut through it, there was a strange low-pitched shriek that built from deep within the tree, and then it spread out. The branches shuddered and fell still.

Gavin looked up at the tree, searching for any sign that would tell him why trees were able to move like this, but he saw nothing. He rumbled forward, getting out from underneath the branches.

All around him were other battles.

He found Rayena and Brandon backing away from another tree. Gavin darted forward, using their distraction to get beneath it, and he drove his blade into the trunk.

The tree shrieked, and it turned toward him. He spun again and shoved the blade into it. With one jab after another, he could feel the tree slow.

Then something swatted him from behind.

Gavin tumbled, coming to land in a clearing near one of the bralinath trees. Thankfully, he hadn't landed on it, as he didn't know whether the bralinath tree would allow him to get close enough to touch it. But whatever had attacked him didn't come nearer.

He got to his feet and started forward, when branches swept down, creating a cage around him.

Gavin brought his blade up.

"No!"

He looked up at the shout. Brandon was hollering at him while running and pointing. A branch swung down and slapped Brandon, sending him splaying out on the forest floor. As soon as he crashed to the ground, he looked up at Gavin, eyes wide, shaking his head.

Gavin glanced up. It was only then that he realized why Brandon was yelling the way he was—Gavin was within a cage of the bralinath tree. He lowered his sword, not wanting to attack the tree, though it held him in place.

He turned back to the enormous trunk. It was easily twenty paces around, and the tree towered over the rest of the forest. The branch that had come down to block his exit was as large as some of the other trees near him.

"I don't know why you're holding me, but I need to get out to help my friends," Gavin explained. "If you can release me, I would appreciate that."

He felt foolish talking to a tree, but given what he had seen with the way the other trees moved and attacked, Gavin thought that maybe this was exactly what he needed to be doing. The tree trembled as if it were answering.

Thump, thump, thump.

It was the same steady thumping he had felt before, but there was a different characteristic to it. It seemed to be slowing, fading.

Thump, thump, thump.

It was quieter than before.

Gavin frowned.

Someone shouted, and he turned his attention back to the main part of the forest. As he did, he realized why the sounds were fading.

The trees were moving. Not toward Arashil—they

were retreating. All of them were leaving, except for the ones Gavin had stabbed.

And the bralinath tree had prevented him from stopping their retreat.

Gavin was only able to watch through the branches hanging down around him as the other trees retreated. When they were gone, the bralinath tree's branches lifted and freed Gavin. He stumbled forward, looking for his friends and trying to understand what had just taken place here.

All around him, the forest was quiet and still.

CHAPTER FIVE

"I don't suppose you have any explanation as to what just happened there," Gaspar said to him.

Gavin shook his head. "Not at all."

The forest had fallen quiet, though there was an occasional tremble from someplace deep beneath him. Gavin could feel that strange energy, but he didn't know if it was from the trees or some power that echoed around him.

He stood in front of one of the trees he had stabbed, which hadn't retreated. He could still feel the energy and tension from within the tree that suggested it was trying to move, but whatever he had done to it had prevented it from being able to.

Brandon got to his feet and dusted himself off. Rayena stood near one of the other injured trees, talking quietly with Tristan.

"The forest moved," Gaspar said.

Gavin glanced over to him, nodding. "The forest moved."

"And we fought trees. *Trees.*"

"I'm aware of what we fought."

"I'm just trying to get a point across that this wasn't anything normal."

Gavin chuckled. "I think that if you stay with me, you will find that more and more things are going to be quite different than what you expected before."

"*Trees*, boy."

"I know," Gavin said, clapping Gaspar on the shoulder.

He touched the wounded tree. He wasn't sure if it was going to fight him or try to hurt him, but it didn't do any of that. A tremble came from within the trunk, almost as if it were afraid. The trunk was warm as well—certainly warmer than any tree Gavin had been around. He could feel the energy coursing within it.

He focused on his core reserves, on the El'aras side of him, and he drew power up through him, through the ring, and pushed it into the tree. He wasn't sure what he was doing or why, only that it felt right. But more than that, it was his way of trying to understand. As he continued to push that power through him, he could feel something build. Some part of him echoed up into the tree, and he could feel the tree's injury.

"What are you doing?" Tristan asked, coming over to stand across from him.

Gaspar eyed Tristan warily. Rayena stayed a step behind Tristan, glancing from him to Gavin, almost as though she couldn't decide who she needed to be following. Gavin would've laughed at that if they were not dealing with something else so ridiculous.

"I'm just trying to understand the tree," he said.

"You're trying to understand the tree?" Tristan said. "I think the tree made its intentions with you quite clear. If you want to understand it, maybe you should—"

"The tree didn't make its intentions clear at all. It was only attacking."

He looked over, and there was at least one other tree that he'd stabbed, which couldn't retreat either, but he hadn't cut through the root like he had with this one. It was able to move, though it was doing so incredibly slowly, retreating only about a foot every ten minutes or so.

"Somebody sent these at us," Gavin said.

"Or they decided to attack," Tristan said.

"Have you heard of trees like this before?" He looked to Tristan, then to Rayena, and finally to Brandon, who had joined them. "The bralinath tree didn't want me to harm them any more than I had to."

Was the bralinath tree angry that he had cut through the root system? Gavin didn't know if the tree could be angry, but given that he didn't know much about these trees in the first place, he would have to be careful.

"These are seeker trees," Brandon said. Some of the cheerfulness had returned to his voice. "Though I wouldn't have expected to see them out here. They're quite a ways from their home."

"You've heard of them. Can you tell us anything about them?" Gavin asked.

"All I know is that they're called seeker trees. They're not usually found in this forest. It's possible this place is hard on them."

"Good," Tristan muttered.

"The other trees will choke off their sunlight," Brandon said. "Over time, the trees won't survive. That is, unless the others around them give them space to grow."

"Have you ever heard of seeker trees moving?" Gavin said.

"Well, they are known to migrate. We generally stay away from them. They leave us well enough alone, so we leave them well enough alone. They don't move very far, and they surely don't move very fast, so this is a bit surprising for me."

"They marched toward us. And they were moving quickly."

Not only moving quickly, but they were attacking quickly. Why now? Had somebody known they were here and decided to target them?

They had come out here to test whether the nihilar would follow and attack, so presumably this served as answer to that. But why use trees here and not in Yoran?

Gavin ran his hand along the surface of the tree, feeling the energy within it. It was trembling still, as if afraid of his touch. Then again, he had stabbed it and cut through one of its legs, making it impossible for the tree to escape. He felt a little bad about that.

He frowned. "Where were they going?"

"They were coming after us," Gaspar said.

"But why?"

He focused on his core reserves and the ring, and he let the power flow up through him, through the tree, wishing there was some way for him to understand just what it had been trying to do. As he concentrated on the magic and pushed it out through him, there were no answers for him.

He could feel the energy of the trembling tree, the power so distinctly different than his own. And he could feel something else—a connection that traced away from the tree.

Gavin focused on it, trying to feel for that connection, and when he realized where it was going, how it was flowing, he turned to the others.

"The seeker trees are connecting to the bralinath tree," he said.

"Well, if they are both sentient trees, then maybe that makes sense," Gaspar said.

"None of this makes sense."

Gaspar snorted. "Nope. I'm sure the kid has some explanation for it."

"Any thoughts, Wrenlow?" Gavin asked through the enchantment.

"Actually, I haven't heard of seeker trees," Wrenlow said through the enchantment. "I haven't heard of bralinath trees either. I have a few books here that I'm going to look through, but I don't know if I would come up with anything fast enough to help you."

"So we have just been attacked by trees," Gaspar mumbled once Wrenlow fell quiet. "I don't suppose this is what you would have expected?"

"Not at all," Gavin said. "I figured we would face enchantments. Maybe the nihilar. Maybe sorcerers." He shrugged. "To be honest, I didn't really know what we might encounter, only that I was ready for the possibility that we'd have to deal with something magical. Something to give us an idea about what they were after at the temple outside Yoran. None of this makes sense to me."

Gavin had considered plenty of different possibilities of what they might find, but nothing had included trees. The idea that they had come across trees that attacked them still felt impossible. But he was perfectly willing to acknowledge some of the impossible things that he had encountered these days. Now that his power had continued to grow, it made sense that he was dealing with increasingly challenging things.

But why would everything be accelerating like this?

He turned to Tristan, who was talking quietly with Rayena. He stepped away from the tree and moved to stand in front of his old mentor.

"What exactly were you expecting to happen?" Gavin asked.

Tristan looked up and locked eyes with him for a moment, then nodded to Rayena. She backed away to join Brandon.

Gaspar stood alongside Gavin, and when Tristan glanced in his direction, the old thief shrugged. "I'm not going anywhere. I'm here for the boy."

Tristan sneered. "The boy is not your responsibility."

"He is my friend," Gaspar said, glowering at Tristan.

Gavin found himself chuckling inside. Tristan's

fighting styles were such that he should be able to handle Gaspar with ease, though maybe not. Gavin continually told himself that he wouldn't have any difficulty with Gaspar, but the old thief had made it very clear that he would never bring a direct confrontation with Gavin. If they were to fight, he would do it discreetly. And that was the same way that Gaspar would deal with Tristan.

Gavin stepped forward. "You're still keeping things from me. Whatever it is, I think we need to know. You were training people to become Champions. Why?"

"Because of the prophecy," Tristan said.

Gavin shook his head. "The prophecy that you didn't believe in. There's more to it. And for whatever reason, you're still trying to keep it from me, and you want to shroud your intentions." He looked around the forest, his gaze settling on the tree that had attacked him. The other one had retreated deeper into the forest and had made it far enough away that Gavin couldn't see it easily, though he doubted it had gone all that far.

Tristan frowned at him. "What do you think you've been doing all this time?"

"I've been training to fight, but not to fight trees."

Tristan looked up at the tree, his gaze narrowing for just a moment. "No. You have not been training to fight a tree, but you have been training to handle yourself, mastering every bit of your physical powers, and then your magical powers."

"My magical powers? You haven't done anything with that. In fact, I wouldn't have known that I have any magical powers had you kept me with you."

"But did I keep you with me?"

"This isn't something you've been in control of," Gavin said. As much as Tristan had tried to play it up as if he were somehow in control of events, Gavin couldn't see how that would be possible here. Tristan certainly had ways of influencing him, but not like this.

"No," Tristan agreed. "At a certain point, I had to release you and give you an opportunity to prove yourself. I could not control all of it, though I wanted to."

"I'm sure you did," Gaspar muttered.

Tristan turned to Gaspar, and he frowned more deeply. "You cannot understand what I was doing. You cannot understand the depths of my knowledge, and the depths of my experience."

"And you can't understand—"

Gavin ignored them. Something else had caught his attention. A faint, subtle whisper.

He turned away from everyone else and headed deeper into the forest, into the darkness of the shade. At first the whisper was soft, but the farther that he moved away from Arashil, the louder the sound came, until it was a clear, steady call in his ear. And he understood where it was coming from.

"Anna?"

Her voice had come through the enchantment before, and he kept waiting for her to try to get through to him again. Gavin listened for the sounds of the forest, for birds or insects or animals, but everything around him was still and quiet. It was almost as if the seeker tree attack had completely disrupted everything and changed the energy of the forest.

"Anna. If you're there, answer me."

He couldn't hear her, but he had a sinking suspicion that she needed him. Anna had never called to him like this. That she would do so now, repeating his name, suggested that she needed his help.

Maybe she needed the Champion.

Could the trees have attacked the El'aras?

He would have imagined they had an easier time with the trees than he did, especially given their connection to their own power. But then again, the only reason Gavin had been successful was his connection to nihilar, and not because of the El'aras side of him. The trees wouldn't have listened to the El'aras. Especially if they were commanded by someone.

"Gavin Lorren," Anna said, her voice distant and quiet in his ear.

Gavin focused on the enchantment, and he pushed a bit of his core reserves into it, trying to use enough so that he could speak to her.

"I'm here," he said. "Can you hear me?"

No answer.

He continued to send a trickle of power out through him and into the enchantment. It was only a little bit, but the more he focused that power out of him and into the enchantment, the more he started to hear something shift. The connection between him and the enchantment seemed to solidify.

"Gavin Lorren," she said again. It was louder now.

"I'm here," he said. "Can you hear me?"

"I can."

There was a note of relief in her voice, and that surprised Gavin more than anything else. Anna was the Risen Shard. She was powerful. He wouldn't think an El'aras would struggle with anything, especially not her. He would not expect her to be relieved at hearing his voice.

"I don't know how much time we have," she said. "The enchantment isn't working that well." A brief pause. "There has been an attack."

"I've had some too. The nihilar attacked in Yoran, and I'm not exactly sure what happened in Arashil, but we were targeted by seeker trees."

There was a moment of silence from her end, and he worried that maybe he had not given enough power to the enchantment, or perhaps some part of it had faded. He had no idea how far away she was. She had returned to the main part of the El'aras lands, and Gavin didn't know how far apart they were. It was possible that she could not fully communicate with him.

He tried to pour more power into the enchantment, but he knew if he pushed too much, he ran the risk of overwhelming or possibly even destroying it. He only wanted to give it more energy so that he could communicate better.

"Gavin Lorren," Anna said again.

"I'm still here."

"Seeker trees?"

"They attacked us," Gavin said.

"Then it is moving."

"What is?"

"The danger," Anna said. "You need to be careful."

Gavin's brow furrowed. "Of what?"

"Need to be careful," she said again.

Her voice was faint and crackling, and Gavin had a difficult time hearing what she was saying. He wished he had some way of repairing or strengthening the enchantment, but he didn't know how to do that. Something seemed to prevent her from reaching him.

Maybe someone.

"What's going on?" Gavin asked.

"We have been attacked," Anna said.

"Attacked by what?"

"We don't know."

There was a pause, and in that silence, Gavin recognized the worry he had heard in Anna's voice. Something had targeted her people, and she had no idea what it was. How was that even possible? She was incredibly powerful, and so were the El'aras. Gavin wouldn't expect anything to target the El'aras that they couldn't handle.

"Anna?"

"We have moved," she said.

"To where?" Gavin asked.

"Beyond. The attacks have been moving, but we have not been able to defeat them."

"The nihilar?"

Gavin didn't know if the nihilar had moved from attacking him to the El'aras, or if this was something else. The nihilar—and Chauvan in particular—certainly had the ability to defeat the El'aras, so Gavin could see how their attack was possible, though he wondered if it was something else.

"Not the nihilar," she said, sounding strained. "I do not know what it is."

"Can you fight back?"

"We are not strong enough. There are…"

Her voice faded again. Gavin pushed a bit more power into the enchantment as he tried to reconnect to Anna, but he wasn't sure if he was going to have enough or if there was going to be any way for him to maintain that connection. Nothing seemed to work.

She needed his help. He needed hers as well. Anna would know more about the seeker trees.

"Fires," she said. "Ancient. Nothing like we have seen in some time. The elders speak of the same, but…"

The connection was lost again.

Gavin focused on his core reserves, on the power of the El'aras ring, and he tried to reconnect to her.

"What's causing the fires?" he asked.

"Ancient evil," she said.

Gavin had no idea if she was answering his question, or if she was speaking about something else. At this point, he couldn't tell anything other than the fact that she was responding to him, but responding in what way?

"What ancient evil?"

"Fires," she said again. "Be prepared."

"Where are you moving to?" Gavin asked, deciding to try another approach.

There was silence.

He attempted to try to send enough energy through the enchantment to connect to her, but each time they talked, he could feel something fading.

"Anna? Where are you moving to?" he tried again.

If the El'aras were under attack, shouldn't he get involved?

That was the very reason he had gone after the nihilar in the first place. Gavin had wanted to understand why that would attack the El'aras, to understand the reason behind that violence. The dark threat, as Anna had called it, was an ongoing danger to their people.

"Fires," she said again.

"I understand that there are fires," Gavin replied. "How can I help you?"

"Stay away."

Her command was clear, as clear as anything had been, and he frowned. "I can't stay away. If the El'aras need help…"

Maybe there was another way. The El'aras had to run from whatever was coming for them, but what if they had a place they could go for more help?

"Bring your people here," Gavin said.

"Not safe," she said.

"Why not?"

"Ancient evil."

Gavin had no idea how much of it was her repeating herself and how much of it was this unstable connection between them. At this point, they weren't able to speak to each other easily or clearly. He felt as if all he had to do was find a way to figure out the connection, some way to join the two of them, but he couldn't. And he had a sense from her that she couldn't reach him either.

"Bring your people to Arashil," Gavin said again.

"Dangerous," she said. "Nihilar."

That part was clear.

"I have control of nihilar," he said.

"Control?"

He felt as if he was missing aspects of the conversation, with the stuttering nature of how she was speaking to him and the delay between her responses, but it seemed as though some parts of their communication, and maybe the key aspects, were getting through.

"I have control of nihilar," Gavin said. "And we stopped the attack. We have control of Arashil."

He waited.

When she didn't speak again, he decided to try something else. "If this is an ancient evil and you need help to defeat it, bring your people out. Come to—"

Gavin almost said Arashil again, but maybe that wouldn't be enough protection. There were the bralinath trees here, and that was it. If her people had already left their ancestral home to run from this ancient evil, then any place they went would have to offer something more than what their home did. He would have to promise them a layer of protection that they couldn't get any other way.

"Bring them to Yoran," Gavin said.

"Yoran?"

Her voice came through clear, enough that he could almost believe that she was standing next to him. But then her voice grew quiet again, and Gavin lost track of her words.

"Bring them to Yoran," Gavin repeated. "We can help. We can offer you protection. We can—"

The enchantment faded completely. She was gone.

He tried to put more power into it, but each time he did, he couldn't feel anything different. He kept repeating her name, but nothing changed. Finally, he released his core reserves, and he looked around the forest.

He turned back and saw that the others were there. Gaspar watched him, Tristan frowned, and Brandon and Rayena had troubled looks on their faces.

"The El'aras were attacked," Gavin told them. "They had to leave their home."

"We gathered that," Gaspar said.

"I couldn't hear much of anything, but she mentioned an ancient evil."

"And you told her to come back to Yoran?"

"I did."

"You know what that would mean if they were to do so?" Gaspar said.

Gavin understood. It wasn't that he wanted to cause trouble for the constables, enchanters, or anyone else within the city, but Yoran had been the ancestral home of the El'aras at one point.

"Gavin?"

Anna's voice filled his ears through the enchantment again, though distant and faint.

"Yoran. Coming."

CHAPTER SIX

G avin started back in Yoran's direction, and the others marched alongside him. It was late in the evening, and it might've been easier for them to stay in Arashil for the night, but none of them had wanted to linger near the settlement. Not with the potential for the seeker trees to attack again, regardless of what the bralinath protections might be. There was not the same safety there had been before.

Their enchantments helped all of them move quickly. The forest blurred past so that the tall trees, including the bralinath, gradually spaced out as the five of them made their way toward Yoran, though the trees remained a constant presence the entire time they journeyed. The air smelled of the fragrance of the trees and the dampness of the earth, and there was a constant buzz of insects, though that increased the farther they traveled away from Arashil, as if the insects had avoided the settlement too.

He found Gaspar looking at him every so often, an unreadable expression in his eyes.

"You know what this means," Gaspar finally said, breaking the silence.

Gavin glanced over to Tristan, who was walking next to Rayena. They had been quiet, though Gavin continued to suspect he knew something.

"I know," he said.

"I don't think you do," Gaspar growled. "You just invited the El'aras to Yoran."

"It wouldn't be the first time the El'aras were there," Gavin said. "It wouldn't be the first time recently, either."

"That's not the nature of your invitation."

Gavin breathed out. "If they're facing some ancient evil"—which Gavin had no idea what to make of, other than that Anna had mentioned fires—"don't you think that's eventually going to come our way?"

"Unless it's simply after the El'aras."

"I doubt that's the case," Gavin said. "When has anything only been about the El'aras?"

"What makes you think you can do anything here, anyway?"

Gavin turned to him, and he frowned. "I *don't* have any idea. All I know is that I need to try something."

Gaspar scoffed. "Because of this El'aras woman."

"It's because they're my people."

Gaspar clenched his jaw. "I suppose the enchanters can begin placing protections, and maybe we can get the city ready." He snorted. "I can only imagine what Chan is going to say when he learns you invited the El'aras to come."

"They can offer protection."

"We both know those aren't the protections he wants."

"No, not the type he wants," Gavin agreed.

Darkness had fallen in full, the moon fat as it hung in the sky. It was nearly midnight by the time they reached Yoran. They had made quick time, far faster than Gavin had ever thought possible traveling to and from Arashil on foot. He could have taken the paper dragon or used one of the other stone golems, and he wasn't sure why he had not.

Gavin felt a measure of relief when he found the city intact, with no signs of fighting.

"You can't get rid of this place, can you?" Brandon said. "Everything seems to bring you back here."

"Why do you say that?" Gavin asked.

"Well, it was once a stronghold for our people. A long time ago."

Gavin looked over at Gaspar, who was frowning at him, and he shrugged. "I'm not saying anything else."

"You don't need to," Gaspar said.

He turned to the others. "Get some rest and—"

"Where do you want us to rest?" Tristan asked. "Seeing as how you've decided that you're in control of all of us."

Gavin crossed his arms and stood in front of him. "Where were you staying when you were in the city before? Because I can guess where you were."

Tristan held his gaze. "I was studying."

Gavin snorted. "Studying inside the temple."

"I was. You didn't tell me that you didn't want me to."

That was true. Gavin hadn't really cared. Increasingly, he wasn't sure how much to care about Tristan or how much to worry about what he was doing and what he was involved in. But now, especially with what he had encountered, he no longer knew what to make of it.

"Just get some rest."

"What about you?" Brandon asked.

"I think I could use a mug of ale," Gavin said.

"Oh. I could do the same. Are we going back to that tavern you like? That place is quite interesting. Although the last time we were there, it was quiet."

"I doubt it will be now," Gaspar muttered.

Gavin tapped on the enchantment to try reaching Wrenlow. He had been attempting to get his attention during the walk back, but there had been silence from his end. Gavin hadn't worried. Not entirely. But given what they had fought through and that Wrenlow was supposed to be waiting in Yoran to warn them if needed, Gavin would expect him to be waiting, ready to tell him anything. That Wrenlow was silent suggested that either he was off with Olivia, or something had happened.

"I'm going to the Dragon," Gavin told the rest.

"Then we all will go," Tristan said.

Gavin frowned at him. "You aren't going to cause trouble there."

"When have I ever caused trouble for you?"

Gavin bit back a laugh. He had to be careful not to let Tristan bait him. All of this was some sort of a game to him.

Instead, they wound through the streets and passed some patrolling constables, who Gavin tried to stay clear of. The size of their group was large enough that it would draw the constables' attention, and he didn't necessarily want that until he had a better sense of what he was going to do.

At one point, Gavin passed a tall, twisted bells tree and avoided it. A wall had been built around it, allowing the tree to grow ever taller. There were dozens of them throughout the city, and the people of Yoran had built structures around the trees, which left him thinking of Arashil and the bralinath trees. He doubted that bells trees were similar, but this was also a place of the El'aras.

Some buildings had been toppled during the fighting the city had faced recently, and despite attempts from the enchanters and the constables at rebuilding quickly, it was slow work. There were sections of the city that were more damaged than others, though Gavin found himself drawn to them for some reason. He continued to move quickly, avoiding the crowded areas, which might account for why he was drawn to the destruction—there were fewer people.

Now that they were within the city, he could feel the presence of the enchantments around it, designed to try to limit the use of magic. These days, Gavin had no real restrictions to his power, not the way he once did. He could still feel his core reserves, the power of the El'aras ring, and the nihilar flowing. All of it filled him with a sense of energy and a certain connection from deep within him.

Gaspar leaned close to him. "I haven't been hearing anything from the kid."

"Me neither," Gavin said.

"Wonder why that is."

"I'm hoping it's just about Olivia, but…"

"But what?"

Gavin sighed. "Well, I've been trying to reach Wrenlow on the walk back and haven't been able to, which would be worrisome enough on its own, especially given what we faced. But there's another possibility, and it's one that worries me more than any other."

"You care to fill me in?"

"I'm trying to, if you would just give me a moment." He glanced over to Gaspar and forced a smile. "When I was connected to Anna, I had to push my own power into the enchantment. I'm starting to wonder if maybe I pushed too much magic into it and somehow disrupted the enchantment's power, corrupting it."

"I thought you said your El'aras enchantments can't be corrupted like that."

"To be honest, I don't really know anything about what can happen with El'aras enchantments," Gavin said. "It's entirely possible that they can be or that I can ruin them, though I have no idea how." He tapped on the enchantment. "Can you hear me through this?"

Gaspar shook his head. "You need to be ready to get more enchantments."

Gavin sighed and nodded.

They reached the Dragon. With his hand above the door, he tested for the possibility of power but didn't feel anything. He had found himself doing that more often lately, almost without even thinking about it. He pulled the door open, and the familiar smells of the fire, food, and ale wafted out. The sounds of people talking, and even the terrible minstrel playing his lute, made Gavin breathe out a sigh of relief.

As soon as they stepped inside, the warmth of the place began to surround him. He felt an energy here, along with something else that made it welcoming. He looked around for Jessica, but he didn't see her. Several of her servers made their way through the tavern, women Gavin no longer knew as well as he once had.

The place was crowded, much more so than it had been in quite some time. The last time there had been a crowd like this had been one of the very first nights he had come to the tavern. He hadn't realized just how much his presence had influenced the activity here.

Gaspar shouldered past him, and he stopped in front of a table near the back. He glowered at the two people sitting there, who scrambled to their feet and scurried off.

Gavin joined Gaspar at the table. "Was that necessary?"

"Maybe not, but we needed space and they were in my spot."

"I didn't know you had an assigned table," Jessica said, her voice coming from behind them.

Gavin turned around. Her chestnut hair was pulled back and her apron was covered with a few stains, but the twinkle in her eyes and the hint of a smile that lingered on her lips made her just as lovely as when he had first seen her.

"Quite the gathering you have here," Jessica said, watching Gavin. "You keep coming back." She glanced over to Gaspar.

"Blame me. I keep dragging the boy back. Figure we could use him. If he gets under your skin, I can have him wait outside."

Jessica chuckled. "I think you'd like it if he could get under my skin, but I'm a little more resilient than that. So," she said, slapping a towel down on her leg, "given the way you all look, I have to wonder if there's anything I need to be concerned about."

"Not yet," Gavin said.

Gaspar dropped down into the booth and slid across the seat. "You know what I like," he said, grinning at Jessica.

"If you talk like that to me, Gaspar, you will find that you will not be served in my establishment."

"I'm sorry," Gaspar said, settling his hands on the table. "I would love a mug of ale, tavern mistress."

"That's a little bit better, but you're still testing me."

Gaspar grinned.

The others took a seat, and Gavin looked around the tavern. There was something comforting about it, cozy despite the crowd and the terrible minstrel playing now. When he had been with Jessica, he'd always thought that she chose her music as a way to antagonize him. Maybe she had, or maybe she just enjoyed it. Gavin didn't know if it was his taste in music or Jessica's that was the culprit. This minstrel was strumming steadily, tapping his foot as he sang in his squeaky voice, which cracked at times.

Several people were dancing in front of him, as if they actually enjoyed it.

"Would you stop glowering at him?" Gaspar said.

"I'm not glowering at anyone," Gavin mumbled.

"I see the way you're looking at that poor minstrel. You look like you intend to attack him."

Gavin snorted. "I think Jessica would like that. But I'm not going to attack anybody in here."

Jessica arrived with a tray filled with mugs of ale and set it on the table in front of them.

Each of them took one. Rayena stayed quiet, looking over to Tristan with uncertainty lingering in her eyes. Gavin didn't care for this side of her. She was a confident fighter, and she had been one of his staunchest allies, but now she was a shell of what she had been. She'd lost the rest of the Order, but Gavin didn't think that was what had changed her. He suspected it had more to do with Tristan's return.

Brandon grabbed his mug, leaned back, and took a long drink. All the while, he glanced around the tavern, smiling as he looked at everything. There was a hint of a grin as he did, almost as if this was exactly where he had hoped to be, and exactly what he wanted to be doing.

Gaspar cupped his hands on the mug, and he flicked his gaze until he caught Jessica's attention.

"We need to talk to the kid," he said when she walked over.

"I haven't seen him today," Jessica replied.

"We were talking with him earlier."

"Well, he spends quite a bit of time with Olivia, as you

well know, so I think that if you want to speak to him, maybe you could go visit him there."

Gavin knew better than to do that. "Do you have any way of sending word to him?"

"It's late, Gavin. Just let it wait until morning."

"He might be worrying. The last he heard, we were under attack. He might fear that we're hurt."

"And are you?"

Gavin shook his head. "No."

"There then. You don't have to worry about him. Let him have his night with Olivia. That's the reason he stayed in the city, after all. He wanted to have something normal. Do you want to take that from him?"

Gavin shook his head again slowly. "You know that I don't."

"I know you don't, but you continue to come back here, and the way you keep bringing..." She stopped herself, and she pulled herself up tight, crossing her arms over her chest and clasping the tray against her body. "Enjoy your ale, Gavin."

She turned away and left.

"She's not wrong," Gaspar said.

"I've been trying to leave the city, but things—"

"Things are always going to make it so that you are brought back here. Unless you refuse, you're always going to be drawn back and tempted to return. Is that what you want?"

Was it?

When Gavin had been here before, there had been a distinct sense that he had spent too much time in Yoran.

And over that time, he'd started to feel as if he needed to leave, as though he had no choice but to do so, and staying would only mean that he was bound more and more to the city. There was a part of Gavin—the part that had been trained to move on and not to stay in one place for too long—that had felt as if that were necessary.

But the longer he stayed in the city, the more he had started to feel as if he were a part of life here. And there was something comforting about it.

He had never really had a home.

As his thoughts went in that direction, he glanced to Tristan, who was still quiet, sipping his ale but not really drinking it. Every so often, he would lean toward Rayena, say something to her, before he would sit back up and look around the tavern. At one point, his gaze lingered on Gavin for a long moment.

The El'aras might be his people, but he didn't feel at ease with them. Even when he had been in Arashil, he had never felt as if he had been home.

And that was what he wanted.

Having lived his entire life on the road, having trained to fight, to move from place to place and to be somebody who was meant to keep moving, there was an overwhelming desire to find a place where he wanted to settle. And the more that he thought about it, the more he realized that place was Yoran.

He snorted.

"What is it?" Gaspar asked.

"I've been trying to run from Yoran for as long as I

could. Ever since I got here, I felt like things were conspiring to hold me here."

"It's still doing that, boy."

"It is, but…" Gavin frowned.

Gaspar regarded him for a moment, and then he leaned close. "Don't tell me that you want to stay."

"Would that be so bad?"

Gaspar grunted and took a long drink. "No. And I might enjoy the little bit of entertainment that having you around would bring."

"I wouldn't necessarily bring anything entertaining here," Gavin said. "I have means of traveling now. If I needed to take a job, I could travel away from the city and then return."

"Sounds like you are working through the possibilities to make it work," Gaspar said.

"Maybe I need to."

"Maybe you aren't the type to settle in one place. And I don't want you to feel like you have to stay here because you've been here as long as you have."

That wasn't it, and the longer Gavin thought about it, the more it felt right to him. He couldn't put a finger on it, but as he looked over to Tristan, watching his old mentor, he realized that was exactly what he'd been missing. He had been running from place to place. Even when Anna had come and invited him to learn about his El'aras abilities, he had taken that opportunity to keep moving.

But why? Did he really need that?

"Maybe this is what I need," he said softly.

Gaspar shrugged. "It's going to be… Kid."

Gavin turned in his seat. Wrenlow stood by the table, hair disheveled and an ink stain on his nose. He clasped a book in front of him. A dark-haired woman stood behind him. Gavin hadn't seen Olivia in quite some time, and she was just as lovely as the last time he had seen her. She nodded to Gaspar and frowned at the others at the table with them, before joining Jessica near the back of the tavern.

Wrenlow set the book down, and he dragged over a chair from one of the nearby tables. "I stopped hearing you," he said to Gavin, holding his gaze. "I thought something had happened to you, but the last time I heard you, you were talking to somebody. So I didn't think that anything really happened to you, but I didn't know."

"I was pushing power into the enchantment," Gavin said. "I didn't mean to deactivate it, but I might have."

"It seems strange to me. Then again, I don't really know how to work enchantments, at least not like you have." Wrenlow glanced over to Gaspar and shrugged. "Don't you think that's strange?"

"I couldn't say," Gaspar said, "seeing as how I don't understand the way enchantments are made."

Wrenlow looked at the book before turning and nodding to where Olivia was. "I have some understanding about how the enchanters make them, but I suspect your connection to them is different, Gavin. Maybe you can learn how to do it? If the enchantment is broken, could you fix it?"

"That seems to be an advanced form of magic," Gavin said.

Brandon leaned forward. "Oh, not as advanced as you would think. Not that I have any real facility with it. There are some who study these things. They like to make artifacts where they leave a part of themselves in." He nodded to the communication enchantment that hung from Gavin's lapel. "Something like that. They have their uses, but in our lands, it really isn't quite as useful as you would think."

"Because everybody there has magic?" Wrenlow asked.

"A form of it," Brandon said, "but you know, we don't really have any reason to do those sorts of things. We aren't fighters."

"Not all of you," Gavin said, glancing to Rayena.

She tensed, looking up at him and holding his gaze. Then she glanced back down into her mug of ale. She hadn't taken a drink, from what Gavin could tell.

"Well, you are the Champion," Wrenlow said, "so I would imagine that the power you have access to would be enough for you to create something. But maybe not. Maybe you just need to learn how to control your power, and when you do, you can turn it into..." He shrugged and glanced at the book. "I just don't know. Anyway, I'm glad to see you. When I was told that somebody had come through the barricade around the city, I knew it was you."

"You knew?" Gaspar asked.

"At midnight? And with the threat of magic?" Wrenlow nodded. "I came looking for you. I went to the border first, then to the entrances to the El'aras hall, before finally coming here. It would've been much easier if we had the enchantment." He tapped on one still in his ear. "We need to get this fixed."

"I would love to fix it," Gavin said. "But we might have to wait until Anna and the other El'aras arrive."

Wrenlow's eyes widened. "What?"

Gavin filled him in on the trees, what Anna had said, and why he had needed to pour power into the enchantment.

Wrenlow sat back with his hands clasped in front of him. "So there's an ancient evil, there are fires… and you mentioned that when you were with her before, she talked about a great shadow."

"That was the nihilar," Gavin said.

"What if this is something like that?"

"It probably is," Tristan said softly.

Gavin turned to him. "What do you know?"

"It's not a matter of what I know. At least, not what I truly know. It is what I've suspected."

"And this has to do with the prophecy that you continue to refuse to share with me, the prophecy you believe I'm somehow tied to and need to be a part of."

Tristan nodded slowly. "Again, I'm not exactly sure."

"If I am somehow tied to this prophecy, what is it? What are you trying to keep from me?"

Tristan glanced over to Rayena. "We've been talking about this ever since the seeker tree attack. When Brandon mentioned that, it triggered a memory. Something I read about long ago. There were stories of the forest trees uprooting themselves and running."

"Running from what?" Gavin asked.

"I don't know. But taken with the prophecy I have been able to piece together, along with the roles that you and the Risen Shard play in it, I can no longer overlook the possibility that what we're coming into is a true time of darkness."

Gaspar snorted. When Tristan looked over to him, Gaspar shrugged. "We've been in a true time of darkness my entire life."

"What kind of darkness have you experienced?"

"I don't know. How about sorcerers trying to kill enchanters, enchanters trying to kill sorcerers, the Fates returning to the city and unleashing... Oh. Wait. That was *you* who unleashed the creatures on the city."

Tristan was silent, and he held Gaspar's gaze for a long time before turning back to Gavin. "Regardless. This is a time of danger. A time of darkness. And everything we continue to see tells us that it's building, that there's more coming and we have to be ready for it."

"What do you mean by 'a time of darkness'?"

"A time of the ancient gods," Tristan said.

Gaspar started to laugh, but Wrenlow leaned forward.

"What kind of gods?" Wrenlow asked. "We've heard about Sarenoth, and I've uncovered some rumors of a few others, but I'm not exactly sure what to make of them." He grabbed his book and flipped through the pages. "To be honest, I don't really know what to believe. These days, it could be nothing more than rumors, but rumors, unfortunately, have a way of turning out to be something real." He looked over to Gavin. "I know you want me to be reading through the book you left me, but

I have been, and I haven't found anything useful. Everything I found is tied to the temples, but there isn't anything else. Not in the temples, at least. But other places…" Wrenlow glanced around the table. "There are references of different things. Not necessarily in the book, but in the writing beneath the ground. There are some mentions of something called Grathorl, Var'anlal, and Tibran." He shrugged. "I don't even know if I'm saying them right, but they're in one of the older sections where the language is even harder to read than other places."

"They were the old gods," Tristan said.

Rayena looked up at him, frowning.

"What about the old gods?" Gavin asked.

"He's mentioned their names, and I won't repeat them."

It was a level of superstition that surprised Gavin.

"They ruled these lands, and then something changed." Tristan watched everyone at the table in turn, before settling his gaze on Gavin for a long moment. "I don't know what happened, so you can keep asking, but I don't have any answers for you. All rumors say the old gods warred, gifting some part of themselves to their followers."

"So the gods are responsible for… what?"

"I don't know," Tristan said. He squeezed his hands around the mug of ale, though he didn't take a drink. "Perhaps they gifted the power to the El'aras. To others like them—us. I'm not quite sure."

"You know something more," Gavin said.

"All I know is that the old gods were powerful. Everything you have read from the El'aras is tied to their initial celebration of those old gods. And then they disappeared."

"Completely?"

Gavin thought of what he had learned about Sarenoth and how the Sul'toral somehow were trying to free that ancient dark power. Was this something similar?

"I'm no scholar," Tristan said.

Gavin let out an incredulous laugh. "You have tried to position yourself as something along that line, so you obviously want to be something like that."

"I'm not a scholar, but if the rumors are to be believed, the old gods will eventually escape and grant their powers in full to their followers once again. And then we will see a great violence unlike anything we have seen in millennia."

"Sarenoth?" Gavin asked. He couldn't believe that he was having a conversation like this. It felt ridiculous to him.

"He is but one great power," Tristan said.

"Nihilar?"

"I don't know. It is another power."

"What about the others Wrenlow mentioned?" Gavin said.

"I've only heard of them in passing. I don't know anything about them, and I certainly don't know if there's anything more to the kind of power they possessed. There could be." Tristan shook his head and looked over to Wrenlow with a frown. "Again, I don't really know. I'm no scholar."

Gavin smiled to himself. Tristan continued to say that,

though a part of Gavin suspected that Tristan knew far more than he was letting on. Why was Tristan hiding it from him?

"If the gods are... waking," Gavin said, trying to find the right words for what was taking place and being unsure that he truly had them, "what role do we have in it?"

"We have to pick a side," Rayena said.

She had been silent ever since they had fought in the forest. Truth be told, she had been silent ever since they had left the city in the first place. Gavin wasn't sure whether it was her sudden look of worry or the intensity in her eyes. Either way, there was something about Rayena now that put him on edge. She had been the head of the Order. Of all people at the table other than Tristan, Gavin suspected that she knew things that the others did not.

That mattered.

"Eventually, we will all have to pick a side," Rayena said again. "The El'aras have already aligned themselves with one, but we must be careful of the others." She held Gavin's gaze for a long moment. "If she told you that an ancient evil was coming and mentioned fire, I fear what it is."

"And what is that?" Gavin asked.

"The Ashara have returned."

CHAPTER SEVEN

Gavin rubbed his eyes. He hadn't slept well. Then again, he often didn't sleep very well as he usually wasn't tired enough to truly rest.

Their conversation had devolved into speculation, which wasn't useful for anyone. Wrenlow tried to raise concerns about what he'd heard about the gods, and Tristan ignored him, which only irritated Gavin more. Rayena didn't know anything more about the Ashara, only that they were some ancient threat to the El'aras. Tristan tried to make his own theories but didn't offer much of use. Brandon piped in every so often, before finishing his ale, getting to his feet, and singing and dancing to the minstrel's music.

Wrenlow was quiet after Tristan shut him down, which wasn't entirely surprising. He seemed to be taking in the information, as if he were trying to decide what to make of all of it. He finally got up and told Gavin that he was going to find Olivia, then left the rest of them to continue their conjecture.

Gavin had suspected that rather than going to Olivia, Wrenlow planned to continue his research, since he had access to places within the city that Gavin did not. There were archives that might have some resources, but there was also the El'aras hall and its writing that Wrenlow could use. Gavin had to give him time.

And he had known that he was tired. He needed rest.

More than anything else, he needed to recover and be ready for the possibility that he would have to face whatever ancient evil Anna was dealing with. It was coming. Gavin was convinced it was. The problem was that he didn't know what that meant. The darkness had been the nihilar, and Gavin had gained some measure over it, even if it wasn't control. At least it was an understanding.

Fires, though. That was different.

Thankfully, Jessica had given him a room in the Dragon, and he had slept about as well as he had for the last few weeks. He'd tossed and turned, having strange dreams of flickering flames, with a darkness that seemed to hover over everything. Occasionally, Gavin caught glimpses of smoke that swirled around him, which he assumed was his tired mind creating concern about what they might have to face.

Early morning light streamed in the windows. He dressed and headed down to the tavern, where he found Gaspar already awake. He was sitting at a table, helping Jessica fold napkins.

Gaspar flicked his gaze over to Gavin. "I didn't expect to see you up so early."

"I couldn't sleep," Gavin said.

"You don't need to, not often. The only time I've seen you need much sleep is after you take that powder."

Gavin sniffed. He didn't have enough sh'rasn powder on him anymore. If only he had. He might've taken it during the tree attack.

"Do you think there's really something to what they were talking about last night?" Gaspar asked.

Gavin shook his head. "I don't really know. Not anymore. With everything we've seen, it's possible."

Jessica rested her hand on the table, pausing as she folded napkins. "Gaspar was telling me about what you faced."

"Was he?"

"I didn't figure it mattered," Gaspar said.

"It probably doesn't," Gavin agreed.

"Trees?" Jessica asked.

Gavin shrugged. "I know how it sounds."

"Oh, I very much doubt that you know how it sounds. You faced it, and you probably did just fine."

"I managed to stop them."

"There you go. The great Gavin Lorren. The Chain Breaker."

"You mean Tree Breaker?" Gaspar said with a snicker.

Gavin dropped down into the chair across from them, and he grabbed a stack of towels and began to fold as well. "I've never heard of anything like it before," he said. "Which makes all of this…"

"Believable," Gaspar said.

Gavin held his gaze. "Unfortunately, it does make it believable, doesn't it?"

Gaspar sat quietly for a few moments, then looked up. "Everything keeps building, boy. First, sorcerers that are almost too powerful for us, then the Fates, and then these Sul'toral. And now we are talking about gods. Everything is focused here as well. Why do you think that is?"

"I think some of it was focused here, but the others..." Gavin shook his head. "I don't really know. It doesn't make sense that this would be some sort of nexus for a kind of godlike power."

"Probably not," Gaspar agreed. "Maybe it was just a place where the El'aras had celebrated their god." He sat up, pausing as he picked up a towel. "What about that temple? It was for the nihilar, but what if it was something else to the El'aras?"

"I didn't feel anything in it. I didn't see anything either, but to be honest, it's beyond my understanding. I'm hoping Wrenlow has some breakthrough and can piece it all together for us."

"Well, maybe you, Chain Breaker, need to see what you might be able to discover."

Gavin could look at patterns, and he could use that knowledge to try to understand some of it, but how much of it could he truly comprehend? He didn't have Wrenlow's ability to break things down the same way. His ability to follow patterns was different, but maybe he needed to take on a greater role.

"I will see what I can do," Gavin said.

Gaspar nodded, as if that solved everything.

"He tells me that you told the El'aras to return," Jessica said. "Are you going to talk to the constables?"

"Davel likes it when I give him a warning," Gavin said, thinking about the head constable and what he might do.

"I'm sure that would be best."

"Do you think I shouldn't have?"

She was quiet as she folded three napkins and set them in a pile. Gavin stayed busy as he worked on the towels. He glanced across the table at Jessica, waiting for her to say something more.

Finally, she breathed out a heavy sigh. "I don't know what you should have done," she said. "They are your people, aren't they?"

"My people," he muttered. "I don't know anything about them. Not enough to know if they're *my* people." Maybe he needed to understand that, as well. It was another question that he should ask Tristan about, but it had never really seemed important to him. He had not come to care about who he was, only what he was, and he'd never really thought about where he had come from.

Mostly, it was about where he was going to be. Now that he was coming to terms with the idea that maybe he wanted to stay in Yoran, he had to have a better plan.

"If they are your people, you will need to do whatever you can to protect them," Jessica said.

Gavin sat quietly for a few moments. "I see the danger in having them return to Yoran."

It was not just their presence; it was what the city had

once meant to the El'aras. That was part of the problem. He didn't know how the El'aras might view a return. Anna was one thing, as Gavin had a pretty good idea about how she might react, but the others might not be as calm.

"I don't know about any of this," he said, looking over to Gaspar.

"When they come here, you can get your answers," the old thief said.

Anna would know. And if she didn't, there were others with her who had to know more. It was the other part of the reason that he had suggested they should come to the city. Not because he necessarily wanted the El'aras here or that he wanted them to bring danger with them, but because he felt as if there might be answers.

Gavin got to his feet. "I think I'm going to take a walk."

Gaspar looked over to Jessica, then to Gavin. "I'll come with you."

"You don't need to."

Gaspar held Gavin's gaze for a long moment. "I'm not going to let you go wandering off into some danger again, boy."

"You don't have to protect me from Tristan."

"Who said I was protecting you from Tristan?"

"I see the way you're watching me," Gavin said, "and I know you well enough to have an idea about what you intend. I'm not exactly sure what you think you might accomplish, but—"

Gaspar grunted. "Let's go. You were going to go down to the El'aras temple and see what was there, so I'm coming with you. I know you'd rather bring the kid, but seeing as how he went off with Olivia last night, I think you need to give him a bit more time. A young man like him needs to enjoy himself."

Gavin snorted. "What about an old man like you?"

"I'm not *that* old. And you don't have to worry about that," Gaspar said.

Jessica glanced over to him briefly before turning back to the towels. Something had passed between them, though Gavin couldn't quite read what it was. Why was Gaspar suddenly motivated to come with him? Was there more to it than what he was letting on? Gavin didn't think he could push Gaspar too much, not without upsetting him more than he already had.

Instead, he motioned for Gaspar to follow him. They headed out into the street and made their way through a quiet Yoran. They passed a series of patrolling constables, and Gavin nodded to a couple ones he recognized. Gaspar knew more of them, and at one point, he paused to chat with them.

They passed another bells tree. A bird perched on one of the upper branches, which Gavin always found amusing. The tree's sharp leaves were likely to slice through anything.

They avoided groups of people as they wandered, picking their way through the streets and taking the easiest route. By the time they reached the edge of the city, the sun had fully risen.

"It's a little surprising to me that this is the way you want to go out here," Gaspar said.

"It's more direct," Gavin said.

Gaspar snorted. "It's not. It's probably *less* direct, because you have to weave through crowds."

"What crowds have we seen?"

"Well, maybe not at this time of the day," Gaspar said, "but if you came through here at other times, it would be busier."

"Then I'd go through the tunnels underneath the city."

Gavin passed through the barrier at the edge of Yoran and felt it the moment he did. He looked down at the enchantments situated in the ground that ringed the entire city, and he thought about the amount of work that had gone into placing them. He didn't know whether they would be enough to suppress the sorcerers that might come, though they had encountered quite powerful ones before. It might slow them, at least.

And that might be the greatest benefit to the protections. They could potentially slow an attack and give the constables and enchanters an opportunity to regroup and prepare their additional defensive mechanisms.

Gavin turned, looking back at the city. "How protected is Yoran, really?"

"Is that your way of asking whether the enchanters have offered enough defenses against sorcery?"

"We're talking about powers that might be greater than the Fates," Gavin said. "I've seen the fortress, and I understand that Zella and her people want to defend the city, but how protected is it? Really."

Gaspar chuckled. He pointed to a cluster of weeds not too far from them. "Do you see that?"

"I do."

"Do you *feel* it?"

Gavin frowned, then headed over to what looked like little more than blades of grass mixed with some creeping vines. But as he approached, he started to feel something else. Power emanated from it.

His eyes widened. "*This* is the enchantment?"

"Do you see anything else within it?" Gaspar asked.

Gavin crouched down and began to draw on his core reserves, pushing that energy into his eyes so that he could augment his vision. As he did, he realized that there was something there. Several somethings, really—small sculptures made of stone.

"Golems."

Gaspar motioned to a small group of trees. "Look over there."

The trees had been here the entire time Gavin had lived in Yoran, or at least he thought they had. As he neared, he realized that the trees might've been, but the shrubs between them were obviously enchanted. They seemed to be made out of twisted ropelike vines with sticks woven within them. All of the shrubs radiated the energy of an enchantment. And staggered throughout the little copse of trees was a series of small golems.

"It's like this all around here," Gaspar said. "So if your question is whether the city has a way of defending itself, I would argue that there are mechanisms in place. We haven't had to test it, but you can be damn sure that Davel and the enchanters have been working diligently to ensure Yoran's safety. If there's a threat, they have ways of protecting themselves."

Gavin breathed a small sigh of relief. "I hadn't paid that much attention before."

"It's better defended than any place I've ever seen," Gaspar said, his voice soft. "I can't help but feel a measure of pride at what they've done. They've created so many layers that there shouldn't be any way that people can get through here."

It might be enough to stop powerful sorcerers, but would it stop the power of the old gods? That was what they might be dealing with now. And if not... Gavin didn't know what they would have to do.

"It's impressive," Gavin said.

Gaspar nodded. "It's more than impressive. It would keep pretty much anyone from the Society out, and probably several someones, if they decide to make a full-on assault. I can't say what it would do against somebody like the Fates, but it would certainly slow them down and give Zella and the others a chance to break out her *other* defense mechanism."

Gavin looked back to the city. The semarrl were dark creatures that siphoned power from those with magic, and they were trapped in a box within the fortress. He hoped that Zella would never have to use them, but if it came down to it, Gavin was thankful that she had the semarrl as some way to defend themselves from the kind of power the Fates had.

"All of this is meant to be a delaying tactic," Gavin said.

"Whether it's a delaying tactic or just their way of protecting themselves, *you* had them set this up. It's because of you that they were able to ensure that they have the necessary defenses."

"I created some defenses, but not all of them."

He had also tested the barrier, helping them fortify it and making sure that if there were weaknesses, then they would know where they were. Now these enchantments were buried in the ground so that anybody coming here wouldn't be able to easily see them circling the city, but they weren't completely invisible. There was still the possibility that somebody with enough power would recognize the enchantments and destroy them.

"Come on," Gaspar said. "We were doing something."

"This is something," Gavin said.

"It would be something more if you had a way of adding to it. The others are wrong. If you are El'aras"— Gaspar grinned as he said it—"then having your own enchantments would be beneficial. Can you imagine what it might mean for somebody like you to add to what was already done?"

"I don't have any way of adding enchantments. I've started to understand how to take them over, but adding to them is beyond me."

"Maybe when the El'aras come, you can work on that," Gaspar said.

"I don't have a feeling that's how they want to teach me to use my abilities," Gavin said. "I was with them in Arashil. They were more interested in trying to get me to understand how to call power out through me, using the same way they do, but my connection to my El'aras abilities is distinctly different. It's what defended me against the nihilar, but it also separates me from the rest of the El'aras. I don't know if I'd be able to use the same techniques they do."

"You won't know until you try."

The only person who'd ever really offered him any insight on how to create enchantments was Alana. She'd mentioned putting her power into it, creating a desire, and then commanding the enchantment to take that shape. Gavin didn't know if that would work for him. Knowing what he did about his own El'aras power, he should have taken more time to try to understand it so that he could find a way to create his own enchantments. They would be beneficial for multiple reasons, not the least if he were too fatigued to draw upon his own core reserves. And he might be able to create enchantments that were useful in ways that the enchanters could not replicate.

They continued onward. As they made their way away from Yoran, Gavin found himself looking back and searching for more signs of protections. He found several other clumps of what looked to be weeds, other groups of trees, and other places that he now began to suspect were defense postures surrounding the city. One tilted rock had what looked like a face carved on it, and he could easily imagine Mekel placing that enchantment there, ready for quick activation.

"How would they trigger them?" Gavin asked, suddenly realizing what troubled him.

"That's on Zella," Gaspar said. "To be honest, I wasn't sure it would work, but I think she's tested it several times. If somebody attempts to come through the barrier without having the appropriate clearance, the enchantments will activate."

"They would just simply activate like that?"

"I don't know if there's anything *simple* about it," Gaspar said. "From what I understand, a matter of intent is involved. I don't really get it, and they haven't been able to explain it to me. It has something to do with enchantments added to each of them."

"Wait. There is more than one enchantment on each of them?"

"Several," Gaspar said. "There's the primary defense enchantment, but then they have something else added to it—one that lets them activate it, one to allow them to detect intention, and..." He shrugged. "To be honest, I don't know all the keys to it. I just care that it works."

Gavin nodded in appreciation. This was more than he had ever believed possible with enchantments. There were places in the world where the people believed that enchantments were inherently weaker than anything a sorcerer could do, but it had been Gavin's experience that this wasn't the case. Everything he had seen about enchantments, and especially the kind that had been used in Yoran, suggested that they were incredibly powerful. The enchantments Mekel made had helped Gavin defend himself against Jayna when she had attacked. Her Toral power was unlike that of sorcery, far greater than anything they had dealt with while in the city.

Gavin and Gaspar reached the series of rocks that created the opening down into the temple, which obscured the entrance and made it nearly invisible. As Gavin looked back at the city, he wondered if the entrance being hidden even mattered.

Gaspar clasped him on the shoulder. "You don't have to keep looking back there like that."

"I can't shake my concern," Gavin said. "Ancient evil, fire, gods... All of that seems impossible to even fathom."

Gaspar scoffed. "It *is* impossible to fathom. But you've seen even more impossible-to-fathom things in your time since coming to Yoran."

"As have you."

They started toward the temple and descended the stairs.

Gavin felt a surge of tight energy around him.

He froze, then quickly reached for the El'aras dagger. It was glowing grayish blue.

The last time it had done that was in the forest.

He spun and looked behind him on the stairs, half expecting to see seeker trees coming out of the nearby forest and marching toward him, or perhaps converging on Yoran.

There was nothing.

"What did you detect?" Gaspar asked.

It was a measure of the trust that had formed between them over the years that Gaspar didn't hesitate. He didn't even question that Gavin had picked up on something.

"Look at the dagger," Gavin said.

"If it's not the trees…"

"If it's not the trees, then it's sorcery."

And then Gavin saw it.

Power—an orange glow that was building.

And it was coming toward them.

CHAPTER EIGHT

The orange glow looked like a fireball. That was the only thing Gavin could comprehend.

He darted forward and immediately began to draw upon the El'aras ring. He tried to think about the lessons he had learned during his time with the El'aras, wanting to prepare himself for an attack. Drawing energy through the ring should be fairly straightforward. There was nothing complicated about it. There were no patterns involved like there was for the rest of the El'aras, and it was certainly not the way sorcerers demonstrated their magic.

Gavin simply created power and pushed it outward. The advantage of the El'aras ring was that it was incredibly strong, and it allowed him to connect to something far greater than he could with his own core reserves. Not that he had endless supplies of power, though. There were limits. Even with the ring, he had to be careful not to exceed what he could do.

But for now, all he needed was to deflect that fireball.

Gavin let his power blast outward. The fireball struck the barrier he had created around him, and then it sizzled, fading completely.

He sprinted forward.

Gaspar stayed next to him. "What do you think we have here?"

"Probably a sorcerer, but I don't know why they would come at us like this."

His mind went to the different sorcerers they had dealt with so far, including the Fates. Maybe they had grown tired of waiting to get their revenge for what Gavin had done. Or maybe they had sent someone else on their behalf.

"Unless they know there's something here," Gaspar said.

"Unless they know," Gavin agreed.

As he raced, he could feel the sorcery beginning to build again. The sensation was like a tightness along his skin, and the El'aras dagger shimmered more brightly than before.

"We have to defend the temple," he said.

The nihilar had attacked Yoran not all that long ago, using some strange enchantment that had drawn that dark energy, but Gavin still didn't have an answer as to why. They were after something, but he had no idea why they'd come out here or what they might have been after.

He grabbed for his El'aras sword. Against a sorcerer,

he wasn't sure if the dagger or the sword or his own inherent El'aras abilities would be most effective, but these days, he increasingly felt more comfortable having the blade in his hand.

He squeezed it and pushed power out from him, through the ring, and into the blade. It glowed with the strange gray energy that was a combination of his El'aras abilities and the nihilar that filled the ring.

A burst of heat came from behind him. A part of Gavin's mind locked onto the concern about fire. There was that threat Anna had mentioned about ancient evil and fire, but he didn't have time to process it much.

He had to react.

He spun, driving his blade forward, thinking that he might catch the sorcerer. But he was gone.

Somewhere near him, Gaspar grunted. "They have me wrapped in those stupid bands of power!" he shouted.

If their communication enchantment had been working, then perhaps it would have been easier to hear Gaspar, but otherwise it sounded as if he were trying to call through muted energy.

Gavin raced toward the sound of the old thief's voice and found him standing in front of a sorcerer. He tried to carve at the red rope that worked its way up and around Gaspar, but it did nothing. It was almost as if his blade didn't matter against that kind of magic.

Instead, Gavin focused on his own power.

He needed control.

It was what the El'aras had been working with him on, trying to get him to understand the control within himself and trying to get him to master his own magic. But Gavin had not had the time or the ability, so even now, as he tried to summon that power, he couldn't feel whether he would be able to call enough to him.

He tried a different approach instead.

He simply blasted his magic outward. His burst struck the sorcerer and sent him tumbling back. He slammed into stone with enough force that Gavin heard the stone crack. Gavin darted at him, planning to finish the sorcerer off with a single blow, but the man stepped forward and sent a wave of power outward. It twisted up Gavin's legs and wrapped around him, constricting him. He had felt something similar so many times before, and he immediately grew angry. He called power up from within himself and pushed it through the ring and through his core reserves.

The bands bulged, but they didn't release him.

That's new.

Gavin was the Chain Breaker. He hadn't expected that anybody would be able to contain him now that he had the power of the El'aras ring, especially infused with the nihilar as it was. But somehow, the sorcerer did.

The man remained quiet as he stared at Gavin, as if Gavin were merely there for amusement and not anything else.

Gavin could overwhelm this man. He *knew* he could.

He pushed power out from him again, but he encountered the same resistance that bulged against him and then constricted downward. As it bulged, he flew forward and tried to stab his attacker.

But the sorcerer disappeared.

It was as if he folded, using a similar technique as Chauvan.

Gavin spun. Gaspar didn't look like he was in any danger, but he needed to be careful.

"Any ideas?" Gaspar shouted.

"He's more powerful than most sorcerers. Maybe like Jayna?"

"Wouldn't she have warned you if she sent somebody here?"

Gavin shrugged. "I don't have the sense that she sends people. I have a feeling she's trying to fight people like this."

A dark sorcerer.

When he had dealt with Jayna, he knew she had been working against dark sorcery and hunting its users, so he knew there were sorcerers like that in the world. Gavin had never really differentiated between them before.

"Well... Oh." Gaspar grunted again, and bands of red light began to work their way around him once more.

They started to snake toward Gavin. As soon as they struck, Gavin immediately drew on the power of his core reserves and pushed outward through the ring. He worried about overusing his power, knowing he had to be careful about how much power he drew so that he could continue to defend himself.

He raced toward the sorcerer, only to find that he was gone again.

Each time that Gavin tried to get to him, he couldn't. The sorcerer was too fast.

But it wasn't just speed. It was the way he was calling on power. He was somehow folding himself, doing the same thing Chauvan did.

Nihilar.

This was a sorcerer, but he was using nihilar. That would explain why Gavin's technique was not as effective as it should have been.

He kept himself close to Gaspar. He didn't know if the old thief needed his help, but he wouldn't abandon him. Gaspar had managed to escape from his bindings.

Gavin circled around him. "Did you see where he went?"

"You're asking me? I'm having a hard enough time staying on my feet here. I thought maybe you saw him."

"I didn't. He's hiding. And he has the ability with nihilar."

Gavin struggled to see the sorcerer, and the only thing he was aware of was the sudden burst of magic near him.

It came from behind.

He turned, holding onto the power from his core reserves and the El'aras ring, and he let it continue to build. The energy surged up through him, and it exploded outward.

The magic washed over the attacker.

The effect was faint and subtle, but Gavin felt where the sorcerer was.

He drove his fist forward, El'aras dagger in hand. He jabbed at one attacker, then another. Each time he did, he felt something fighting against him.

But he also felt power building.

At first, he wasn't exactly sure what it was, only that he was aware of the energy continuing to rise within him, as well as the power building around him. He held his hands out, prepared to block, and felt the wash of energy as it was unleashed.

"I'm going to need your help," Gaspar said.

Gavin realized that he needed to offer more than just help.

Gaspar couldn't handle anything like this with his enchantments. The power was incredible. Gavin had never felt anything quite like it before. He had faced plenty of sorcerers before, but none like this.

"I'm using everything I can," Gavin said. "Nothing seems to be working."

"What kind of sorcerer is it?" Gaspar asked.

"I'm not even sure it's sorcery."

"If it's not, then what is it?"

Gavin couldn't answer. There was nothing Gavin could do. The only thing he could focus on was the way that power was filling him. He had felt it before, but not only that, he had *seen* it before—something within the power that struck and the fireball of energy that was exploding toward him.

Gavin held his hands out and braced himself, trying to trace out one of the El'aras patterns Anna had taught him, needing to have enough strength. He had to draw upon the energy of the El'aras ring and add all he could of the nihilar. He pushed power out from himself. His magic slammed into the strange burst of energy the sorcerer was using.

Gavin withstood the attack, but a blast struck him, sending him staggering back. He collapsed and tried to get to his feet. Gaspar raced toward him but got tangled.

"We need to get help," Gavin said.

"What kind of power do you think can help us?"

"Maybe Tristan?"

And Rayena, Brandon, or any El'aras who could fight a sorcerer.

Even they might not be enough.

Gavin needed enchantments.

He reached into his pouch, grabbed several of Mekel's stone figures, and hurriedly activated them. They rumbled to life, taking on their enormous size. One of them looked like a lumbering giant, another like a massive wolf, and the third like a lizard. All of them were designed to protect, and he hoped they would be able to attack.

Gavin braced himself by holding onto his power and connecting to the enchantments. He had to hope that the combination would work. He had to link the power of the enchantments and mix it with the power that came from his core reserves and the ring. He felt a strange energy around him, and he had to find some way to resist it.

"It's time to regroup," Gavin said.

He took up a space in between the enchantments, giving them a chance to do what they needed to. Gavin hoped the enchantments were powerful enough to withstand what was around them, but he didn't know. He drew upon the power within himself and the energy that connected him to the El'aras ring, and he felt the faint tremble of the nihilar buried within it. The combination should be enough.

He looked over to Gaspar. "I think—"

An explosion of power ripped stone free, and one of the enchantments shattered, Gavin's awareness of it torn from his mind. He hadn't even realized that the enchantment was linked into his mind that way, but he felt the weight fade from his consciousness with its sudden disappearance.

With little more than that, a sorcerer had ripped that connection free?

Gavin couldn't even fathom that kind of power.

He focused on different fighting styles, thinking about what might work here. Against sorcery, the simple fact of him being the Chain Breaker generally made a difference. But drawing on his core reserves and the El'aras ring was not going to be enough.

They weren't alone.

There were multiple sorcerers here.

He aimed the El'aras dagger at one of them and flicked it, sending it tumbling. The dagger pierced through a cloud of what Gavin had thought was the sorcerer, but they had folded themselves, and now there was nothing.

Another burst, and stone shrieked.

A second golem was ripped free.

There was no pain, just an awareness of what happened and the way that he was now separated from it. He tried not to think about how *he* felt that discomfort, but at least he understood what Mekel spoke of when he lost enchantments. There was a separation, even if Gavin didn't feel it quite the same way.

Another burst of energy came from nearby, and Gavin turned.

Could it be yet another sorcerer?

He had thought that he could handle any single one, but they had disabused him of that idea. But they weren't simple sorcerers. He was trained to handle many fighting styles, but this was something different. This was more than just a fighting style. He was dealing with sorcery and violence.

Another blast struck from somewhere else, and then the third stone enchantment exploded.

This one was painful when it was ripped free. The awareness shredded through him, tearing away his thoughts and every part of him that connected to the enchantment.

He staggered, but strange bands of magic constricted around him, holding him in place. Power built around him.

Gavin tried to surge out of it.

He could hear Gaspar saying something, but he couldn't make sense of what it was.

Gavin tried again. He could see little other than a faint cloud of dust around him, a hint of smoke that swirled, making it so that he could see nothing.

The distinct energy bands worked their way around him. He could feel each one as it twisted and turned, squeezing him. It was more than Gavin could rip free from. He was the Chain Breaker, but not as powerful as three sorcerers.

Gavin had had better luck against the Fates.

Which meant that these were more powerful than any sorcerers.

Were they Toral? Or worse—Sul'toral?

Gavin had faced a Sul'toral only once. That power was considerable, and perhaps it was similar to this, though he didn't remember it since others had fought with him.

He continued to struggle against those constricting bands. They worked up from his feet, around his thighs, and then squeezed his chest, making it so he could not breathe.

Something started to shift, and power pushed down on him and crushed him.

Somewhere nearby, Gaspar cried out.

Gavin tried to think through different techniques that Tristan had taught him, but nothing fit with what he faced now. There had been many times when Tristan had bound him in rope or chains, forcing Gavin to find a way to break free, but this was different. And it was different than any magical attack he had tried to break out of before.

He had the ring. He had nihilar.

He was the Chain Breaker. He was El'aras. And he was the Champion.

The pressure continued to build, squeezing him down, almost as if he were folding.

And then there was blackness.

CHAPTER NINE

The blackness lingered, and it seemed as if it did so for an impossibly long time.

Gavin fought against it, and he could feel the energy squeezing down on him. He strained, trying to overwhelm that pressure. It was building on him, crushing him, crumpling him. It was unlike anything he had ever experienced before.

As he felt that pain collapsing down on him, he struggled against it, searching for some way out. He had to find a way to get free, but all he felt was pressure, and all he saw was the darkness.

And then it faded.

The darkness eased rapidly, and then there was light all around him. Hot air gusted down upon him, which stunk. The bitter, foul aroma mixed with something acrid, something else that smelled like rot, and another stench he couldn't quite place.

"Get up," a voice said.

Gavin rolled, realizing that Gaspar stood next to him.

"What happened?"

"Gods if I know," Gaspar said.

Gavin scrambled to his feet, sword in hand, ready to fight.

But there was no sense of the sorcery around him. He spun in place, looking for the attackers and the clouds that suggested that the sorcerers were still here.

His blade didn't glow. The energy around him faded, and the air... That was the most distinct difference.

It had been rapid, almost impossibly so. He was fully aware of the change, and fully aware of how the power swirled around him. And yet, there was something here.

Gavin realized that the landscape had shifted.

The ground was barren, with no grasses, no trees, nothing like what had been there before. He didn't see the pile of boulders that indicated the opening into the underground hall. The only thing he was aware of was the shifting wind.

That and the hard, arid ground.

"Where are we?" Gavin asked.

"I was hoping you might be able to answer that. What happened back there?"

Gavin looked down at his legs, half expecting that he would have been broken in half, especially given that he felt like he'd been folded. But he seemed to be fully intact. The pain he had experienced seemed to have faded the moment he'd appeared here.

"I think they sent us somewhere."

"They? I only saw one sorcerer," Gaspar said.

"We only faced one, but I think there were three. At least, there were three distinct bands around me." He looked over to Gaspar. "And you were by me, so…"

He didn't know whether they had attacked Gaspar because Gavin was there, or if they had targeted both of them. Either way, Gavin knew they had to find some way back. But first they had to figure out where they were.

"Does anything here strike you as familiar?" he asked.

"Nothing. Never seen anything like this. You're the one who's traveled the most."

"I've traveled, but nothing like this."

"Did you know they could teleport like that?"

Gavin shrugged. "Chauvan disappeared on us before, so I knew there was a possibility they could travel like that, but I had never gone through it before."

And if it was possible, then why wouldn't more sorcerers do that? It indicated that the sorcerers' powers were even more significant than he had thought.

"I wonder who we faced," he said. "If I'm right, then those were Sul'toral."

Gaspar clenched his jaw. "But you defeated a Sul'toral before."

"I did, but I had help."

It had been the combination of the Champion and the Shard. Gavin didn't have that now. He might have access to his El'aras abilities and the ring and some connection to the nihilar, but he didn't have more than that.

"Anna gifted me some of the power of the Shard when I fought him before."

"But you have some other connection now."

"Some other," Gavin said. "But not enough. Not nearly enough."

If they were Sul'toral, that would explain why he and Gaspar hadn't been able to stop them. That kind of power was more than he had ever imagined before, and he had struggled against one. With three...

Gavin hadn't stood a chance.

It was almost enough to make him believe in the old gods that Rayena had mentioned. It had to be more than just Sarenoth, didn't it? Maybe there were other gods that could provide that kind of power.

"What now?" Gaspar said.

"Now we have to figure out where we are, and then we can figure out how to get out of here."

"What about your enchantments?"

Gavin reached into his pouch. He had the paper dragon, along with some of the other enchantments he had been given, so maybe they could use those. He tested the dragon, then started to activate it. Something within that enchantment seemed to fight him. Some part of its power felt as if it was resisting.

He tried to draw on more from his core reserves and the El'aras ring, but even as he did, there was too much pressure against him.

Finally, he shook his head.

"It didn't work," Gavin said. "I don't know if I used too much strength trying to fight off the sorcerers, or if there's something in this land that makes it so that my power doesn't work the same way. Either way, it didn't work."

Gaspar frowned. "I thought your ring power was limitless."

"Not exactly limitless, but far more than I normally have on my own. Even in that, I've come close to running out before."

When Gavin had been with the El'aras, he had access to sh'rasn powder, but he didn't have that any longer without Anna. Now he had to use his own core reserves, the ring, and whatever enchantments he could activate.

They couldn't linger here, though. There were three powerful sorcerers—and possibly Sul'toral—just outside of Yoran. They'd had little difficulty with Gavin. What would happen if they brought the fight into the city?

Gavin tapped on his enchantment. "Wrenlow."

There was no answer.

He had damaged the enchantment, and he knew there was a danger in that. He called on his core reserves and once again felt as if there was some barrier to him reaching his power. It felt similar to how he did when he drew on too much, as if his own core reserves were fading.

What about the nihilar?

He could still reach that power, couldn't he?

The ring had the energy of the nihilar trapped within it. Gavin didn't know how to use that energy exclusively, though he could feel it, and he thought that maybe he could tap into that power and use it. He'd never attempted to separate it out, never thought to draw upon only the nihilar. As he tried, he felt that power build. Would it actually work?

It started to fade, and then it disappeared, leaving him with nothing.

"That doesn't work," Gavin said.

Gaspar grunted. "Then we walk."

Gavin didn't like being gone that long with the danger near Yoran, but what choice did they have? He looked up at the sky, toward the hazy clouds obscuring the sunlight, and saw no sign of anything to guide him. He didn't know what direction he would need to go in.

He pursed his lips. "I don't know if we have to go north or south, east or west."

"We'd better figure out where we are," Gaspar said, "and then we can figure what we need to do to get out of here. Maybe as you recover, your connection to the enchantments will recuperate enough that you can activate them."

"What about you?" Gavin held out the dragon to him.

Gaspar took it and clenched his jaw as if he were trying to do something, but nothing changed within the enchantment. Finally, he handed it back to Gavin. "I think it only responds to you."

"It's an enchantment. I'm not exactly sure it matters who activates it."

"But it's one that Alana made for you. I don't know much about them, but I do know that there is something about the way that girl does it that's different than others."

Alana did have a different connection to enchantments, and she had a unique way of using them. It was possible that Gaspar was right.

Gavin tried again and again. Each time he attempted to trigger the enchantment, there was no response. Finally, he gave up and stuffed it back into his pocket.

He sheathed his sword and his dagger and looked over to Gaspar. "I guess we do have to walk."

"What about your other enchantments?"

Gavin had several others on him, including those for strength, speed, and stone skin.

"I have some, but…"

He focused on the one for strength, and he pushed off in a jump. It carried him up into the air higher than he would go without it, but still not as high as he would've expected from the enchantment.

"So the enchantments are limited as well," Gaspar said.

"It seems that way."

Gaspar frowned deeply. "How many do you have on you?"

"Maybe a dozen," Gavin said.

"Same. Our enchantments are limited, we don't know where we are, and we don't know how long it's going to take for us to get back. We should preserve them."

"I agree, unfortunately."

It made sense to avoid drawing on that power at this point, until they knew what they were dealing with.

He spun in place, and a dark cloud overhead caught his attention.

Not a cloud.

Something flying in their direction.

Gavin pointed. "I don't know what that is. Some sort of—"

The thing turned toward them, then shrieked as it dove.

"I guess that answers that," Gavin muttered, withdrawing his sword again.

They might need to use their enchantments sooner than he realized.

He braced himself. Next to him, Gaspar had his knives out, which likely wouldn't be as useful as something with a longer reach. They would have to find Gaspar better weapons.

As the creature dove, it gave Gavin a chance to survey it. The thing was enormous, with a wingspan about ten feet across, with a long, sharp head, a whiplike tail, and talons that looked like they could shred them with barely a scratch.

"Avoid anything sharp," Gavin said.

Gaspar grunted. "I generally do."

"Maybe we need to run."

Gaspar stared for a moment and then nodded. He took off sprinting.

They hurried away from the creature. It shrieked again, and Gavin hazarded a glance up as it dove directly toward them. Once it neared, he rolled to the side and jabbed upward with his sword.

The blade met some resistance. It was similar to what Gavin felt when he tried to call on his core reserves or draw energy through the ring. He shoved harder, wondering if this was just what it was like to fight without those core reserves and to have to use only his own strength.

The sword went into the creature's belly.

It wrapped its wings around Gavin, who pushed off, drawing through his enchantment for strength and finally managing to get free. He yanked back his blade, shook some blood off, and staggered. He felt strangely wobbly, which was odd, given that he didn't think he was hurt.

"Did it get you?"

Gaspar's voice seemed to come from a great distance. Gavin looked around and then stumbled again. Gaspar grabbed him and kept him from falling.

"Boy?"

"I don't think it got me."

"Something isn't right," Gaspar said.

"I don't know," Gavin managed to get out.

"It's this place. Nothing here is quite right. You look like you're going to fall over."

"I feel like it too."

"Do you know why?"

Gavin shook his head. "Can't tell you that. All I can say is that…"

He staggered forward once more, and this time the fall wasn't so much of a threat—he *did* fall. Gaspar tried to help him get back to his feet.

Gavin looked up, smiling tightly. "Things aren't working quite right, Gaspar."

"What happened?"

Gavin blinked, and his vision cleared for a moment, but little more than that.

Everything was blurry. He looked down at himself, half anticipating that he'd see some massive bleeding wound. There had to be some terrible injury to leave him with this kind of reaction. Gavin saw no blood. He just felt strange, as if he had taken significant damage.

He looked up at Gaspar and tried to clear his vision.

"It wrapped its wings around me," Gavin said. "But I got free."

"You got its blood on your hands," Gaspar said.

"I got... *what?*"

"Blood. We have to get it off of you. Take off your cloak."

Gavin peeled off his cloak and was only distantly aware of Gaspar blotting at his hands, face, and neck. He even seemed to dig into Gavin's ears. When he was done, Gaspar teetered for a moment, stepping back and dropping the cloak.

"Damn, boy. It's the blood."

Gavin could feel the wooziness starting to ease, and the blurriness that had been obscuring his vision finally lifted a little bit.

"Blood?" he said. He still struggled to comprehend what Gaspar was saying to him. The dizziness faded, though not completely. Part of him remained off, but he couldn't quite place what it was. Something had affected him.

"You need to get up," Gaspar said.

Gavin stumbled as he attempted to get to his feet, everything within him feeling numb.

"We don't know how much time we have before

another attack comes," Gaspar said. There was an edge to his voice, and a note of seriousness that wasn't always there. It was mixed with concern. "I need your blade, boy."

Gavin closed his eyes for a moment, and he focused on the parts of himself. His core reserves. The El'aras ring. The nihilar. As he focused on all that, he could feel some bit of him return again. It was as if that emptiness had started to fade and evaporate. The dizziness eased even more, and Gavin began to work past it, finding a sense of relief.

Finally, he took a deep breath and let it out slowly, then opened his eyes and looked back at Gaspar. "I think I'm better."

"Good. I'm not so sure I want to take those things on by myself." Gaspar chuckled, glancing to the sky. "Not saying I could, either."

"I've never experienced anything quite like that before. I don't even think I was injured."

"You've seen that you don't have to be injured to be affected by certain things. It was almost like I was—"

"Enchanted," Gavin said.

Gaspar shook his head. "I was going to say poisoned, but maybe enchanted. Can't say that I know." He had Gavin's cloak on the ground, and there was a smudge of the creature's blood on it.

"I don't want to leave the cloak behind."

"You want to carry it, even knowing that it might affect you again?"

"It's El'aras made," Gavin explained.

"I don't care if it's made of gold, I just know how it affected you."

"I'm not sure it was the cloak, or what was on my hands, or…"

Gavin just didn't know. And he wasn't about to abandon his cloak. He didn't know what the weather was going to be like here, out in the open in a place where he had no idea what they might encounter.

He took a cautious step forward, testing to make sure that he didn't stumble again, and was thankful he didn't. He crouched down and began to fold the cloak, wrapping the blood-soaked section into the middle until he formed a bundle where the blood didn't penetrate.

"You get to carry that, boy."

Gavin shrugged. "When we find water—"

"You mean if?" Gaspar looked around. "A place like this looks too arid to have much water. If we find any, we're going to want to drink it, maybe find a way to store it. We don't have much in the way of preparations."

The suddenness of the Sul'toral attack had caught them off guard. Neither of them was ready for a long journey. Gavin was always prepared for a fight, but this felt like something else entirely. They had no food or water or any supplies. They had a limited number of enchantments, and this place seemed to be dangerous. And worse, they were short on time. The sorcerers would reach Yoran and attack. Gavin didn't know how long the city's defenses would protect the people, but he doubted it would be indefinite.

"Let's get moving," Gavin said, struggling to spit out

his words. It felt like his tongue was too thick for his mouth.

"I want to stay away from those creatures." Gaspar glanced at the sky. "If you see anything…"

Gavin snorted. Those creatures were easy enough for them to see.

They started walking. He kept the cloak folded underneath his arm, tucking it against himself. At one point, he thought he saw another shadow move across the sky, but they paused and waited until it was gone. Gavin didn't know how those creatures detected prey—if they were aware of movement or if they hunted by sight—but felt it was best just to give it time.

They moved so steadily that it felt as if they were making slow progress, though Gavin didn't know how much of that came from the fact that he had been using enchantments to move more quickly lately. Some of it could also be tied to this place and whatever resistance it had to him drawing on his core reserves and other forms of magic.

The landscape was bleak, and everything felt empty to him, leaving him wondering where they were exactly. In the distance, he caught sight of a set of tall, thin trees that looked irregular, as though they had dried out. It was the first change in the scenery so far, and Gavin wasn't sure if he should head toward them. The trees seemed as if they had been poisoned in some way, but maybe they had just baked in the heat of the sun.

"Have you ever heard of any place suppressing magic like we've experienced?" Gavin asked.

"Not that I know of," Gaspar said.

"I haven't heard of anything like that before, either. I think it would've been useful knowledge to have when I was first learning how to fight."

"It seems to me that Tristan didn't want you to have all the knowledge you could," Gaspar said. "I've now spent a little time around him. Unfortunately, I feel like he knew exactly what he was doing. He kept things from you. There are not too many reasons to hide information from a person who's growing in their skills. Either he thought it was the best way to train you, or he worried what would happen if you learned so he wanted to maintain control over you."

Gavin looked over to him. "You say that as if you have some experience with that."

"I have experience with men who think they can hide things. It's not always for your benefit. Most the time, it's for *their* benefit."

"I had that same feeling."

"When I see you around him, I don't see that same fighter," Gaspar said.

"What are you getting at?"

"Well…" Gaspar paused, and Gavin had the sense that he was trying to pick his words carefully. "You don't seem to me like you're questioning him as you do most people."

Gavin wanted to argue with him, but maybe Gaspar was onto something. He was too close to all of it. When it came to Tristan, he did have some issues. Maybe that was what Gaspar was trying to get at. He wanted Gavin to recognize his blind spots and be prepared. Or maybe it was more than that.

"You think that all of this was to somehow benefit Tristan."

Gaspar grunted. "And you don't? A man like him doesn't do things for altruistic reasons. He's been trying to find the so-called Champion for years, but for what reason?"

He fell silent, and they neared the broken forest in the distance.

"You have to start to look at what benefit he might have from all of this," Gaspar said. "There's no doubt in my mind there's a benefit to him, and it's just a matter of understanding what it is, what he thinks to gain from it, and why he chose you. Once we figure that out, then you can start to piece together what to do."

For so long, Gavin had thought that it was a matter of Tristan just trying to train him, but perhaps Gaspar was right. If Tristan had been after something else, something more than just the Champion, he might still be holding something back from Gavin.

"First, we have to get out of here," Gavin said.

Gaspar scoffed. "We do, but maybe we need to figure out where *here* is so that we can do it."

He pulled something from his pocket. For a moment Gavin thought it was going to be a knife, but it wasn't. Instead, it was a small cylindrical enchantment. Gaspar tapped on it, as if he were trying to find some rhythmic pattern he could use, or somehow summon, but...

"You're calling to Imogen," Gavin said.

"If I had many other options, I'm not sure I would. I just wanted to try anything we could."

"Are you sure you should?"

Gaspar shrugged. "I know she is off with her brother to lead him back to the Leier homeland, but I'd like to at least speak to her. The last time I really had a conversation with Imogen was after her brother had killed a Toral—"

"What?"

Gavin hadn't heard the story. But then, when he had returned to Yoran, he hadn't been focused on what Imogen was up to. When he had left, he'd believed that Imogen was going to leave. She had needed to find her own way. After completing her quest of stopping the hyadan and destroying the keystone, she had needed purpose.

"I didn't tell you?" Gaspar shook his head. "No. Damn. I guess I didn't. Well, he attacked a Toral."

"By himself?" Gavin asked. That didn't strike him as being like the young man he had seen. Imogen's brother was skilled, like most of their kind, but not as skilled as she was. Gavin had a hard time thinking that even Imogen would take on a Toral on her own.

Gaspar nodded. "By himself. I have a sense that Imogen wasn't too thrilled with it. She left with him. She felt as if he needed help. I don't know what she thought she could do, but she seemed to believe that returning to her homeland, and to her people, would give her some way of getting through to him."

"And now you think you can reach her?"

"I've tried to communicate with her periodically,"

Gaspar admitted. "I told her that I would leave her alone and let her find her way, but the longer she's been gone, the more I find that I want to know she's doing well." He looked up at Gavin. "Does that make any sense?"

"You care about her. Of course it makes sense."

"I don't care about her like that," Gaspar said.

Gavin shook his head. "You don't have to explain it to me. She's a friend. I have friends. Well, now I do. I understand."

Gaspar regarded him for a long moment. "I suppose you do, boy."

Gavin watched as Gaspar continued to tap on the enchantment, but from what he could tell, there was no response. Besides, with everything around them seeming to suppress any enchantments and any magic, Gavin couldn't help but feel as if there was something here that tied them differently to this place.

"Has she responded?"

"She's never responded. Most of the time, I try to tell myself that it's because she's busy doing whatever it is she is doing and that she's needed where she is. And that she's safe."

"Most of the time?"

Gaspar took a deep breath and then let it out slowly. "Most," he said. "Sometimes I start to question whether something happened to her. She's with her brother, and I saw the look in his eyes when he was here. You only knew him for a little while, but after you left, he seemed different. I've known men like that. He had the look of murder in his eyes. He wanted to chase those he blamed for his position in the world."

Knowing what he did about the Leier, Gavin understood what that meant—chasing after sorcerers.

But that wasn't it. At least, that wasn't all of it. Timo had wanted to chase after more than just sorcerers. He'd been upset that Gavin had been the one to stop L'aran, a Sul'toral.

"Even the two of them shouldn't be able to take on a Sul'toral," Gavin said.

Imogen was skilled with her sword and could handle herself. He had seen her take care of sorcerers with little difficulty, but going against a sorcerer was different than going against a Sul'toral. That would be out of her depth.

"She knows," Gaspar said, "which is why she tried to get her brother to return to their homeland."

"And then what will she do?"

Gaspar frowned. "I don't know."

As they neared the trees, Gaspar finally put the enchantment back into his pocket.

What Gavin would have given to have that team back together. When he and Gaspar had traveled with Rayena, Brandon, and Tristan, they had been a competent group. But there was something about having Gavin's old team together. Gaspar. Imogen. Wrenlow. Gods, there were others aside from Tristan and the El'aras that he imagined would be far more capable at fighting alongside him.

He pushed that thought aside. It was time to focus on what they needed. They had to find some way out of this place, but as they searched, Gavin began to wonder if that would even be possible.

He tapped on the communication enchantment again, whispering Wrenlow's name, but there was no response. He lowered his hands, and then he felt something. It was a hint of power.

Sorcery.

He looked over to Gaspar, then turned his attention to what he believed to be the north. Away from the forest.

"What is it, boy?"

"Well, if I'm not mistaken, I just detected sorcery," Gavin said.

"Let me guess. You want to go toward it?"

"Considering how we've been wandering aimlessly until this point, going toward anything we can find is probably in our best interest. Especially since we have no idea what's here or how to get out of here. Maybe we need to go just so we can figure out if there's going to be some way to escape."

Gaspar regarded him for a moment, then nodded. "I don't like it, but I'm starting to think we don't have much of a choice."

They would find the sorcerer, or someone else who could use magic, in this wasteland, and then they would force that person to help them return.

If nothing else, at least they now had a plan.

CHAPTER TEN

The air crackled with energy.

Gavin had slipped on all of his enchantments, at least all that would fit, so that now bracelets circled both wrists, rings adorned several fingers, and a necklace with a small medallion rested against his chest. He could draw on the enchantments, but only faintly, and he worried that if he didn't have enough power, he might not be able to handle a sorcerer.

But then, he had handled sorcerers before without knowing about his magical abilities. There had to be some way for him to defend himself against what was out there and what was coming, so he had to think that if they could at least get to the sorcerer, then they could figure out some other way.

Gaspar had done the same with his enchantments and now had both knives in hand. He moved with a bit more fluidity than before.

"You should be careful calling on your enchantments too soon," Gavin said.

"Like you're one to talk. As soon as you put those on, you started to stride forward as if you were filled with your power again."

"I wasn't trying to use the enchantment."

"You may not have to try," Gaspar said. "Just having them on you changes things."

Gavin looked down at what he wore. Most of them were simple metal enchantments, and the symbols for the power that had been pushed into them by the enchanters were either exposed or pressed against his skin. He found that the ones with the enchanted symbol pressed directly to his skin were far more potent than the others. He ran his hands along a few, which were cool to the touch despite being wrapped around him.

"Still," Gavin said.

Gaspar glanced over to him. "Let's say this is a sorcerer. Maybe even one who sent us out here. Are you ready to take that on again?"

"I'm ready to do whatever we have to."

"Out there," Gaspar said, thumbing as if pointing to where he believed Yoran was, "you had the full spectrum of your abilities. You weren't limited, not like you are here. You were able to be the Chain Breaker. Do you think you can do that again?"

"I don't know," Gavin admitted. "I'll do whatever I can to try."

He had no choice.

They'd been walking for the better part of several

hours by his estimation. The Sul'toral would have attacked Yoran by now. Even if they managed to get back, it would be too late. Their only hope was to return and see how much damage had been inflicted on the city. He had to hope that its protections would be enough of a defense. If not, the city might already be destroyed.

"We either get through this or die," Gavin said.

Gaspar snorted. "You never do anything half-assed, do you?"

"Not like that."

"Well, maybe your plans are," Gaspar muttered.

"I'm not really making a plan this time."

"And you prove my point."

Gavin chuckled. "Are you ready to make a run at this?"

"You're not giving me a lot of choice in the matter, are you?"

"You don't have to come with me. Maybe you can stay back here by some of those trees. They look pretty."

Gaspar looked over his shoulder at the bizarre trees, his brow furrowing and his frown deepening. "You call *those* pretty?"

"I call them something."

"I think I'd rather go with you."

The sense of sorcery continued to build. Gavin hadn't been completely sure what he had felt at first, but the longer they made their way to what seemed to be north, the more certain he was that it was sorcery. And if it was, the fact that somebody had the ability to use that kind of magic here, in this place that suppressed everything within him, was surprising. If he could learn the trick of it, he could figure out what they were doing and maybe use something similar. If not, Gavin was willing to cut them down.

They reached a small rise, and then the ground trembled.

Gavin grabbed Gaspar and jerked him back.

The stone in front of them started to emerge from the ground.

The enchantment was enormous, appearing as though it were completely made of rocks, but with a detailed face. It had ears that looked like they were made of twigs woven together, as well as dark eyes that seemed to swallow the daylight.

"What the hell is that?" Gaspar cried.

"Some sort of enchantment."

"I have never seen anything like that before."

"Well, you saw something like that when we faced the Sul'toral," Gavin said.

"Not like that. Look at it."

The massive thing towered over them. It had to be over forty feet tall and seemed to radiate a strange sort of energy. The creature moved toward them, and it felt surprisingly appropriate to call it a creature and not an enchantment. In that, Gavin thought maybe Gaspar was right. There was something about this thing that felt different.

It lumbered, but it did so with a surprising fluidity. The thing turned toward them, as if aware that they were standing there.

Then it threw a boulder at them.

The stone was easily as large as Gavin and Gaspar if they were balled up together, and they had to jump off to the side to avoid the blow.

Gavin sprung to his feet and spun around.

"Do you have any suggestions?" Gaspar asked.

"If this is an enchantment..." Gavin frowned. There was something about the way the creature moved that left him wondering whether it really was an enchantment. Enchantments didn't have this kind of fluidity in their movements. This was more like the seeker trees and how they had moved through the forest, impossibly alive, not like enchantments. "We have to disrupt it. That should allow us to stop it."

That said nothing about trying to destroy it. Gavin had no idea if they would be able to. Even with his full abilities, he couldn't. It would be too large. His sword wouldn't cut through it, and even with drawing upon the El'aras ring and the nihilar, he had a hard time thinking he would have enough power to do that.

"I'll follow your lead here," Gaspar said.

"I'm not so sure you should," Gavin said.

He darted, trying to get behind the creature. It twisted and looked down at them, then threw another boulder. The gigantic rock tumbled toward Gavin, who had to jump out of the way again to stay clear of it. If one hit him, he wouldn't survive. His core reserves would heal him in normal circumstances, but with his abilities muted, it was likely that a strike like that would crush him.

"We need to tangle it up," Gaspar said. He was

crouched as if trying to confront some wild beast rather than this monstrosity.

The creature turned toward him, and Gaspar scurried forward and then scrambled between its legs. He moved fast—enchanted fast—and as he raced between the creature's legs, it bent forward like it was trying to reach down.

It fell forward.

"Move," Gaspar said, grabbing Gavin.

"Your plan is to outrun it?"

"I don't have a plan. I thought I would do things the Gavin way. Move."

"If that thing gets up…"

"What do you mean *if*? I didn't kill it. I just knocked it down. Well, it knocked itself down. Now move."

Gaspar had the right of it. If they could keep ahead of the creature, they might be able to knock it down and stay away from it. There was still the danger of sorcery somewhere in the distance, and though he had no idea where it was, he did feel it. It wasn't tied to this boulder monster.

The sound of rumbling began to build behind them once again.

"It's getting up," Gavin said.

"I told you it would, and I also told you we have to keep moving," he said, pushing Gavin along. "The creature isn't down, so just get going."

They raced down the hillside. For the first time since they'd started working together, the old thief managed to run just as fast as Gavin without any prodding. Gaspar needed to be more careful. He had to be drawing on all of his enchantments.

The rumbling persisted, and the air whistled.

Gavin shoved Gaspar out of the way, and they both sprawled to the ground as a boulder came whipping past their heads. Gavin leapt to his feet and charged toward the monster the same way that Gaspar had.

The creature swung one arm toward him. Gavin danced out of the way, then slipped in between its legs. It grabbed for him and managed to wrap a thick hand around him.

Gavin had enchantments, but he dove into the connection that he normally had with his core reserves, along with the El'aras ring power and the nihilar. That combination was there. As Gavin grabbed for that energy, he could feel it building up.

He sent it out from him. There wasn't much, and the power was muted. But even muted, at least Gavin had *something*.

He took his El'aras dagger—it was the only blade he could reach against a creature like this—and jabbed it into the stone monster's hand.

Gavin was surprised when it let him go.

That was a pain response.

This wasn't an enchantment. It was an actual creature.

Gods. What have we gotten ourselves into?

The thing tried to spin, but because it had one hand between its legs, it got tangled up and stumbled. Gavin raced back and reached Gaspar, who was looking at the boulder that had missed them.

"I've never seen anything quite like this," Gaspar said. He rested his hand on the rock. "But it's smooth and warm."

Gavin shook his head. "I'm not sure what this is. It's some sort of creature. When I stabbed its hand, it let me go."

"So that's not an enchantment?" Gaspar pulled his hand free from the boulder and turned to look at the stone monster. "What kind of thing is that?"

"I have no idea."

Facing something like that...

Gavin had trained to handle all sorts of things, but he had never trained to fight monsters or learned how to deal with that kind of power. Having this creature in front of him now left him feeling incredibly inadequate.

Unprepared.

A twisted thought came to him. "I wonder what Tristan would think if he knew I was going to need to use my fighting style to deal with a stone monster like that," Gavin said.

"Why don't you ask him. When we get back."

"If."

Gaspar frowned at him.

The creature got to its feet again and turned toward them.

"Any thoughts?" Gavin asked.

"You said you hurt it."

"Its hand."

Gaspar pursed his lip. "Well, you hadn't attacked

because you assumed it was made out of rock. Maybe it is, but if it's also alive…"

Gavin got what he was getting at. He sheathed his dagger, brought out his sword, and raced toward the creature. This time, he confronted it with a different intention.

Not to run, not to hide, but to find an opening.

Everything had a weakness. The creature had already shown that its hand was sensitive. That meant there was an exposed area.

What about its legs? If Gavin could hamstring it, it might fall. But even that might not work.

What about its head? Mouth and eyes were always sensitive areas, but he didn't know for sure.

The creature swung its hand at Gavin again. He ducked and then quickly shifted direction. He stabbed with his sword. The blade sliced across the creature's hand.

It cried out. The strange, trembling sound sent the stone rumbling all around it.

Gavin felt it throughout his body. It was almost as if the thing were connected to some deeper part of the earth.

The creature kicked. Gavin rolled to the side, springing up and bringing his blade around to try to connect with its leg. His El'aras blade bounced off. It was too hard for even this sword, at least when Gavin didn't have access to his core reserves or his El'aras ring. With those, he wondered if he might be able to pour enough energy into the blade. That might penetrate the creature's stone hide.

Without that, Gavin had to find another opening. He knew he had to target its hands.

The creature spun toward him. When it swiped, Gavin jumped. Again, he didn't jump with nearly as much power as he usually would. As he lunged forward, the air squeezed down on him, as if any energy he was using to fight as he normally did was holding him back. But the blade punctured the creature's palm.

It jerked back again and took a reeling step back.

That was a victory.

As the monster staggered away, Gavin redoubled his efforts. He jumped again, trying to scramble onto the creature's arm, but he could not reach it.

Something struck him—maybe a small boulder—and Gavin went flying backward. Once he rolled to a stop, he leapt to his feet again with his blade held out.

The creature was looking at him.

"It looks like you got its attention," Gaspar said.

"I could use help!" Gavin shouted.

Gaspar grunted. "I don't know that I'm going to be a whole lot of help against something like that. You can go ahead and take it on."

"I have been. Its hands are sensitive. I've been trying to target its eyes and mouth, but everything is too hard to reach."

"Let me try something."

"What are you—"

Gaspar didn't give him a chance to finish and went

racing toward the creature. When it spun toward him, Gavin feigned moving in one direction, before darting forward and twisting between the creature's legs. Gaspar rolled, and as the creature reached for him, he dodged and then stabbed with his El'aras sword.

The stone monster tumbled. It curled into a ball and went rolling forward, and it eventually came to a rest.

Gavin sprang into action. Now that the creature was down, he didn't have to jump quite so high to get into its range. He hurried, wanting to get to it before it began to get to its feet, and he darted into its field of view. When it turned toward him, he slammed his blade forward to try to catch the stone monster in its eye. It turned its head at the last moment. Gavin's blade landed on the side of its head and went into its ear.

The shriek that thundered was overwhelming.

Gavin tried to pull his sword out, but it was stuck, and he wasn't fast enough.

The creature stumbled to its feet, the blade still sticking out from its ear. Gavin leapt back, unsheathed his El'aras dagger, and just stood there watching.

The stone monster was shaking and shouting in ways that made the rock around Gavin tremble. It hurled massive boulders that seemed to come out of nowhere, sending them streaking through the air.

It shook its head violently. Then it grabbed at the sword in its ear.

Gavin winced, afraid the blade was going to snap in half, but the creature managed to snatch the end of it. It shrieked again as it pulled the sword out, then threw it down to the ground.

Gavin hesitated. He needed that weapon.

The stone monster continued to shriek. Boulders rained down, appearing out of nowhere. Somehow, it seemed as if this creature had power over rock, as if it were simply generating stones and hurling them. It wasn't grabbing boulders from the ground at all.

Gaspar looked toward Gavin, a question in his eyes. There was a small break in the attack, and Gavin used that as an opportunity to race toward his blade. The creature turned toward him, fully aware of where he was.

Gavin froze.

The creature shrieked again.

Gavin held his dagger up and yelled at the top of his lungs.

The creature continued to shriek at him, but Gavin yelled back. He cried out until his voice went hoarse, waving his hands in front of him as he did.

"What are you doing?" Gaspar said.

"I'm trying to sound threatening," Gavin said.

"You sound like a maniac."

"I'm hoping that it will be afraid of a maniac."

Gaspar joined him. He yelled and waved his hands in the air, daggers clutched in his fists. He shouted, screamed, and they made as much noise as they could.

Gavin started to laugh. Now he truly felt like a maniac.

Finally, the stone monster started backing away from them. As soon as it gave them a bit of a reprieve, Gavin retrieved his sword. He held it carefully and waved it like he had with the dagger, feeling as if he had lost his mind.

Gaspar started laughing too. The two of them shouted and screamed at the stone monster, trying to appear threatening to a creature that towered over them at nearly five times their height.

Then the creature turned and lumbered off.

Gavin took one long breath, then sank to the ground, panting heavily.

"Gods, that worked?" Gaspar said. He sheathed his daggers with a flourish.

"Well, we have rock monsters that aren't enchantments, magic that's holding us here, and who knows what else we might have to deal with."

"Didn't you say there was a sorcerer up here?"

Gavin had almost forgotten about that, which was dangerous. He got to his feet, still holding his El'aras blade. "There is a sorcerer. And we have to deal with them."

Maybe not deal with them entirely. If they could convince the sorcerer to help them, that might be enough.

They made their way up a steep hillside. They didn't go far before they paused again. In the distance stood another enormous figure—another stone monster.

But that wasn't what caught his attention. A person was fighting it.

That was where the sorcery was coming from.

"Does it look like they're trying to kill it?" Gaspar asked.

"Only one way to find out," Gavin said.

"You want to go *help* the sorcerer?"

"Help? Gods no, I just want to go and get some answers."

Gaspar groaned. "This is another one of your plans, and I don't like it any more than I like any of them."

Gavin chuckled.

They started forward, toward the monster, toward the sorcerer, and hopefully, toward answers.

As they ran, Gavin was increasingly uncertain that they would find any answers. But he wasn't going to stop.

Yoran needed them.

CHAPTER ELEVEN

The ground trembled again as if the creature knew they were coming toward it.

Gavin could detect sorcery all around him. It was a distinct sensation, the feeling of power building from someplace up ahead, and the kind he wished he had the ability to access. He couldn't tell why this sorcerer could reach for their magic, nor could he tell what kind of magic they were using, only that they were trying to wrap spells around the creature's legs.

"That's not going to work," Gavin said, looking over to Gaspar.

"How do you know the sorcerer isn't going to stop *that?*"

Gavin shrugged. "I was just commenting. So, which role do you want? Maniac shrieker, or the person going after the creature's hands?"

"I think I would rather be the maniac shrieker at this point. And you are far better with that sword than I am."

"I don't know. I was a pretty good shrieker."

Gaspar let out a laugh.

There was a nervous energy between them, both of them giddy with surprise at having survived the last attack, but they didn't have much time. The creature grabbed the sorcerer.

Gavin raced forward. He called on the power of the enchantments, knowing it would drain them. As soon as he reached the creature, he lunged with his blade. He stabbed at its open hand, and the thing cried out, shrieking much like the last one did. This one wasn't nearly as tall—only about thirty-five feet. The last one had been stocky and massive, whereas this one was more slender. Maybe this was a female stone monster, though Gavin didn't know if they had genders.

He slammed his blade up again, trying to catch the creature in the palm. Gaspar started shouting as he did so.

Gavin knew he also had to be ready for the sorcerer's attack, but there wasn't any. Instead, magic began to wind up the creature's legs, snaking up from the feet and wrapping around them as if constricting them. Gavin had seen this spell from many different sorcerers, and it seemed to be a baseline use of power. Could this be one of the Sul'-toral who had sent them here in the first place?

Maybe they should let the stone monster attack.

He danced back, taking a quick survey of everything around him.

The sorcerer had the hood of their cloak up, and a

flash of red hair hung loose. Gavin's gaze immediately went to their hands. There was a ring on one finger, which glowed a faint red.

"Jayna?" he said.

He would bet anything that he was right. The last time he'd seen her was in Nelar.

Is that where we are?

Gavin knew the lands around Nelar. These weren't it. The problem was that he didn't know *where* they were.

"We can talk when all this is over," the familiar voice said. "But right now, I'm having a little trouble with this creature."

"You just have to look big and threatening," Gavin said.

"I have to do *what?*" She pulled the hood of her cloak back and looked at him with dark eyes. Her skin looked burned, and some of her hair even looked charred.

"You have to look big and threatening," Gavin repeated. "They respond to that. I don't know what parts of their bodies are sensitive, other than hands and ears. I tried stabbing the creature in the eye, but—"

"You tried fighting this with a sword?" She laughed, and Gavin shrugged.

"I'm just telling you—"

Gavin twisted to the side as a swing came toward him. He jabbed upward, trying to connect his blade with the stone monster's hand, but he missed.

Nearby, Gaspar was still shouting and waving his daggers in the air. He was doing a great job of sounding like a maniac, and Gavin wanted nothing more than to laugh with—or at—his friend.

Jayna flicked her gaze to Gaspar. "You brought some-body like that out here?"

"I thought we were talking after this is over."

Jayna shook her head. She raised her hand, and the ring started to glow softly. She clenched her jaw and gritted her teeth, and then a band of red power slipped out from her. The magic worked its way around the creature's feet, wrapping upward until it reached its chest. From there, the bands split and moved up either side of its head, and then they jabbed into the creature's ears.

The creature shrieked, stumbled back, and then collapsed. As it cried out, it battered at the ground with massive fists and kicked over and over again.

"You don't have to kill it," Gavin said. "Just scare it."

"It's going to chase us again," Jayna said.

"We don't know that it will."

She released her sorcery, and it faded.

The monster trembled for a moment before the kicking stopped. When it got up, it sat for a moment and watched them. Then it shrieked again.

Gavin raised his sword and took a step toward the creature while shouting and waving his blade. Jayna joined him, holding her hands up as she shook them from side to side, looking almost as crazed as Gavin. With burns on her face and charred hair, she looked even more maniacal than him or Gaspar.

The stone monster scrambled to its feet, then lumbered away.

Gavin breathed out a sigh of relief.

"I can't believe that worked," Jayna said. She sunk down to the ground, rubbing the back of her neck.

Gavin looked over at Gaspar, who was watching the creature's back as it disappeared.

"What happened?" Gavin asked Jayna.

"You saw what happened. The damn thing came across me, and I did my best to stay in front of it, but they're almost impossible to hold. Every time I thought I had my spell wrapped around it, it would slip out. I had no idea how it could do that."

"That's not what I'm talking about," Gavin said. "Where are we?"

Jayna looked up at him. "What?"

"I mean, where are we?"

"What are you talking about?" Jayna got to her feet and wobbled for a moment. "Damn. I need water."

"Do you know a place that has water?"

"I can find it, if that's what you're asking about. The real challenge is purifying it enough so that it's safe to drink. But I should be able to do that."

"Does your magic work here?" Gavin asked.

"Sorcery?" She shook her head. "Not really. I have to use my other connection, and even that's a bit twisted. I've been trying and have gotten better control over it, but it's not quite what it should be." She motioned toward the distant form of the rock monster that was still lumbering away from them. "You saw what happened."

"It seemed to me that you had pretty good control over your power just then."

"That was the best I've had in quite a while," Jayna said.

"And the pain…" She shook her head again. "Well, it's too much for me. There are times when I can't even tolerate it."

"What kind of pain is it?"

Jayna watched him for a moment and looked as if debating how much to tell him. "There's pain when I try to draw on my Toral connection. It always hurts, but not like that. Coming here has changed it. It's a struggle in a way that it normally should not be. It's augmented it."

"Augmented your power?" If that were the case, then maybe they could get out of here.

"Not the power," she said, her voice dropping to a whisper.

"Water?" Gaspar prompted.

Jayna turned away, and she headed toward the broken forest.

"See?" Gaspar said to Gavin.

"I never said you were going the wrong direction," Gavin said.

"Well, I just wanted some confirmation that maybe I have good ideas from time to time."

Gavin chuckled. "And I will give you all the confirmation you need, especially when it comes to you finding water in a magical and dangerous land that suppresses our power and is filled with rock monsters."

Gaspar nodded. "That's all I want."

Jayna looked from one to the other. "I don't remember the two of you acting like this before. What happened?"

"I think it was the blood of some dark creature," Gavin said, realizing that had to be true. He and Gaspar both were being a little strange. Then again, not only had they survived a strange creature that had poisoned him with its bizarre blood, but they had also lived through fighting two stone monsters.

There had to be something to that, though Gavin didn't know what it was. These creatures seemed significant, as did the number of them that they had already encountered. But why?

"What kind of creature?" Jayna asked.

Gavin spread his arms and flapped them as if he were a massive bird. "Some enormous black-winged creature. Had a dangerous tail."

Jayna furrowed her brow. "How did you survive?" She seemed genuinely interested.

"My sword," Gavin said, holding the blade out.

"Interesting. Even I haven't tried to take them on. It's not the blood, though. It's the saliva."

"Saliva?" Gaspar said. He looked over to Gavin and laughed. "You get kissed by some bird?"

"At least I'm getting kissed," Gavin said.

Gaspar scowled and turned away. They'd been teasing each other quite a bit lately, so it surprised Gavin that he would react that way. What had he missed?

"Saliva," Jayna said, catching Gavin's attention. "If the creature's saliva gets on you, it has strange effects. I'm not sure about all of them, but it does cause disorientation and confusion, sometimes delirium. Always weakness." She shook her head. "That saliva can be used in certain spells."

Gavin frowned as he tore his attention away from

Gaspar. "What kind of spells would use that? Who would need that kind of power in their magic?"

"Dark spells," she said, then strode away from them.

Gavin hesitated for a moment before making his way to Gaspar. "Listen," he said, seeing the irritation on Gaspar's face. There had been a time when he wouldn't have bothered addressing it, but they were friends now. "I didn't mean to upset you."

Gaspar clenched his jaw, looking as if he were trying to swallow something foul. "It's not you. It's all of this."

"No one would blame you for getting upset. We shouldn't even be here."

Gaspar shook his head. "And I said that it has nothing to do with that. Well, maybe some of that. I would much rather be sitting in the Dragon, sipping a mug of ale, and not worrying about magical creatures trying to kill me. But this is where we are, and we have to deal with what we have to deal with."

"There's the attitude I was hoping you would have," Gavin said, flashing a smile but receiving a scowl in return. "Okay. So you're not ready for joking."

"It's Desarra," Gaspar said.

Of course. Why hadn't he been smart enough to piece that together? Gavin had seen signs. He knew that something was going on between the two of them. Before Gavin had left Yoran, Gaspar and Desarra had been practically inseparable. But they hadn't been together since Gavin had returned. Something had happened.

"The two of you aren't together anymore, are you?"

Gaspar stared straight ahead and shook his head. "No.

She..." He swallowed again, a sour expression on his face. "I don't know if it's because of something I did or if it's because of what she saw in my interest in working with you, but she decided that she didn't want to be part of it." He finally looked over at Gavin. "Ever since the constables started to incorporate the enchanters back into the constabulary, she hasn't really done well."

"Has that strained things between you and Wrenlow?"

Gaspar frowned at him. "Why would I take anything out on the kid?"

"Because of Desarra and Olivia..."

"That's their business, has nothing to do with me. But Desarra, well, I think it was hard enough for her when I returned. And we tried it. We really did. But both of us have changed." He let out a sigh. "She settled into her life, and I sort of settled into a different one. I'm a different person than she knew all those years ago."

"We all change," Gavin said.

"For so long, I couldn't imagine anything more than getting Desarra back," Gaspar said, his voice quiet. "I pictured the two of us having a life together again. That we would have a chance to live freely, the way we had never managed to do before." He held Gavin's gaze. "I never expected to have that chance. I knew better. I was a thief who had gotten mixed up in magic, and then..." He looked at the ground. "Well, none of that matters. When we needed her, she was there for me. And then later, we tried. We rekindled things, and it just didn't feel right. Not for her. Not for me. I think we both tried to force it."

"What happened?"

"She got angry," Gaspar said.

"When?"

"Shortly after Imogen left. She told me I should've gone with her."

"Why?" Gavin asked, knowing that he had to be careful here. But he started to suspect.

"I don't know," Gaspar said. "She said I was moping and that I needed a purpose. And she even made a comment that Imogen needed me, and I needed her." He waved his hand. "I can't tell you any of that. Not really."

"Why didn't you go with her?"

Gaspar looked over to Gavin. There was a hint of darkness in his eyes, a flash of irritation, but then it faded. "She needed to find her own way. Much like I needed to find my own. And you needed to find yours." He snorted. "It seems like the only one who really knew who they needed to be was the kid."

"He just wanted to have a home, and to have somebody to love," Gavin said.

"Pretty much," Gaspar said. "And he's done a good job of it. He's happy. At least, that's how it seems to me. That's what matters. The kid should have that happiness."

"And maybe Desarra saw that?"

"Can't say," Gaspar said, shaking his head. "And if that's what it is, then maybe it's for the best."

They fell silent, following Jayna through the trees, and Gavin wondered why he hadn't asked Gaspar about this before. He was Gavin's friend, somebody who had willingly come with him on a dangerous mission—and Gavin hadn't even questioned why he was willing to leave the person he cared about to do so. But then, Gaspar had done it several times. As Gavin looked over to him, he found him twisting a knife in his hand, flipping it from one finger to another and catching it. Gavin realized that, for as long as he had known Gaspar, he had always been willing to throw himself into a fight. Whether or not it was his fight, Gaspar was willing to join.

Maybe that was what had bothered Desarra more than anything else.

Jayna looked back at them. "Are the two of you coming? I don't know how much longer I'm going to be able to walk this slowly."

"If you have some way of enchanting us to help us walk faster, go ahead, but we don't have our enchantments."

She frowned, flicking her gaze to the ring on his finger. "You have *that*, don't you?"

"It's being suppressed," Gavin said.

"Strange," she muttered.

She turned away and continued to make her way toward the trees, and Gavin and Gaspar followed. The trees parted and revealed a dried grass valley that dropped down below. Far beneath them, Gavin caught sight of a pool of glistening blue water. Jayna stopped.

"Just a warning," she said. "Getting down there isn't going to be easy. As we get closer, there will be other creatures we'll have to get past."

"Creatures like the stone monster?" Gavin asked.

She shook her head. "Not quite like that, but near enough. Either way, they're dangerous. And you're going to need to figure out a way to get past them and not get killed."

"Sounds easy enough," Gaspar said. He pulled out both of his knives again, and he twisted them with skill.

"It sounds easy, but you'd be surprised," Jayna said. "I nearly died trying to get to that pool the very first time I came here. But once you're there, it's easy enough to defend."

"Why?" Gavin asked.

"As far as I have been able to determine, there isn't much water around. All of these creatures eventually end up here, though not at the same time. They seem to come in shifts that they have mutually agreed on so that they aren't battling each other, but we don't have that advantage."

"So we'll have to fight the creatures in order to get to the pool, and then we will have to defend it," Gavin said.

Jayna nodded but didn't explain anything more.

Gavin followed her with his sword unsheathed. Without his core reserves and his El'aras magic, he wasn't sure how well he would handle the creatures. At least he could feel some power. It was faint, and not as potent as it should be, but there was something there.

"You said you can't use sorcery?" he asked.

She glanced over to him, but she held her hands out from her, as if ready to unleash power. "Not traditional sorcery. I use some of the same spell patterns that I do typically, but I have to draw on my Toral ring. It isn't quite the same, and the power I'm able to summon through the ring isn't nearly as much as what I can use with sorcery and Toral power combined normally. Something here is changing that."

"I feel as if it's muted," Gavin said.

Jayna nodded. "Muted. That's a good way to put it."

"The enchantments we brought with us are muted as well."

"Anything of power seems to be," she said. "It is a dangerous place."

They'd traveled farther than he had realized. He didn't know what had happened to them or where they'd ended up when the Sul'toral had sent them here, but increasingly, he suspected that it was much farther than he had believed before. Even when they got out of here, how long would it take for them to return to Yoran? Gavin had the paper dragon, but would that work?

"Where are we exactly?"

"Near as I can tell, this is some world in between," Jayna said.

"What do you mean, a world in between?" Gaspar asked.

"It's a place in between our world and that of greater powers. We shouldn't even be here, to be honest. I'm surprised you are. I wouldn't have come had I not needed to, but…" She shrugged. "I needed to."

"Why don't you explain a little more about what this world is really."

"What did you feel when you were brought here?" Jayna asked.

"We weren't really brought," Gavin said. "We were sent."

"No creature could have sent you here."

"It wasn't a creature. It was sorcerers."

"Sorcerers shouldn't be able to come here," Jayna said, frowning. "It doesn't work for them. They don't have enough access to power." She paused and looked down across the valley. "In order to do it, they would need access to something greater than what they normally do, and even then it shouldn't be enough." Jayna twisted the pale red ring on her finger, her jaw clenching for a moment. "Not a sorcerer, then, which means—"

"We think it was a Sul'toral," Gavin said. "Maybe even three of them."

"Working together?" She tapped on her chin and pursed her lips. "You know, there are times when I wish I had Char with me. He would understand this."

Char. Gavin remembered that name. He was the other sorcerer Jayna worked with.

"How did you get here?" he asked.

"I came here."

"Why? If you know what this place is and how it separates you from magic, why come here?"

"I didn't have a lot of choice. I came here after Eva—"

Before she had a chance to finish her answer, a high-pitched shriek echoed around the valley. The dried grasses in front of them started to rustle.

Jayna pointed toward the water. "Be ready. These are particularly nasty."

Gavin held his sword, but he wasn't prepared for what appeared.

A small creature streaked toward them. It looked like a

ferret, with stripes along its fur. When it opened its jaw, fangs started to elongate.

Jayna whipped the familiar red bands of magic around it, catching the creature in midair and holding it.

Gavin darted forward, sweeping his blade through the spell and the creature.

The thing shrieked as the blade carved through it.

"Neat," Jayna said. "I wasn't able to do that. It's hard enough just to hold them, especially here. I tried to trap as much power as I can, but when I'm here, it feels like there's something trying to hold me back. Despite everything I've done to figure out ways to blast them, my Toral power doesn't work like that here."

"Because we're in someplace in between?" Gaspar asked.

Jayna rotated her ring and made a pattern with her hands. A bit of power seemed to flow from her as she did. "Didn't I just tell you that?"

"You did," Gaspar said. "But all of this is absurd. It doesn't make any sense."

"You had better get used to it. We have more to deal with."

The grasses continued to rustle. There had to be more of those creatures coming toward them.

"Well, old man," Gavin said, which elicited a scowl from Gaspar, especially because Gaspar was barely ten years older than him. "Are you ready to fight?"

Gaspar took a deep breath, squeezed his daggers, and nodded.

CHAPTER TWELVE

Gavin was covered with the creatures' blood as they marched toward the pool. He was experiencing a different kind of fatigue than he'd been feeling lately. It had been a long time since he'd felt the level of bone-wearying exhaustion that worked through his body right now. The feeling almost overwhelmed him.

He needed access to his core reserves. If he had sh'rasn, maybe it wouldn't be so bad. That powder would help replenish and restore him. When he'd fought the small creatures, Gavin had defaulted to his old fighting styles. There was a familiarity to them, but it had been a long time since he had fought unenhanced.

Perhaps this is necessary.

It was a strange thing to think about, but there was a certain freedom in fighting while using no magic, no core reserves, no enchantments. And he had found himself flowing forward, carving through the strange creatures.

Jayna had helped. She would wrap one in power, and Gavin would stab it, spin, and catch another as it leapt at them. Only a few had managed to get close to them.

Gaspar had been surprisingly effective as well. With his enchantments—and Gavin was convinced he was using his enchantments to the fullest—he'd managed to stay in front of them. The only time a creature had gotten through to Gaspar, he had flicked a dagger toward it, piercing it quickly, but not before it had snapped its jaw around his arm. Gavin had checked on him, but Gaspar must've been using stone skin because he wasn't injured.

By the time they reached the water, everybody was ready to rest, but Gavin didn't know if he could. He could see the undulating movement of the grasses behind them, and given what Jayna had said, the creatures would continue to try to press forward for the water.

"You're going to have to give me a moment here," she said. "I can purify it, but it's going to take some time. And I don't know how long it will last."

"What do you have to do to purify it?" Gaspar asked.

"The water is probably fine, but I figure that it's safer to be certain, given that I don't know where we are and what kind of power is in this place."

"What would happen if we drank it?"

Jayna shrugged. "Can't say. I don't really know, and I don't really want to find out. All I'm looking for is to make it through this. I need to get to Eva and get her out of here."

"How do you do that?"

"I have to find a key."

"A key?" Gavin asked.

"Well, supposedly, they are scattered, but tied to each person trapped here. In this place, they can be impossible to find. At least easily. But..." She shrugged. "Once you find the key, you can use it to bring yourself back."

"What if the Sul'toral don't want us to go back?"

"They might be able to restrict it," she acknowledged. "I'd be surprised if they had that much control over this place, especially seeing as how it's a world in between. Their power doesn't hold quite as well here, but they probably wanted you to come because *your* power doesn't work as well here either. They might not be able to kill you," Jayna said, regarding Gavin with a frown, "but they wouldn't have to here. There are plenty of other things that can do that job for them."

"I had the feeling they could have killed me," Gavin said. "They were incredibly powerful."

"Maybe there was a reason for sending you here. You might have believed them to be incredibly powerful, but they might have felt the same way about you." She motioned to his ring. "And it's possible that they needed to weaken you so that they could separate you from that."

"I don't think they care about the ring," Gavin said. But then, maybe they did. There were El'aras who cared about the ring, and so did Chauvan. Someone might want it.

"Well, depends on the kind of power you have with it," she said. "It's not Toral, or even Sul'toral. It's some other kind of power. Maybe the other Sul'toral think they can add another connection to an ancient."

She spun and hurriedly formed a glowing red ball,

capturing a creature that had leapt at them. Gaspar stabbed through the spell and punctured the creature's side.

"As I said, they want the water."

"And if they get it?" Gavin asked.

"They aren't going to take it from me," she said. "Or from you. You are going to help me stop this."

He was reminded of his first encounter with Jayna. She was powerful. Almost impossibly so. That was the first time he'd ever faced a Toral, and she had challenged him in a way that almost no others had before.

He had been challenged much worse since, but she was his first glimpse of greater powers in the world. The Fates were certainly dangerous, but they were a danger that he could make sense of. Sorcery with extreme power and control. Gavin had understood that he might not know the spells they used or how to defeat them, but he had recognized the way they used their power. When he had threatened them, they'd reacted the way he'd expected.

Jayna, with her Toral ability, had been different.

Not only her, though. Eva as well.

Jayna crouched along the shore, tracing a pattern of triangles, irregular lines that seemed connected, and several other oblong and odd-looking shapes. When she was done, she leaned back and pressed her hands on either side of the pattern. Power flowed from her ring, out through the patterns, which also began to glow. When the energy formed, she sent it streaking out from her and into the water, where it settled like a haze on top of the water's surface. It was a reddish discoloration, though it was only a faint color, not a solid red.

"What happened to Eva?" Gavin asked.

"She came here for understanding," Jayna said. "Or she was drawn here. I don't really know anymore. I felt her need, though."

"What need was that?"

"She's trapped."

"Like we are."

"Eva isn't trapped quite the same way," Jayna said. "She came here looking for answers about her power. That's all she's really been wanting. I came after her because I was worried about her."

"So she is or isn't trapped?"

Jayna shook her head. "I don't know. I thought I could help her, but now I've been here for a while and haven't been able to find her."

"How long is a while?" Gaspar asked. His back was to the water, and he continued staring straight ahead of him at the grasses. There was movement, but nothing else had come out.

"A few weeks? Maybe months? I don't know. Time is a bit odd in here."

"How do you know?"

"You just do. You can feel it, can't you?"

"We haven't been here that long," Gavin said.

"Are you sure about that?" Jayna asked, glancing back at him. "How do you know? Like I said, time is odd here."

Gavin hoped he hadn't been here that long. Maybe they still had time. He didn't think they did, but what if time really was odd enough that it gave them an opportunity to get back to Yoran in time to stop an attack?

"We need to get out of here as quickly as we can," Gavin said.

"Well, we'd better hope time is slower here. Or is it faster?" Jayna frowned, and she continued to push her power out over the water. Finally, she stopped. The haze persisted, but it began to lower into the water, causing everything to bubble faintly. She smiled at Gavin. "See? There you go."

"What am I supposed to see?"

"I've purified the water."

Gavin looked at the pool. He had no interest in drinking from it. He had no idea what it might do to him. Maybe nothing, but he'd seen the haze.

"What happened to your ring?" he asked.

It wasn't something he necessarily cared about, but it looked different than the last time he'd seen her. Normally, her ring had a white stone, and that was how she connected to her Sul'toral and the power he possessed.

"We modified it," she said in a matter-of-fact tone. She crouched down next to the pool, cupped her hands into the water, and brought it to her lips. She drank and then leaned back. "It's bloodstone. Have you ever heard of it?" Jayna looked back at him.

Gavin glanced at her ring again and shook his head.

She sighed. "That's too bad. I was hoping you might know more. Quite a few people have heard of it, but not many people *know* about it. It takes on power, and it's unlike anything I've ever seen before. I fused it with the ring."

"And…"

"That's all there is to it. If I didn't have the bloodstone ring, I don't know how much I'd be able to do here." She looked at Gavin's finger. "And without that, you might not be able to do much here either."

He twisted his own ring. He hadn't been able to take it off ever since it had bonded to him. "So your ring holds additional power?"

"Something like that. Bloodstone is unique. It makes enchantments stronger, changes them. I'm not exactly sure how to make it, though, but I do think it is tied to Eva and her kind…" She trailed off for a moment. "I know she's out here—I just can't find her."

Jayna wasn't going to leave Eva behind. Gavin could see that.

And they couldn't stay.

"We might have to go in a different direction," Gavin said.

"What direction is that? Where do you think you are?"

"We don't know."

"I've told you that you are in a world in between," Jayna said. "There isn't any other place for you to go. Everything here sort of winds back around. You can walk for hours and you won't go anywhere. It's sort of how this place works."

"Then how do you expect to find Eva?" Gavin asked.

"Because we're not the only ones moving," she said. "She's moving, and…"

Gavin looked at her and realized she was keeping something from him.

"What else is it?"

"I don't know how much to tell you," she said.

"Because you don't think we can handle it?"

Jayna shrugged. "It's more because I don't know how much I can trust you."

"You know I'm not some dark sorcerer," Gavin said.

"Oh, I know that." Her gaze drifted to his ring again. "But you have power, which means you're going to have to pick a side."

It was so similar to what Rayena had said. What had he missed?

Ancients. Gods. That was what they were talking about. And Gavin wondered if there was a way for him to know which side he needed to choose. He wondered if there was a side *to* choose.

"You have to know there's something coming," Jayna said.

At one point, Gavin would have believed that she was talking about the nihilar and the dark cloud that posed. Now he didn't know if that was the case, or if there was something else—something worse. Anna had mentioned fires, but even that didn't feel right. Power was coming, and a fight would come with it. Maybe he did have to choose a side.

"And what side have you chosen?" he asked.

"I'm not changing what I'm doing," Jayna said. "I've been dealing with dark sorcerers, dark creatures, and now other dark threats, so I fully intend to handle myself. I've found plenty of dark sorcerers and, unfortunately, rot within the Society."

"What kind of rot?"

"Oh, the kind that leads the Society," she said, waving her hand dismissively.

"The Fates?"

She frowned at him. "You know of them?"

"I think most people who have some experience with magic know about the Fates," Gavin said.

"You might be surprised. But yes. The Fates."

"What happened with them?"

"The Society was founded by the Sul'toral. The Fates were part of it. I was tasked with removing dark sorcerers, which ultimately led me to trying to deal with the Sul'-toral. Unfortunately. And now I'm chasing down the kind of power I don't really understand, trying to keep myself sane as I stand on the precipice of light and dark." She flashed a smile as she looked over to Gavin. "What about you? What do you intend to do?"

He breathed out a heavy sigh. "I haven't really thought much about it. I've been trying to understand what I am, the power I have, and—"

"I doubt you're going to have much time for that."

Gavin wasn't sure what to make of Jayna and what she had been telling him, but maybe she was right. He didn't have time to try to understand himself. All he could do was fight.

She turned to the water, cupped her hands, and took another long drink. "The water is fine. You can have some."

"Are you sure?"

Jayna laughed. "I wouldn't be drinking it if I wasn't. It's fine for now. I don't know how long I can keep it that way. The change won't last forever. If you're going to drink, you should do it in the next few minutes. Otherwise, I might have to purify it again. It takes quite a bit out of me when I do it, so I don't like to do it that often."

Gavin knelt in front of the pool and looked at the water. There was still a hint of red coloration to it—the bloodstone influence. He had no idea whether there was anything to worry about, but Jayna seemed unconcerned.

Finally, he took a deep breath, cupped his hands in the water, and took a drink.

It was warm. He'd expected that, given how the water had seemed to boil, but it wasn't hot. He took another drink, and when it washed down his throat, it did rinse away some of the thirst. A part of him expected that something terrible would happen, but nothing changed. Just a warmth that washed through him.

He looked over to Gaspar. "I think it's safe."

Gaspar regarded Jayna for a moment, and she chuckled. "You don't have to drink. You're not going to hurt my feelings. I don't know how much water you have on you, and as I said, time is strange here. You might be able to last longer than we realize."

As Gaspar crouched in front of the water, he muttered something that Gavin couldn't quite hear. He took a long drink. Gavin did the same, drinking until his belly was full. He could live without food, but he needed water. And if time was strange here, maybe water would be all he needed.

"You stay near this watering hole?" he asked.

"Near enough," Jayna said. "I venture off from time to time, looking for Eva and laying out markers that will help me track her, but I haven't found anything."

"Do you have any way of holding water?"

"Do you?"

Gavin shook his head. "Not particularly. Without having any enchantments—"

"I can't make them either," she said. "At least, not that I've tried. I haven't really attempted too much. This place takes so much out of you that it's difficult for me to attempt anything."

"Why does it?"

"I don't really know. I think it's because this place is in between, buffering our world from that of the ancients."

"You used that term before," Gavin said. "What do you mean by that?"

"They are ancient powers. Some call them gods, but I'm not exactly convinced that's what they are."

It kept coming back to the gods. That was what he had learned about in Yoran, and what they were dealing with now. What kind of gods did he have to fear?

"Like Sarenoth?" he asked.

She nodded, though a hint of concern washed across her face. "Something like that. There was a time when I believed that Sarenoth was a dark god, but I am not sure that's the case anymore."

"Then what is he?"

"A means to power," she said. "At least, for those who chased such things. They trap his power and can call on even more magic. That's what the Sul'toral do."

"What about you?" Gavin asked.

He knew her power was tied to a Sul'toral, which meant that she was linked to one of the gods—Sarenoth.

But Jayna was unique even among the Toral, he thought. And she wasn't evil. She had always felt as if she were fighting on the same side as him.

"I'm connected differently to that power," she said.

"Not to a Sul'toral?"

"Yes, still a Sul'toral," she said. "But, at least from what I've been able to tell, I'm connected to a different kind. Though maybe I'm not. I don't really know." She shrugged, and she turned her attention back to the water. "Not much time left," she said, and she took a long drink. "Did you get what you needed?"

"I might take a little bit more," Gaspar said. Once he did, he sat back and looked over to Gavin. "It seems to be clearing my head. I felt off."

"You are off," Gavin said.

"You're the one who let that creature lick you."

"I didn't let it do anything. It crashed into me. I was lucky enough to survive."

"Well, you might have to deal with even worse while you are here," Jayna said.

"I don't intend to be here much longer," Gavin said.

"Then you had better get looking. I don't know what's involved, but there are said to be keys. They are tied to each person's magic." She looked to Gaspar. "Sorry. If you don't have magic, then you have to be brought out by someone else. And if you stay, I think this place will eventually kill you. At least, that's my suspicion. Most of these creatures keep attacking. I don't think any of them are native to here, either. I've been trying to get a sense of the rules of this world, but I just don't know what they are."

A key.

And it was going to be tied to his magic?

The grasses were still moving, and there was a strange undulating quality to them that suggested that creatures were out there and moving toward them. They likely didn't have too much time before something else tried to attack. Sooner or later, something would come for the water.

How long would he be able to fight?

Jayna's words stuck with him.

Eventually, this place would kill them.

Gavin had always thought himself strong enough to be able to survive almost anything. He had withstood countless attacks. He had handled powerful magic. This place felt different. There was considerable danger here, not only because of the types of creatures that existed but because of how this place suppressed his magic.

"If we stay together, it might be easier for us to find a way out, but I'm not leaving before I find Eva," she said.

"What happens if you find her and she doesn't want to come with you?" Gaspar asked.

"It's a possibility. She's been trying to understand who and what she is, and I've wanted to offer whatever help I can, but it's difficult." Jayna whipped her head up. "I think it's time for us to go."

Gavin looked around and realized the ground seemed to be moving again, as if something was coming toward them. If they stayed, they would have to fight. He wasn't sure that he wanted to keep fighting these creatures endlessly. He unsheathed his sword, watching the ground as it shifted and moved, and he could feel an energy here as well.

Jayna twisted her ring. The red magic flowed from her, racing across the ground. "This is new. I can feel something, but I don't know what it is. I don't like it." She glanced at Gavin. "It's only happened since you came. I wonder what changed."

"You know, she's not completely wrong. I don't like it either," Gaspar whispered to Gavin, shaking his head. "But unfortunately, she might be our best bet at getting out of here."

As Gavin watched Jayna move forward, he noticed that she still had more power than he would've expected. A hazy red glow swept through the grasses.

"We find my key, and then we can get out of here," Gavin said.

"You make it sound so simple," Gaspar said.

"Simple is a good plan."

"If that's your plan, then it's not simple. Or good. Or a plan." Gaspar grunted and started after Jayna.

Gavin turned his attention back to the water. The color had changed, the red haze fading into more of a blue.

They had to find his key, figure out how it was tied to him and this place, and then he and Gaspar could escape.

The only real hope he had was that time was different here. Hopefully, they could still get back to Yoran before it was too late.

CHAPTER THIRTEEN

They reached the broken trees again. The ground had been changing for a while, though there were still dried grasses, boulders that reminded Gavin of the rock monsters, and stunted shrubs. How much of these were native to this place, and how much had been drawn here much like the creatures—and Gavin and Gaspar? One of the clusters of trees reminded him of the bells trees, which seemed fitting for this place. Not all of them did, and the broken trees certainly did not seem the same.

Jayna paused and peered backward.

"What are you looking at?" Gaspar asked.

"At that," she said, nodding back to the pool of water. "It feels to me like there's something to it that I should be able to understand, but I don't know what it is." She shook her head. "There are plenty of situations where my spells don't hold, but what happens there is unique, even for this place."

"Why?"

"Because it's like I'm placing an enchantment. Maybe that's not it, though. An enchantment would be permanent, and in this case, it was definitely not permanent. But as I place it, I can feel it starting to shift, as if it's somehow ignoring my direction." She shrugged. "I don't really know how to explain it any other way, only that I can feel that something about it is not quite right. It's like it's trying to fight me."

"And you don't feel that when you place an enchantment otherwise?" Gavin asked.

"Not particularly," Jayna said. "You have to know what it's like to place an enchantment, though. You have that ability."

Gavin squeezed the hilt of his sword. "I'm still trying to understand my abilities. If I can place enchantments, then that isn't something I know much about."

She pursed her lips. "Surprising."

"Why is it surprising?" Gaspar asked.

"Because you're El'aras, right?"

Gavin nodded slowly.

"That's what I thought," she said. "But not like any El'aras I've seen before. Most are skilled, but you... Well, you're something different. And I'm surprised Eva didn't react as strongly to you the first time we met. She wanted to help you, which I wasn't expecting, given what I know about her and what I know about the El'aras."

"Why?" Gaspar asked.

"Because it's Eva," she said.

Gavin shook his head. "I'm afraid I don't really know what that means."

"She's one of the Ashara."

Gavin froze. Ashara. He'd heard that before. Rayena had mentioned them.

Jayna kept going as if Gavin had not heard. "You don't know what that means. Okay. That's interesting, though maybe it shouldn't be. I didn't know about the Ashara until recently either. Now that I do, it doesn't help me all that much. It just helps me know what she is and gives a name to things."

He tried to shake himself from the surprise. He wasn't about to reveal what he knew.

"So that name is—"

"It's the name of her people," Jayna said. "Eva doesn't know much about them. She lost her memory before the two of us met. She's been trying to get it back the entire time I've been working with her."

"They use smoke?" Gaspar asked.

Not smoke, Gavin suspected. Fire. That was what Anna had mentioned.

"You really don't know?" She glanced over to Gavin. "How don't you know?"

"Because we don't have the same experience you do," Gavin said. "And we haven't been around Eva that much."

"You fought her. You fought alongside her, and you would've seen the kinds of things she can do."

"We were mostly concerned about the kinds of things you could do," Gavin admitted.

Jayna shrugged. "I was never going to hurt you. I don't even know if I can."

"Oh, you definitely could hurt us," Gaspar said with a grunt.

She nodded. "Well, Eva learned more about her people and where they were from, and it seems that some key to understanding all that moved here." Jayna reached into her pocket and pulled something out that Gavin couldn't see, then twisted it in her hand. "Not that we can really understand what it is, or why, or how. But she didn't talk about it either. Eva didn't really know. I tried to get her to help explain, but she's always been distrustful, if that makes any sort of sense to you."

"It makes some sense," Gavin said.

"We're trying to figure out what she knows. That's why I've been looking for her. And why she came here. She thought that she might regain some of her lost memories."

"Will she know how to find these keys?" Gaspar asked.

"I don't…"

Jayna stopped and stared off into the distance, then sprinted off.

Gavin watched her go.

Ashara. An enemy to the El'aras. That was significant.

"Is she going to be like that the whole time we are around her?" Gaspar asked.

"I don't know what to make of her," Gavin said. "She wasn't like that the last time she was around us, but she *was* trying to kill me quite a bit of the time. Now she's different."

He hurried after Jayna, but she was putting too much

distance between them. The landscape shifted, though Gavin started to see a series of tall, burned trees.

He slowed and looked behind him. "Didn't we just come from here?"

Gaspar nodded. "I think we did."

"She did say that things are unusual in this place."

They finally caught up to Jayna, who had paused in front of the trees.

"What was it?" Gavin asked.

"I thought I saw smoke, but then it was gone," she said, her voice soft. She looked behind her and then straight ahead. "It was here. I saw it, I felt it, and… I can still feel it. At least, I can feel it somewhat."

"If it was smoke, does that mean Eva was here?"

"Eva, Asaran, or any of the others."

"Who?" Gavin asked.

"Another Ashara," Jayna muttered. She waved her hand as if to explain it. "But why here?" She headed into the trees. "I've already looked here. I have spent countless hours looking here."

"I thought you were looking for the keys."

"Partly the key, partly Eva, and partly any of the others," she said, glancing back at him before turning her attention to the trees. "I'm not exactly sure what this is. It has to have something to do with the Ashara."

"If it does, then you shouldn't be here," Gaspar said. "None of us should be."

"Would you abandon your friend?"

Gaspar glanced over to Gavin. Gavin expected one of Gaspar's usual remarks, the retorts he used to make fun of Gavin, but instead he just shook his head. "I would not."

"I didn't think so. You've been with him every time I've seen you, and even though you don't have the same power, you come. It's sort of like me and Eva."

"Only she has power of her own," Gavin said.

"I told you that she's been struggling with her memories. She doesn't understand who she is. What she is." Jayna moved toward the trees. She started mumbling something, though Gavin couldn't tell what she was saying.

"I don't know if she's going to help us, boy," Gaspar whispered.

"There are keys here," Gavin said. "We find the keys, and then..."

"And then what?"

Gavin didn't know. He reached the center of the burned trees. As he stood there, he became aware of something unusual. It felt like sorcery, but sorcery with a strange edge to it. It was something that Gavin couldn't quite place a finger on, only that he was distinctly aware of it.

"Can you feel that?" he asked Gaspar.

Gaspar shook his head.

He looked toward Jayna, who was sending a layer of the same red haze over everything. Her bloodstone power. It seemed to float everywhere around them and drift downward, and he could feel it. She seemed to have far more magical connection than Gavin thought possible in this place.

What about his own power?

He reached for his core reserves. Gavin had not attempted to do so in quite a while. As he did, he recognized some faint energy of his core reserves and then began to focus on that by drawing it through the ring. The power responded to him in a way that it had not since he'd first come to the strange land. Maybe it was just that he hadn't used it in a while. Something about it felt different, though.

It took Gavin a moment to realize why. Whenever he called on his core reserves normally, he had to draw the magic up through him, the same way he did with his ring. In this case, he felt it as if it were pushing down through him. Some of that was the pressure he felt all around him. What if he didn't fight it and instead tried to draw power in that direction?

He let that pressure guide him.

And he felt it.

He pushed down, rather than pulling up.

It was like trying to redirect the flow of his own blood.

But it wasn't quite the same.

Perhaps it was because he'd been trained the way he had. His magic was something sensed within him, unused until he needed to tap into it, not like the other El'aras who connected to their power continuously. Gavin didn't need to have that power at all times. He'd learned to function without it.

Gavin hesitated, focusing on that energy, and he squeezed it downward. It was almost as if his power were the reverse of his normal connection—inverted. If he could figure out some way to draw on it, he might be able to call his own magic once again. There were creatures drawing on their own power. He had seen it. There had to be some way to access that.

Why would it be inverted, though?

He had seen how the Sul'toral had folded, and he had felt that power collapse inward as it compressed him. He had tried to fight it, but what if that was a mistake?

He looked over to Gaspar. "Can you feel anything?"

"What am I supposed to feel? Other than the awfulness of this place. It's like it's squeezing me."

"Exactly," Gavin said.

What if he could fold himself? He'd seen how the Sul'toral had done it. If he could replicate that, maybe that was the key to escaping. They obviously had some way of pushing him here, but it was more than that. He had thought that the folding was some way of traveling as well. They had mastered some aspect of it, and by folding inward, they could move without walking.

But it wasn't just the Sul'toral.

Chauvan had done the same thing. He had disappeared. He had transported from one place to another without walking. What if the key was somehow using this space?

A place in between.

A place where magic didn't work quite right.

He tried reversing it but couldn't fold himself the way he thought he needed to. The idea seemed sound, though.

"I found something," Jayna said.

Gavin stopped trying to invert his power. He turned

back to her as she sent the sweeping red magic away from her. He wished that he understood what she was doing, but he did not know what it was, only that she sent her Toral magic through this strange forest.

But he recognized something.

"I can feel something here. It's an echo," Gavin said.

Jayna looked over to him. "What do you mean?"

"Keep doing what you're doing."

She continued to manipulate her Toral power, that reddish haze swirling around her, and Gavin felt some aspect of it that was different. She was pressing it down toward the ground, probing.

Downward.

That had to be part of this. As Gavin joined her with his own magic, he could feel the way hers worked. It was like the haze was trying to press *through* the earth. He had felt something similar when he was tapping into his magic, trying to understand the way that that was working.

He closed his eyes again and focused.

Gavin squeezed downward.

He could feel something.

Inverted.

That seemed to be the most important part of this.

Beneath him was something incredible, powerful. And yet he couldn't access it. He was aware of it, though. Gavin attempted to add additional aspects to it but failed.

He opened his eyes. Jayna was clenching her jaw, and she held her hand out. Power streaked from the ring, spreading across the ground in a faint cloud of pale red and squeezing downward.

"What's she doing?" Gaspar asked.

"I think she feels what's beneath us," Gavin said. "But I don't know how she can access it. I can't."

Jayna glanced over to him. "If you can feel it, you can access it."

"I don't know how."

"You need to form an enchantment," she said. "That's what I'm trying to do, but it's fighting me."

"What kind of enchantment?" Gavin asked.

"Anything. Place your mark on it."

He snorted. "I don't have a mark. I don't even know how to place an enchantment."

"It's different for each type of magic user," she said. "With sorcery, there's usually a matter of trying to create a pattern, infusing that pattern with power, and then holding it there." She was giving him a lesson while continuing to maintain considerable power. He could feel the energy she exuded as she did. "But then there's a different kind. The dular, or enchanters, use their own kind of magic. It's different than sorcery. It's somehow intrinsic to them, but I'm not exactly sure what they do as they create their enchantments. Some emotion, from what I've heard, but it's also a matter of desire."

Emotion.

He'd heard that before.

"And the El'aras are even more different," she said. "To be honest, I have no idea what they use, only that whatever power they tap into is something unique. The El'aras like to believe that their power is more natural than others, but I suspect all power is ultimately natural. It's just how you access it, isn't it? Everything seems to overlap."

Jayna fell silent, and Gavin wondered if she was right.

"You know what you have to do," Gaspar said to him. "You've done it before."

"I haven't done anything with an enchantment before. I can tie myself to it..."

That was what it was.

He'd done something similar before, but he didn't know if there was anything here that he could do now. He could link himself to it if the power worked for him. There had to be some power here, but as he pushed on it, he felt it moving the wrong way. He tried to control it, but drawing that energy through him and through the ring felt awkward.

He needed to succeed.

He could do this.

Gavin pushed downward, and he felt something beyond himself.

Then he felt the strange enormity of the power beneath him. It was like a forest. It was like he could feel trees stretching outward, and there was something familiar to them.

He recognized these trees.

Bralinath.

But they were wrong.

Inverted.

Gavin focused.

He channeled power out from him, and he tried to touch one of the bralinath trees. He'd never tried to touch that power, warned by the El'aras that it was dangerous to do so. He didn't want to damage the bralinath. All he wanted was to see if there was some sort of connection.

He felt resistance. Gavin pushed against it, straining downward rather than trying to draw his core reserves up through him, and the resistance faded.

He touched the bralinath. Not only that, but he left his mark. There was a moment, little more than a flare, and then he was thrown free. The energy dropped out of him, and he staggered and landed on his backside.

Pain exploded within him.

Gavin sat motionless, fighting the urge to scream. He had no idea what had happened. He had no idea what he had done. Something, though. He could feel it. Now he just had to understand it.

CHAPTER FOURTEEN

G avin struggled to get to his feet. Everything felt strange, but more than that, everything hurt. He fought to feel for the energy that was here, knowing that there had to be something, as he had felt the way his own power had probed down toward the bralinath trees and left an etching behind.

He could feel a connection to magic. It was different than what he felt when he was connecting to enchantments in any other place. In those cases, there was a tie to some part in his mind, which allowed him to control those enchantments, but he was also aware of when they shattered and broke. It seemed to borrow energy through him and his core reserves, and all he had to do was push downward and toward the bralinath trees to reach for that kind of a connection.

"What did you do?" Jayna said. Her Toral power flowed toward him.

Gavin ignored it. "I felt something. Maybe it's my key." He tried to get his mind back in order, but everything felt off. He was aware of some energy here that he had not noticed before. That seemed significant to him.

"What did you do?" she asked again.

He looked at the trees around him, paying her no mind. "These are bralinath trees," he said. "Or they are the roots." He wasn't sure. The idea that they were somehow upside-down bralinath trees seemed impossible, but that was the impression he had.

"These are burned trees," Jayna said. "They're from when the Ashara passed through here. This is what was left."

"I'm not exactly sure that's true," Gavin said. "What did you feel when you were pushing downward?"

"I couldn't feel anything. I felt you try to reach through what I was doing. I almost had the key."

"I don't know if this was *your* key."

"What?" Jayna said.

Gavin shrugged. "I don't quite know how to explain it. And to be honest, I don't even know if it's right or not. But this is tied to me. To the El'aras. It's one of the sacred trees of their people. *My* people, I suppose."

"And how is that?"

"I don't really know," Gavin said. He looked over to Gaspar, expecting him to say something, but he was quiet. "All I know is that this feels like a bralinath tree."

"I can try to link to the key again," Jayna said.

"I don't know if you need to. I did."

Her brow furrowed. "You did what?"

"I linked to the tree."

"You should not have been able to. Not with what I was doing," she said, though she trailed off a little bit at the end as she did. "Why?" she asked, frowning. "Why were you able to do that?"

"I don't know," Gavin said.

And he didn't. But at this point, he wasn't sure it mattered.

"If we assume that this is one of the keys, we need to find the others."

"I've told you that I've been looking," Jayna said. "But it's not just about finding the keys, it's about finding Eva."

That was the case for Jayna, but for Gavin, it was about getting out of this place, returning to Yoran, and saving the people he wanted to save.

But they couldn't just leave Jayna.

He looked at Gaspar, who nodded to him. "Let's find her and the keys, then get out of here."

Jayna said nothing as she turned and started walking.

Gavin focused on the energy of the trees, and he was still aware of it even as they moved away from the forest. It was a distant sort of awareness, faint and vague, but the farther they went, the more Gavin was certain of what he detected. The more they traveled, the more it felt as if that energy was drawn away from him, as if the bralinath trees wanted him to maintain a connection, the key binding to him.

He spied Gaspar watching him.

"You look like you're working on a problem," Gaspar said.

"If this is the key, I'm not exactly sure how we use all of them," Gavin said. "She said there were three."

"That's what she claims."

"And she said that each of us has our own key. If the bralinath trees are mine…"

It made sense, as he was El'aras and the bralinath trees were tied to the El'aras. What kind of key would Jayna have? Gavin watched as she marched away from them.

He shook his head. "I'm just thinking… Gods, I don't even know what I'm thinking. I'm just trying to come up with what they might be doing."

"What do you think it might be?" Gaspar asked.

"I didn't expect to tap into an enchantment. If that is what it is. But I'm not sure the bralinath trees are enchantments."

"Then they are the key. Part of the key is trying to understand the way you do it," Gaspar said. "Enchanters are not the same as you. You've been thinking about the way Alana uses her magic, but her way is different than yours. It has to be."

Gavin nodded. "I know."

"And sorcery is different. Can't say that I know much about how sorcery works or how they create spells, but I do know that the kind of magic they touch is quite a bit different than the kind you use. Yours isn't so much…" Gaspar waved his hands in the air like he was simulating patterns, then gestured to Jayna. "Not the way hers is. Even hers isn't the same as most of the sorcerers I've met. Hers is more of a power tied to that ring."

"At least it is now," Gavin said. "But when I fought her

before, she was using a mixture of sorcery and her connection to power."

"So you have different kinds of power and different kinds of connections to magic, which means that you have different ways of enchanting. But in all of them, the key is the same, isn't it? You're trying to tap into power to hold it in place. That's all you're intending to do with it."

Gavin chuckled. "I never would've expected you to be someone trying to puzzle out how to use magic."

"I'm just trying to make sense of it. And in this case, there isn't much to make sense of. At least, not that I can tell." Gaspar frowned. "Not with the kind of power we're dealing with."

"Why are you trying to help me puzzle it out?"

"Maybe I can help you figure out how to use your power."

"You're just saying that so I don't have to go back to the El'aras," Gavin said.

"Do you even want to?"

It was a loaded question, and one that Gavin didn't have a good answer for. When he had left Yoran, he had done so because he had believed it was the only way he could learn what he needed to about his power, but increasingly, he wondered if that was even necessary.

"I don't know," Gavin said. "They've been trying to teach me how to use my power, but I have come to understand that what I can do with my El'aras connection is quite a bit different than what they do with it. Tristan trained me to use what I've now come to learn as my El'aras magic differently."

"Just because of how you have drawn on your own power," Gaspar said. "But your kind of power is unique to you. At least the way you call on it. If there's nothing else that Tristan did for you, at least he helped you understand how to hold onto your power and not use it unless you need to. That makes you different than the El'aras. I suppose they know that too."

"Anna knows it."

"Does she understand you?"

Gavin arched a brow. "What kind of question is that?"

"It's a fair one," Gaspar said. "Well, I think it is. Does she understand you?"

"I think so."

"And if she does, *what* do you think she understands?"

Gavin shrugged. "I don't really know. She understands the kind of power I can use, and she understands the way I draw on it, and—"

Gaspar shook his head again. "I don't know that she does. I think she wants to use you, the same way others want to use you. Understanding you is different. Understanding you is letting you be the person you are supposed to be."

"Who's to say what I'm supposed to be?" Gavin said. "I've been looking for that person ever since I realized Tristan was trying to turn me into something."

"Odd," Gaspar said with a laugh. "Mostly that you're still looking for yourself after all these years."

Gavin could still feel the connection he'd forged to the trees, and he held onto that awareness, recognizing a benefit to having that connection. It bonded him to something else. Strangely, the longer he kept that connection, the more he felt the power within him. It was different than it normally was.

How much of his core reserves could he call on if it came down to it? Maybe with the connection to the bralinath trees, Gavin could do more than he had before. Fighting might require that he do so. But that wasn't how he wanted to use his core reserves. What Gavin needed was to figure out some way to fold himself—and Gaspar— to break free of this place. He knew it would involve using the power of the bralinath trees, but he had no idea what that would entail.

Gaspar glanced to Jayna. "We should keep up with her."

She was moving across the rocky landscape, and then she paused. Gavin waited, worried that she might've encountered another strange creature, not wanting to come across one of the stone monsters again, though at least they knew what it would take to scare them away.

"Tell me if you see any signs of the key," Jayna said. "I've been looking for Eva for what feels like an eternity, and I finally catch flashes now that you are here? It doesn't make sense. Why now?" She looked around. "And why have the attacks changed now?"

"Had you been fighting with the rock monsters before we found you?" Gavin asked.

"No."

They stopped on the ridgeline and gazed down at the valley with the water. Gavin peered behind him. The broken trees were closer than he thought they should be, especially given how far they'd been walking, and he was again aware of that connection that bound him to them. On the far side of the ridgeline, he saw a different landscape. Everything was bleak, dark, but there were no signs of trees, just broken rock. It looked as if a massive monster had stormed through, shattering all the stone and life that had been here.

Gavin pointed. "How do I get over there?"

"I've tried," she said. "Every time I start walking, I end up back here."

"Is something holding you here?" Gaspar asked.

"Something, or someone, or some power," Jayna said, shrugging. "Can't say that I know. And though I've been trying to fight through it, I haven't been able to. I came here voluntarily, but I don't know what's holding me here." She frowned as she stared off into the distance. "Maybe we went in the wrong direction."

She started down the hillside, fighting through some of the strange weasel-like creatures that jumped out at her. She did not struggle with them nearly as much as she seemed to before, though Gavin suspected that the last time she'd fought them, she'd been weakened by her fight with the stone monster.

Gavin was forced to use his sword a few times, as was Gaspar, but it was an easier journey down than it had been the first time.

They paused at the water. Jayna crouched and started to trace a series of patterns.

"I thought you said it took quite a bit of energy to enchant the water," Gavin said.

"It does, but it's going to get dark soon."

Gavin looked up at the sky and frowned. "It looks light."

"I told you, things are different here. Can't say that I know what it is or why it is, only that everything seems a little off here."

She finished tracing a pattern, and the red haze began to flow outward over the water. When she was done, she leaned back on her heels and rested, then took a drink once the water finally stopped sizzling.

Gavin took a seat, and he pulled the enchantment out of his ear and tapped on it.

"Is it broken?" Jayna asked.

"It's an El'aras enchantment."

She snorted. "I can see that. What happened to it?"

"I don't know. I might have pushed too much power through it to connect to one of the other El'aras when we were separated by a long distance. It didn't work."

"Can I see it?"

Jayna held her hand out, and Gavin reluctantly handed the enchantment over, though he justified it by reminding himself that the enchantment didn't work for him anyway. Not anymore. She ran her fingers along it, and the red glow came from the ring and worked its way around the enchantment.

"I recognize some of the symbols, but I can't tell if anything is damaged," she said. "It's El'aras, so it's possible that I wouldn't know anything about it. I'm pretty good with figuring out sorcery enchantments, especially those I'm familiar with, and I've gotten even better with under-

standing dular enchantments. But since this is El'aras..."
She handed it back to him.

"If we can fix it, I hope I can reach my friend."

"Even if you can fix it, I'm not sure you can hear
anything here. I don't know where *here* is, so I don't know
if an enchantment would reach. It depends on how much
power you can pour into it."

The sky darkened rapidly. Gavin stared up at it.

"I've never seen anything like that before," Gaspar said
to him, wiping a sleeve across his face after taking a drink.
"Maybe she's right. Maybe we are in some other place."

"Some other place. Some other power. Maybe somebody else's control," Jayna said with a frown. "And if we
are, I don't know what it might be."

"What do you mean?" Gavin asked.

"Well, we were talking about the ancients and how
they have their own kinds of powers, and they can gift
those powers if they want to. But I don't know if we're
somehow trapped in one of the ancient's realms."

"Why would there be a place like this that the Sul'toral
can access?"

"You don't know that they were Sul'toral," she said.

"I saw them. They were. I've only fought one other like
that before."

Jayna sat quietly for a moment. "If that's correct..." Her
tone suggested that she wasn't convinced. "Then we are in
a place of Sarenoth. I have connected to his power, but
only indirectly."

"How do you manage that?" Gavin asked. "I thought
you were afraid of the dark power."

"It's not entirely dark, I've learned. Sarenoth is a balance of dark and light. When I call on the power, there is cold and heat and pain and relief," Jayna said, shaking her head. "I have to find a balance." She breathed out. "But this can't be a place of Sarenoth. Eva wouldn't have been drawn by it."

She got to her feet and paced.

Gaspar dropped down on the ground next to him. "Something has got her goat," he muttered as he took another drink. "She keeps going on and on about this Sarenoth."

"It's the power of the Sul'toral," Gavin said. "And when I suggested that we might be in his realm, she seemed especially bothered by it."

"What if this isn't his realm?" Gaspar asked. "I mean, we're talking about gods here, aren't we? I know she wants to call them ancients, but they're gods. And if they *are* gods, don't you think they would have more important things to do?"

"Other than returning influence to our world?"

"Influence, sure, but maybe that's not what they're after." He looked from Gavin to where Jayna was pacing. "Gods. There are sorcerers who tap into some greater power. Maybe this is just some construct of their making. This might be some enchantment they created."

"Just to trap us?"

"Well, it has her trapped here," Gaspar said, nodding toward Jayna. "And now you. How many others like you are trapped in something like this? Or in this exact place? She mentioned her friend, and we know how powerful she is, so it's entirely possible that they have trapped anyone who's too powerful to deal with."

That was a possibility Gavin hadn't given much thought to.

"They wanted to get us out of the way," he whispered.

"Maybe, but maybe they still need you for something. If this is meant to weaken you in some way…"

"Or to force us to link our power to them," Gavin said.

"What was that?"

He could still feel the bralinath trees and how he had connected to them, even if he didn't really understand what it was that he had done. "What if they're trying to coerce us into connecting to them, to use us so that we allow ourselves to be connected?"

"This is some ploy to draw on your power?" Gaspar said.

"Draw on ours or others, or maybe this is how they consolidate different kinds of power."

Unfortunately, the idea fit with a thought that had been bothering him. Why trap him rather than trying to kill him? They hadn't tried that yet. Given how easily they held him here, he suspected they could kill him if they wanted to. Only, they hadn't.

If this was some way of gathering power, it would make sense.

"Keep working on it, boy. Figure out something with that enchantment of yours. You broke it, but that doesn't mean you can't fix it. And then get us out of here."

Gavin cupped the enchantment in his hand as he turned it over, wondering if he might be able to fix it. If he could, he could reach Wrenlow and maybe understand what was happening outside of this place. Maybe he could even get help.

"Be ready," Jayna said, breaking his concentration. "We have another attack coming."

Gavin got to his feet. He didn't want to fight, but that might be how they would have to spend their night.

CHAPTER FIFTEEN

It turned out to be just as long a night as he was afraid of.

Gavin found himself sleeping in fits and starts. Nothing more than that, and certainly nothing with any sort of consistency. He was still tired when daylight began to build. He had no idea if it was truly morning, or if whatever time this place seemed to recognize simply shifted, waking him again.

Jayna sat with her legs crossed, hands resting in her lap, her head bobbing forward. She had her hands wrapped around her ring, as if holding onto it and afraid she was going to lose something within it.

Gaspar lay curled on his side, facing the water, but he was still sleeping.

For his part, Gavin needed to stretch. He got to his feet and moved as quickly as he could away from the others so he wouldn't disturb them. He unsheathed his sword and studied the blade. The markings along it demonstrated the El'aras component to it, but there was something else there that he thought he might try to understand. If he could understand something from the El'aras enchantments, he might be able to re-create them somehow. The sword was certainly an enchantment, but it was no doubt a higher level than anything else he'd ever seen before. If he could figure out what the El'aras had done to place enchantments into the sword, maybe he could learn how to make them, not just link to those that already existed.

The writing formed patterns that he thought he might be able to understand if he focused on it, though Gavin had not taken the time needed to fully understand the El'aras writing. If only he could reach Wrenlow, he might be able to talk it over with him. Without Wrenlow, Gavin had to treat it like any other pattern. The sword wasn't the only enchanted El'aras item he had on him.

He sheathed the sword and pulled the dagger out. Gavin traced his finger along the writing but couldn't tell anything from it. It could simply be El'aras artisans placing some lettering along the surface, as if leaving some part of themselves behind.

It reminded him of what Alana had told him. She, along with the other enchanters, always spoke about putting something of themselves into the enchantments they made. From the way Jayna had spoken of them, there was an emotional component to it, and you had to add that element into the enchantment for it to take hold.

When he had worked with the enchanters, he didn't have the sense that they used much emotion. At least, Alana didn't make it seem as if she put too much emotion into her enchantments. What she described was something different.

When he pushed some power out from himself, he felt a bridge between him and what he intended to enchant. It connected him and linked him, which would be no different than placing part of himself into it. Maybe what he attempted was not nearly as complex as what he had believed.

He heard something behind him.

Gavin spun, dagger held out, ready for another attack. Nothing moved.

The others were sleeping, and he wanted to let them keep doing so. Gaspar needed his sleep. He didn't know how much rest Jayna required, but she looked to be sleeping soundly as well. Which meant this would be up to him.

He slipped forward, looking for what had made the sound nearby. He picked his way through the grasses and up the slope, before looping back to the water. When he reached it, he stared for a moment. He couldn't drink it without Jayna using her enchantment to purify it, though Gavin didn't know if it was dangerous for him to do anyway.

The air was warmer than he remembered the day before. When he'd been fighting, it had felt warm but not hot. Now there was heat.

As he turned, he noticed smoke.

Ashara. Eva.

He backed toward Jayna, keeping his gaze on the smoke. He nudged her. She awoke with a start, immediately raising her hand, which caused Gavin to jump away from her. He pointed in the direction of the smoke.

Jayna got to her feet carefully and turned, looking up the valley slope.

"How long has it been there?" she whispered.

"I just noticed it. I felt the heat first."

"You *felt* it?" She was staring at him, though he wasn't sure why that seemed to surprise her.

"I felt it. I don't know if that means anything, but I can feel something out there."

"Maybe it's not her," Jayna said, her voice quiet.

"You thought she would come?"

"She comes with smoke, but not usually heat," she said. "None of them do. I think they use it, but heat only powers them, though I don't really know how."

Gavin found himself watching her, questions coming to mind, but he wasn't sure what to ask. There was so much more to Eva than he had known. What he'd heard from Anna about the Ashara had suggested that there was fire. Which meant that Eva would be tied to fire.

"We should follow, whatever it is. And if she finds another key, maybe you can use that to leave," Gavin said. And then he could use his key for him and Gaspar to escape.

He gazed at the smoke. It hadn't moved and seemed to

just hang there, which was a strange thing to realize. It didn't catch any of the breeze, or shift or shimmer or do anything he would've expected.

It was just smoke.

"That's not the same as what I've seen from her before," Gavin said.

He took a step toward it, and the smoke began to fade, which caused him to freeze.

"I've seen smoke like that, but not quite so thick," Jayna said. "Elements are similar, but not the same."

Gaspar joined them. "What is it?"

"We were just talking about the smoke out there in the distance."

Gaspar snorted. "You're talking about smoke? Do you expect it to do tricks?"

"Yes," Gavin and Jayna both said at the same time.

"Maybe it's just fog."

"I'm not exactly sure that it is fog," Jayna said. "I haven't seen anything like that in the time that I've been here."

"So you are convinced this is Ashara," Gavin said, and she nodded. "What can you tell me about them?"

He knew what he had heard from Rayena, along with what he suspected Anna might say, but Jayna would have a different perspective.

"What do you want to hear? The Ashara are another kind of power. I suppose they are similar to the El'aras in how they have a natural type of magic."

Gavin remembered what he had seen when he had faced Eva before. He had never fought her himself, but he did remember the smoke and the unique kind of power she possessed. He had never considered the possibility that her kind of magic would be because she was some historic enemy of the El'aras. Though if they were both ancient powers, perhaps that made sense.

"Natural magic as opposed to sorcery?" Gaspar asked.

"Like that," she said. "Sorcery is tied to a natural magic, but it also is tied to more of the natural magic of the world. You use a series of patterns, a collection of items, and sometimes even speak certain words, all to gather power together. The most impressive sorcerers all have knowledge. It's not a matter of collecting power so much as it is experience and an understanding of how to use that."

"And then there are the Sul'toral," Gavin said.

"I've told you that the Sul'toral were the very first sorcerers. They learned about magic. They founded the Society. And then some of them burrowed within the Society to hide," she said, and Gavin sensed her hesitation to share anything more with him. "But they tapped into a greater power. They used that of Sarenoth, or we believe they did, to ask for something greater."

Gavin glanced down at her ring. "And you?"

"I don't serve Sarenoth," she said quickly.

"Are you sure?"

Jayna twisted her ring as she looked over to him. There was a hint of darkness in her eyes. "I don't *serve* Sarenoth. I told you that there is a balance that has to be found. There is power, but the kind of power I use is different and unique. I'm not entirely sure how to describe it, only that I feel both light and dark. Which suggests to me that Sarenoth is both. Maybe the bloodstone changed the connection I have to the ring and to the power I can draw, but it doesn't change me."

He was still watching the smoke. It hadn't done anything different, but he kept his gaze on it, concerned that it might eventually shift or move. When it did, he wanted to be ready for where it would go. There had to be some purpose for the smoke to linger like that, though Gavin wasn't sure what that would be.

"Do you think Sarenoth wants you to use that power?" Gavin asked.

"I think all of the ancients want us to use their power because it gives them strength," Jayna said.

He pulled his attention away from smoke, but he kept it at the periphery of his vision. "Wait. How does drawing on their power give them strength?"

Jayna shook her head. "It's not the same kind of strength. At least, it's not the way you would normally conceive of it. But accessing the ancient power in what we normally consider to be our world gives those ancients strength in our world. It gives influence. Without that, what would they have?" She shrugged and fiddled with her ring, and a hint of power began to flow from it. "Think about what you have experienced with the Sul'-toral. Before they were active again, had you known of any Sarenoth power?"

"I had never heard of Sarenoth before I met you. Then again, I had never heard of Sul'toral either. You're suggesting that the Sul'toral drawing power from Sarenoth gives him strength?"

"Perhaps," Jayna said. "Or maybe it's just that having somebody use his power permits Sarenoth to still touch the world. With enough connection and enough people using that power, those ancients can influence even more."

"Which means we are fighting a proxy war," Gavin said.

"I suppose it's something like that."

Gaspar snorted and looked at Jayna. "What about you? Using this power means you are helping."

"I'm using the power to stop those who want to use it the wrong way. I'm not sure I'm any better, but I don't chase power for the sake of it. At least, I never have…" She glanced down. "Sometimes I wonder."

"What do you wonder?" Gavin asked.

"What will happen when this is all over."

Was Gavin any different? He didn't chase power for the sake of it either. He had never wanted to have El'aras magic, and he had never wanted the nihilar power. And that was not all that different than how Jayna drew on the magic of Sarenoth.

He had seen that power used before, he had seen the danger of it, and he had seen the way the El'aras viewed it as a great shadow. Now that he had access to that power and could somehow use it, did that mean he had somehow turned evil? He didn't feel that power trying to influence him. He wasn't chasing it simply for the sake of power, something he felt that Jayna shared with him. It was more about using it to stop something worse.

"I understand how you feel," he said.

Jayna twisted her ring, and a faint haze of pale red energy flowed from her. "I don't care if you do. You do what is necessary for you, and I have done what is necessary for me."

Gavin let out a small laugh. "I'm going to be ready for whatever we have to face, but I think the war has already started."

"You're wrong," Jayna said, her voice soft as she looked at the smoke.

"How?" he asked. The El'aras wouldn't have moved if the war hadn't forced them to. They wouldn't have given up their ancestral home unless they had needed to. And the Sul'toral wouldn't have come to Yoran unless there was some plan to attack.

"The war never stopped."

Jayna started forward, and the smoke immediately began to move.

He followed, but Gaspar grabbed his wrist.

"She isn't making sense," Gaspar said.

"Unfortunately, I think she is."

"If that's the case, then I'm not sure this is what I want to be a part of."

Gavin met Gaspar's eyes. "I'm not sure we have much choice at this point. I think we have always been a part of it. Think about what has happened in Yoran."

"Yoran wasn't part of some magical war," Gaspar said.

"Even in the last few decades, the city has been a part of something greater," Gavin said. "Sorcerers versus enchanters, and even earlier than that, sorcerers versus the El'aras. The war has been ongoing. We just haven't known who was really involved."

He continued to follow Jayna.

She paused where the smoke had been. It had lifted, and now there was nothing more than a residual energy. Gavin strained for his core reserves and felt a faint hint of magic, but he didn't try to invert it as he had before.

Jayna traced her hand in a pattern, red light flowing from her ring, and she swept around the area where the smoke had been.

"Will that permit you to detect the Ashara?" Gavin asked.

"Them, or their passing."

"If she was here, why wouldn't she have come to you?" Gaspar said.

Jayna shook her head. "I'm not convinced this was Eva."

"Then who else?"

"She's not the only Ashara who was here. There was another in Nelar that she had known before, or thought she had known. They've been hiding, though I don't know how many of the Ashara remain."

"Because they battled with the El'aras," Gavin said.

Jayna watched him for a moment and then nodded slowly.

"What if she decides to fight me?"

She shrugged. "That might be a different matter. I can't say she won't view you as El'aras. She's changed. When you saw her last, she was in the midst of trying to regain some of her memories. She has. Not all of them. We don't know what happened other than one of the Sul'toral attacked her. She was lucky to survive, but she's still working through recovering what she can. Most of her memories aren't there."

"What happens if she remembers and decides that she wants to kill the El'aras?" Gavin asked.

"This is Eva."

That wasn't an answer. And as he watched Jayna, he realized that she didn't have much of one.

"We can keep moving," she said. "I can follow this way."

She walked along the valley edge but didn't head up and over to where Gavin would see the trees. He could still feel the bralinath, though he wasn't sure how much of that was tied to the enchantment he thought he had placed to link them, and how much was tied to the fact that they were just bralinath trees. He didn't know. It was possible that he was feeling that connection, rather than anything else.

"I've been feeling a few scattered surges of the Ashara," Jayna said, moving along the ridgeline. "I'm not exactly sure what it is I'm feeling or why, only that, every so often, I detect a hint of something here."

Gaspar stepped toward her. "What something?"

"There was a trace of smoke. It might be tied to the Ashara, but I'm not confident."

She paused again, the power flowing out from her leaving a reddish haze hovering over everything. It lingered for a moment, and Gavin was aware of the power she used and how she pressed it downward. He could feel that coming off of her, and he did not know quite what to make of it, only that the presence was distinct.

And then it began to fade.

Jayna started off, though she continued to twist her Toral ring and send power flooding out from her the way it had from the very beginning. Gavin and Gaspar followed her, staying quiet as they did. She would pause periodically, turning as if to try to detect something around her, before moving onward.

"We seem to be getting close," Jayna said.

"What if she doesn't want you to follow her?" Gaspar asked.

"I don't know. She knows I want to help her, but I don't know what she might do."

"What if she decides to attack you?"

Jayna shook her head. "She won't."

"But what if she does?"

"Then we have to remind her we're trying to help."

She moved forward again, saying nothing more.

Gavin wanted to be ready. Jayna might be confident about Eva, but he knew better than to pretend there was no possibility of danger. He might not feel anything, but that in itself posed a danger. He was aware of how the bralinath trees pulled on him, but it was subtle. He had to be careful.

Jayna paused again. "Damn," she muttered. "Look at where we are."

Gavin turned around. Everything was off in this place, but it did look like they had been circling around the top of the ridgeline and hadn't made any progress. "We're walking in a circle?"

Jayna breathed out a heavy sigh. "Apparently. I told you this place is strange. I've been trying to get a handle on it, to understand what this place is and what it's trying to do to us, but I haven't been able to."

"So we've been making a circuit around here?"

"Pretty much." She stopped and held her hand out, and the same red glow began to flow away from her. "But I'm determined to figure out what it is and if I can find a break in it."

"You really think you can?" Gaspar asked.

"I haven't so far, but maybe with the two of you here, we might be able to find something different. I just don't know."

She took a seat and looked away from them.

Gaspar held one of his daggers and flipped it from one hand to another, as if he were readying for a fight that only he could see. "What do you think?" he asked Gavin.

Gavin pursed his lips. "I have no idea. We can reach the trees, but we can't reach this other place?"

"There has to be some way to get across."

"Unless there is no *across*." Gavin stared, trying to figure out what to make of it. "What if there is nothing beyond here?"

"Or we're going out the wrong way?" Gaspar asked.

Gavin frowned deeply. Maybe Gaspar was right. They had followed the ridgeline and been up on the other side, but what if they tried walking around the water?

He started down the valley again, ignoring Jayna as she

called after him. When he reached the edge of the water, he began to circle it. He did so slowly, but by the time he was about halfway around, he could feel something pulling on him.

At first, he thought that maybe it was just his imagination and that there wasn't really anything there, but the longer he walked, the more certain he was that something was pulling on him. He focused instead on the enchantment he had placed to link him to the bralinath trees. He pushed downward, drawing his power in a different way, and then took a step.

Everything seemed to blur.

Gavin froze.

"Gaspar," he said.

"I'm here, but you are indistinct. It's like you're standing in some sort of shroud."

"Get Jayna."

Gavin didn't dare move. He had no idea what would happen if he continued to step through this, but if he were to transition past whatever was blocking them and into something else, he wasn't about to do it alone.

As Gaspar brought Jayna over, Gavin still felt the pull, a strange sensation that seemed to drag on him as if it were tugging him.

Gavin resisted the urge to fight it.

"Stay by me," he said. "I think this might be how we can get out of here."

"What did you do?" Jayna asked, the irritation in her voice suggesting that she thought she should be able to do the same.

"I'm not sure. But stay close, and we can see what else we might be able to do."

Gavin didn't say anything. At this point, the only thing he did was try to hold onto his connection, and he stepped through whatever shroud was trying to keep them in this place.

CHAPTER SIXTEEN

The shifting pool of water remained constant, even as he stepped through. Gavin was aware of how it lingered next to him, and he could practically feel the water pressing on him, as if the pool itself were causing some of this.

That's something to consider.

Having seen the changing power within that pool of water, Gavin had to wonder if perhaps it was somehow connected. Maybe everything in this place was linked, much like the bralinath trees were. They connected to him and seemed as if they were connected to this world, but what if there was something more to it?

Could they be drawing power from him?

Or perhaps they were channeling power *to* him by drawing it out of this world.

Gavin didn't know. It didn't strike him as if they were siphoning any power for him or even from him, only that he had felt something more ever since he'd connected to them.

Jayna crouched down. "This is new." A faint pink haze began to sweep away from her. "What did you do?"

"I used the enchantment I made. At least, that I think I made." Gavin didn't really know if he had made anything or if he'd simply modified it the way he had in the past. That, at least, felt like the kind of power he possessed.

"It feels different," Jayna said.

Gaspar joined them. "Do you see any smoke?" he asked.

"I don't—"

A gigantic snakelike creature shot toward them out of the grass.

Gavin unsheathed his blade in a fluid movement and swung it toward the creature, instinctively grabbing for his core reserves and the power of the El'aras ring. There was the strange resistance with his core reserves, but if he pushed it the other way...

The snake lunged at him, snapping massive jaws, and Gavin barely avoided it.

He sprung to his feet, and a tail with long spikes darted toward him. He twisted and felt one of the spikes graze past him, just missing him.

"Try to hold it!" he shouted at Jayna.

Jayna jumped on the snake, stabbing a dagger into its side and slashing along the length of the creature. The snake thrashed, but Jayna continued to slide all the way along its body, until she reached the tail. She bounced off

—obviously using magic, given how fast she moved—and landed next to Gavin.

"Haven't seen a creature like that in a few years," Jayna said.

"When I was outside of Yoran, we used to come across strange things like that," Gaspar said, backing away from it. Was he scared of it? "Maybe not quite like that, but similar enough."

"All you have to do is split them down the middle. They don't have a heart or an easy place to target, but if you gut them, you can keep them from attacking. They might take a little while to die, but they will. Eventually," Jayna said.

Gavin regarded Jayna with amusement. "I never would've taken you for someone to handle a snake."

"There's a lot you don't know about me." Jayna knelt in front of it. "Back when I first started serving my Sul'toral I encountered these more often. I didn't ever learn what these are called, but they are dark beings."

"This one just felt like a creature," Gavin said.

"That's strange."

Gavin snorted. "And what about any of this isn't strange?" He spread his hands out and gestured around him. "We're trapped in a magical prison. Up until recently, we were walking in circles, following some hidden magical path that kept bringing us back to the same place. Everything about this feels bizarre."

"Maybe there's a way we can activate a doorway," Gaspar said, looking from one to the other. "Jayna, you said something about a key, but Gavin said something different. Assuming we are now in another place and dealing with another kind of power, what if there is a different key here? Gavin used the key in his place, so now we need to find one here."

"Maybe," Jayna said. "But it doesn't fit with what I understand of this world."

"How much of it can you really understand?"

Maybe what Gavin needed to do was to focus on the bralinath trees and see if he could use them to fold himself up and draw himself down. That was what he had done before, hadn't it?

He tried, but it didn't seem to make a difference.

They made their way along the slope, with Jayna leading them. Gavin continued to try pulling on his connection to the bralinath trees, but something didn't feel quite right. It was almost as if that connection were muted. Since stepping through the shroud, some part of it had changed.

They kept walking in what seemed like a circle.

Jayna had her brow furrowed as she marched quickly. She twisted her ring, and pale red magic flowed out from her, before settling onto the ground. Each time she did, she would pause and focus, as if she were detecting something from within the power she was holding onto. Then she would release it and move onward.

"I don't know that we're going to find anything here," Gaspar said. "We have to start preparing for another possibility."

"And what possibility is that?" Gavin asked.

"That we might be stuck here."

Gaspar kicked at a stone, then walked away from them.

Gavin picked the stone up and studied it. Whatever they had been doing wasn't working, which meant they needed to try something else. They had a limited amount of time. He didn't know how long, not in this place, but he believed there was a limit. Frustration surged, and he tossed the rock.

When they'd made a complete circuit, Jayna pointed to the fallen form of the snake they'd killed. "We made another loop. It didn't feel like it, but there it is."

Gavin looked up toward the ridgeline. There had been bralinath trees in the other place. Maybe there was something similar here. When he said as much, they followed him up the slope, though Jayna had fallen silent. Almost sullen. Gaspar wore a pensive look, but he didn't argue.

By the time they reached the ridgeline, Gavin wasn't expecting much. He paused for a moment, listening for any sound of movement around him, worried that another creature would try an attack, but nothing came.

That reassured him more than it probably should.

Even still, Gavin felt unsettled. Gaspar had a pair of daggers in hand. He had to be nervous as well. Gavin shared that feeling, not just because of the strangeness around them but because of what they had already dealt with. He expected to find another monster at every turn.

"We've already dealt with one dark creature in this place," Gavin said, looking over to Jayna, "but have you seen or felt any others since you've been here?"

"Everything I've seen could possibly be one. All of them are just regular creatures that have been twisted."

"I haven't seen that many dark creatures in my travels."

"Then you've been lucky," Jayna said. "I have seen countless."

He thought about the hyadan, but even those weren't *truly* dark creatures. As far as he knew, those were manifestations of magic—dark magic, possibly, but not true dark creatures. And they had been created by sorcerers.

"Anything can be twisted for a purpose," Jayna explained. "Eventually, if the wrong creature comes across the wrong sorcerer or magic user... It depends on the creature, as well as the power they have intrinsically and whether they can be twisted or tainted. Dark sorcerers use pain and suffering in what they refer to as a festival." She shook her head and scoffed. "They use this to power weapons, dark spells, and the kind of magic I don't completely understand and that I have no interest in understanding anymore."

"What about things that are created with magic?" Gavin asked.

"They are more like enchantments than anything else," she said. "I haven't dealt with those as often." She frowned. "Though it seems like you have."

Gavin nodded. "More than I would've cared to."

"It surprises me that you haven't dealt with dark creatures."

"I think it's the kind of magic we associate with. I tend to deal with sorcerers who use enchantments, and you tend to deal with dark magic."

She smiled, and a blur of movement behind her caught Gavin's attention.

A stone monster.

It lumbered toward them quickly.

Gavin nudged Gaspar. "Are you ready to look big and frightening?"

Gaspar turned, taking in the creature moving toward them. It was just a single stone monster, but they knew how dangerous it could be. "Again?" he said with a sigh.

As the thing neared, it slowed and regarded them differently than the ones in the other realm. It was almost cautious. This one was tall and slender, much like the second stone monster they had faced...

It *was* the second one, Gavin realized.

Jayna surged forward, slashing power from her ring. The creature shrieked, a strange and hollow sound that echoed before it spun and stomped away. She and Gaspar chased after it, waving their hands in the air.

It would be amusing if it weren't for Gavin's sudden curiosity. The creature moved faster than he could follow. At least, faster than he could follow without access to real power. The thing took enormous strides and tore across the ground, leaving them behind.

When Jayna and Gaspar returned, both of them were laughing.

"We could have followed it," Gavin said.

"Why would you want to?" Jayna asked, turning back, a hint of a smile on her face. "I can't believe that worked, though. When you guys found me, it wasn't the first time I'd run into those things."

"That's the exact same one you were fighting," Gavin said.

Gaspar's eyes widened.

Jayna frowned. "Are you sure?"

"If I know my stone monsters, that's the exact same one," Gavin said.

And if it was, that meant the creatures had some way of traveling between where they had been and where they were now.

Gavin looked back. The creature was nowhere in sight.

"But I've gone that way," Jayna said. "You've gone that way with me."

Gavin nodded. "We have."

"And if that was tied to them…" She twisted her ring. Gavin had the sense that she did that when she was thinking, or perhaps she called on power to help her think. Maybe there was some spell to help her organize things in her brain. "Could they have some way of connecting to both realms?"

"It seems that way. We should follow where it went."

Gavin didn't understand it, only that there had to be some way for the creatures to go between places. If the stone monsters could do it, then maybe Eva and the others with her were able to do the same thing.

Gaspar said nothing, though Gavin had a sense of his discomfort.

They started off. The air was warm here as well. Gavin looked around, wondering if maybe there was a sign of Eva or the other Ashara, but he saw nothing. Just bleak landscape all around them.

They turned toward where the bralinath trees should be. Gavin could still vaguely feel the faint connection he had formed with them, along with the trees themselves, but he didn't feel it nearly as strongly as he had before.

"This is where those trees should be," he said. "Maybe they don't exist in this place. But in the other place, they were the key."

He strode forward, focusing on his core reserves. When he had been in the other realm, he had felt something, and he'd noticed that there was some power there, even if he couldn't fully understand it. The bralinath trees had allowed him to tie into their power.

There was nothing here but a flat white stone near what would have been the center of the trees. He crouched down, tracing his hand across the stone. It was cold. Almost painfully so.

Could this be the key?

Gavin focused on the power within him and tried to push it down. In the other place, pushing downward like this had made a difference and permitted him to connect to the trees. In this one, though, there was resistance, and he detected nothing else. Maybe he couldn't link to this key.

He looked up. What about Jayna?

He motioned for her to join him.

She froze when she reached the stones. "How did you find this?" she whispered.

"I don't know. I just saw it."

She licked her lips, and her face went pale.

"What?" he said.

"You said that the trees were on the other side and that, somehow, the trees were something you could connect to?"

"Right. There's going to be a key. When I got near the trees, I felt like I could link to them. I tried that here, and I couldn't."

She knelt down and reached her hand out toward the stone, but she held it just above the surface. "It's dragon stone. At least, that's what it was colloquially called. I don't know what it's truly called, but it's dragon stone. This is what the Toral rings are made of. You have to imagine it without the bloodstone around it, though. But I would bet my life that this is dragon stone."

"Then you have to connect to it," Gavin said.

She shook her head and looked up at him. "Why? I wouldn't be able to reach this place without you, and—"

"You wouldn't have been able to reach it, but you didn't come here on your own. You chased Eva, right?"

"I did," she said, her voice a soft whisper.

"And what was she doing?" Gavin said.

"There was a place outside the capital. We were working there, dealing with the Society," Jayna said. "Something opened. Eva called it a conduit. She seemed to understand it better than she let on, and when it was fully open, she used it. She thought she needed to come here for answers. And maybe she did. But when she stayed away, I followed. Then we got stuck when the conduit closed."

"Do you think the conduit was trying to connect to some power in this place?" Gavin asked.

"You've seen it," Jayna said. "There is no power in this place. I don't know what they intended, only that whatever it was means that there is something here, something out there, and there is an attempt to link them."

"Another way of drawing on Sarenoth?"

Jayna shrugged. "Maybe."

"If that's the case, I don't know that opening it makes sense," Gavin said.

"Then she doesn't have to do it," Gaspar said, stepping forward. He looked at Jayna. "You don't have to do it. I see that look in your eyes, girl." Jayna arched a brow when he called her *girl*, but Gaspar pushed on. "I know how a person looks when they're scared. You don't have to reach for the wrong kind of power."

"It's my magic," she said. "I used to think that it might corrupt me, but the more I used it, the more I understood that there are aspects to the power that can corrupt, but there are also aspects to it that don't. I told you that it requires balance."

"How much power do you want?" Gavin asked.

She looked at him but said nothing.

"Some people chase power," he said.

Jayna nodded. "Some people. Not me. I only wanted to help people. My brother, primarily. He was lost. And now I finally know what happened to him. Once I get Eva out of here, then I can help Jonathan and…" She sighed. "It doesn't matter."

"What happened to him?"

"He's a thief. Dealt with magic. Probably the kind that ended up getting him in trouble, and now he's in prison.

I'd love to help him out, but I'm not even fully sure which prison he's in. I thought he was dead. At least, I feared he was." She shook her head. "Enough of that. That's not why we are here."

She clenched her jaw and then crouched down, pushing her hand toward the stone. As she did, the stone seemed to ripple. Gavin had no idea what it was doing or why it was rippling, only that it seemed like there was something coming after it.

He watched.

But she only held her hand in place.

"I don't want to push too hard," Jayna said softly.

"Then don't," Gavin said.

"If we want to get answers, I have to, don't I?"

"We can find answers another way."

"Can we?" She bit her lip. "I don't know if we can. I think we need to do this. And I need to do this. You already connected to your side, and now I think I need to connect to mine, mostly so we can understand whether there is something here we can use."

"We already know there's something here," Gavin said. "And for you to force your way through it…"

He didn't know. If she was truly connected to Sarenoth, there was a real possibility that anything she might do might cause harm to them. He wasn't going to say that to her, mostly because he didn't want to offend her, but it was a fear he had.

She swallowed again, and as she did, she pushed her hand down. When it made contact with the stone, she gritted her teeth.

"It's cold," she said. "I... It's cold." She let go for a moment, took a deep breath, and then pushed it down again. Jayna squeezed her eyes shut. Gavin couldn't tell what she was doing. "I can feel it," she said. "I can feel... Well, I don't exactly know. I can feel something."

She held her hand in place and continued to push, letting that power flow outward from her.

And then her eyes flew open and went wide. "I feel it. There." Jayna jerked her hand back.

"What did you do?" Gavin asked.

She licked her lips, and she leaned back. "I don't really know. I could feel something. It felt like I needed to link to something, but I'm not exactly sure what it is." She frowned, and she closed her eyes briefly. "And now I can still feel it. Again, I don't really know what it is, only that there is some presence in the back of my mind."

"An enchantment," Gavin said.

She looked over to him. "I think so, but I don't know why."

"To be honest, I don't either. I'm not sure if it's something of this place or if it's meant to be a representation of the ancients, as you call them, or... if this is some sort of trap."

"If it's a trap, then we just triggered it," she said.

Gavin shook his head. "No. I already triggered it. You were just doing what I suggested."

"What if it is meant to hold us here?"

"I'm less concerned about that and more concerned about using it to harm those we care about who aren't inside the trap."

All of this felt strange to him, but Gavin couldn't help but feel as if he needed different answers. They had to keep looking.

"You said there were three keys," he said.

Jayna nodded. "That's what we were told before we entered."

"What if there are more?" He looked around. "What if there are many more, and what if there are more realms like this? There are more than three ancients. So this would be Sarenoth, and what I connected to would represent the El'aras. That means there would be keys for other ancients."

Or worse—these weren't keys at all.

If that was the case, what did all of this mean? Gavin felt as though they did not truly understand what they needed to.

But it was worse than that.

They didn't have the time to piece it together.

CHAPTER SEVENTEEN

J ayna continued to make a circuit around the dragon
stone, and Gavin left her to it. He wasn't going to be
able to do anything here. He might be able to still feel
the bralinath trees, and he might be aware of some other
power, but he couldn't tie himself to it the same way she
could.

Gavin didn't know if his power could connect here,
but increasingly, he thought he needed to better understand if it could and if it did.

Ancients.

That thought stayed with him. Jayna believed that all
of this was tied to some ancient power, which would
bridge them to something greater. If this was a realm of
Sarenoth, and where Gavin had ended up before was a
realm of the El'aras, then what about others? He knew of
the Ashara, but how many were there?

Not only had Jayna mentioned more, but Tristan had

also named other ancients. Gods. What if they were all focused in certain places like this?

Gaspar looked over to him. "This seems to have gotten more complicated."

"This has always been complicated," Gavin said.

"You've got a great power. Now you've got something else. And we're still trapped."

Gavin nodded. "Very much. You've summed it up quite nicely."

"We don't have a whole lot of time," Gaspar said. "I don't know what it's like outside of here, but if time is passing differently, we can't linger too much longer. We need to get back to Yoran to make sure we can help. If it's not too late."

Gavin looked over to where Jayna was now crouching next to the stones, holding her hands in front of them. She frowned as she traced a pattern with her fingers. Was she working with sorcery, or was she using her Toral power? Or was there something else to it?

"What if we aren't supposed to?" Gavin asked.

"I think *we* are, but I'm not so sure about her. She came for a different reason. She said she's after her friend, but what if there is something else that brought her here?"

"I don't think she's lying to us about Eva," Gavin said. "Unfortunately, I'm not exactly sure that helping Eva is really in my interest either."

"Because she's Ashara. Just because the Ashara and the El'aras are enemies doesn't mean that you have to make them your enemy."

"I know. But we already know that there was fire attacking the El'aras."

"What if that's tied to what's here?" Gaspar asked.

Gavin frowned. What if it was?

They needed to get out so they could find answers.

"And there's something else, boy. What if she doesn't want to leave?"

"Jayna or Eva?" Gavin said.

"Both."

"Well, then I think we have to leave them here."

The idea of leaving Jayna behind didn't sit well with him. She had helped them, and though he knew that she had her own agenda, so did he. And Gavin increasingly felt as if he had to help her escape, mostly so that they could find a way to fight together.

He turned his attention to her, watching her for a few moments. "I still don't know why she was in the El'aras realm."

"It's obvious, isn't it?" Gaspar said.

Gavin glanced over. "What about it is obvious? When it comes to any of this, nothing is obvious."

"Her reason for being there. She already told you. Her friend and the Ashara have some grudge against the El'aras."

"Maybe the other Ashara, but not Eva."

Or maybe there was another reason.

Gavin watched Jayna. They would help her find Eva, but they also had to be prepared for the possibility that things might take a dangerous turn.

"If we find Eva, we have to be ready for the possibility that she might try to attack," he said.

"Normally, I would give you pretty good odds," Gaspar said with a shrug. "Well, at least even odds. She was powerful when we saw her before. Still, you've also grown in your power, and you certainly are more competent than you were before." He offered a hint of a smile. "But in this place, diminished as you are, I'm not sure it's an even fight, the way it was before."

"I don't think it was ever an even fight," Gavin said.

"You have been talking about enchantments with Jayna for a while," Gaspar said. "Now I think it's time you start working through that piece of the puzzle. If you can reach the kid, we can let him know what's going on. And we can hear what has happened to them."

Gavin turned his attention to the rock. "I've been worried about breaking the enchantment beyond repair."

"So practice."

"That's not going to be easy here," Gavin said, shaking his head. "Besides, I don't really know what I need to do with enchantments."

"You've just got to keep working with it and try different things," Gaspar said. "I know this place is strange for you, but that doesn't mean you can't do it."

Gavin knew he needed to try something. Maybe he could bind his connection to the stone. What would he make?

"Alana says that she just tells the enchantments what she wants to do."

"And what about the sorcerers?" Gaspar asked.

Gavin looked over to Jayna. "It sounds like they make a series of patterns, and there's a matter of intention behind it, but also something else. To be honest, I'm not sure what it is."

"So, you aren't a sorcerer, and you aren't really an enchanter, but maybe it's a mingling of the two." Gaspar motioned to Gavin's sword. "That's an enchanted blade, isn't it? What do you have on it?"

"Symbols and patterns in the writing. I've already tried to interpret it, but I can't. I don't know if understanding it would even allow me to use it more effectively. Anna once told me that my lack of understanding of my El'aras side limits me."

"But it also *benefits* you," Gaspar said. "So now you have to embrace the El'aras side. If that's the side that will allow you to make enchantments, then you have to use what you know. Try using some pattern you're familiar with and pushing part of you into it."

It was a reasonable thought.

"Even if I know the right pattern, I don't know that I will be able to fix the enchantment," Gavin said.

Gaspar stared at him. "Just try it, boy."

Gavin sighed and pulled out the dagger. He started carving, cautiously at first. He thought about different enchantments he might place, patterns he had learned from Anna and the others, and he settled on one that seemed most fitting. It was a pattern designed to pull power into it but also explode power outward. He traced the pattern of inverted triangles with a looping swirl around it.

When he was done, he looked at the stone. Now it just looked like he had made a rough carving of it.

"I don't think this did anything," Gavin said.

"Have you added some part of yourself into it?" Gaspar asked. "You just have to give it a try."

Gavin smirked, and he focused on his core reserves, the El'aras ring, and the power that came through it. Given that it was muted in this place, he didn't know if it would matter, but he tried anyway. He pushed through him, calling on some power, and it flowed. But as he pushed outward, he recognized that something wasn't quite right. It was a mistake.

In this place, it wasn't a matter of drawing power out of his core reserves as he had been trained to do. He had to do the reverse—a strange concept.

He was skeptical as he held onto the stone and pushed downward, but he began to feel something shift. The markings he had made on the stone started to glow. Gavin continued to use the strange connection to his core reserves, and the way it linked him to the bralinath trees in this unusual realm.

Power flowed.

And it stayed.

He stared at it. He could feel the energy within it.

It had worked. He had done it. He had made an enchantment.

"What did you do?" Gaspar asked.

Gavin held it out. "Well, we can see if this works."

"And if it does?"

"This took quite a bit out of me, so I don't know if it's going to be effective."

He tossed it, activating it as soon as it rolled across the ground. A brief explosion was followed by the immediate compression of energy.

That wasn't what he was expecting. Even the enchantment worked the opposite of what he had anticipated.

Gavin stared down at it for a moment. "I sort of thought it might do something else."

"I suspect it will be the opposite of what you intend," Jayna said, joining him. "I've been trying to work through things here, and that's the only answer I have."

Gavin looked over to her. She didn't seem surprised that he had managed to make an enchantment or that he had created an explosion.

"Something like that," he said.

"Everything is backwards here. Even the enchantments are backwards."

"I'd love to figure out some way to use my existing enchantment," Gavin said, pulling it from his ear. "I want to connect to my people."

Jayna leaned forward. "When you showed it to me before, I recognized that symbol. It's the same one that sorcerers use. I have a friend who knows how to make similar enchantments, and his uses a similar mark." She pulled what looked like a coin out of her pocket and held it up, twisting it from side to side. "He figured out how to adapt a tracking enchantment into something that can allow communication. But do you see this? The marking is not altogether dissimilar."

Gavin glanced from her coin to his El'aras enchantment. "You think we can use that to fix this?"

"I don't know. Like I said, everything is unusual here. Backwards. Maybe if we can find an inverse of the marking, I can help."

"Would you?" he asked, holding out the enchantment. He didn't love the idea of giving it to her, but he also wanted her help.

She took it carefully, then reached into her pocket and withdrew a piece of metal, which she scraped across the enchantment. "I'm not sure that layering atop an existing enchantment will work. I don't have as much experience with that—"

"It works," Gavin said.

Her eyes widened. "You've done it?"

"I have seen it."

"It's more a matter of layering on top of an El'aras enchantment," Jayna said. "That's not something I've done before. It's not something I've even considered doing before."

"If the symbols are similar, what does it matter?" he asked.

She nodded slowly. "Maybe you're right." She handed it over to him once she finished. "I tried to invert the pattern. I don't know if this is going to work, but theoretically, it seems like it should make a difference, especially with what we've noticed in this place. Besides, I've done something similar elsewhere. You just have to reverse the pattern to get the opposite effect. In this case, if it's a matter of communication..." Jayna glanced at the enchantment, shook her head, and muttered to herself. "Why didn't I think of this before?" She looked up at him. "It should connect."

Gavin squeezed his hand around it. As he had with the stone, he focused, concentrating on what he could detect coming through the ground and through him. He started to push, aware of that energy, and the more he pushed, the more he could feel that building.

He had to use it in a way that was different than what he normally did. But as he did, he felt something grow warm in his palm. He opened his hand and looked down at the enchantment. With a frown, he held it up and turned it over several times.

"It seems like it's working," he said.

"Keep going," Jayna urged. "It's my experience that you can't release an enchantment in the middle of trying to add a connection to it. If you do, it will fail. Unfortunately, when an enchantment fails, I'm not sure you can try again."

Gavin continued to concentrate, and he found the muted resistance against him difficult. It was hard for him to hold onto that power, hard for him to feel any real energy, hard for him to do much of anything. But he kept trying.

The muted energy was there, and as he continued drawing on it, he recognized that it was tying him to the bralinath trees. And though they were not near him, he could feel that power.

Gavin summoned that, and he pushed all of it into the enchantment.

It continued to glow.

Then, finally, it was done.

He stared for a moment. He could see that the metal had taken on a different hue, and it was still warm, though not like it had been when he'd been trying to power it.

He tucked it into his ear, took a deep breath, and tapped on it. "Wrenlow?"

"Gavin?"

Gavin's heart leapt at hearing Wrenlow's voice, but it quickly sunk as he recognized the panic in it.

"I'm here," Gavin said. "We're trapped. We're trying to get back. I know there's an attack on the city."

"There's a *what*?"

Gavin's brow furrowed. "Didn't the Sul'toral attack the city?"

"I don't know what you're talking about." Wrenlow's speech sounded different. Strange. Almost as if it were coming through a tunnel, which it might have been. Maybe the connection folded their voices the same way Gavin and Gaspar had been folded to transport them to this strange place.

"Gaspar and I were attacked by three Sul'toral outside Yoran," Gavin explained. "We were sent to some magical prison, and we can't escape. We've been here for the better part of two days—"

"Two days? I just saw you last night."

Gavin's heart hammered. Jayna had told him that time moved differently here, but he didn't think it would be so different or that they would have that much time.

But they did.

"Then listen carefully," Gavin said. "There are three Sul'toral just outside the city. They're near the El'aras ruins, and they attacked Gaspar and me. I don't know what they're up to or what they're after, but they were able to use power to force us into some magical prison. I'm not sure if they can do the same thing to anybody else, but you need to get Davel and the others mobilized and prepared to defend the city. They're coming."

"If you're sure about it," Wrenlow said. "I think there's something else coming. The El'aras."

"What?"

"Davel is here with me. He was looking for you. I didn't know where you went, Jessica was gone, and I couldn't find Gaspar, which now makes sense. But Davel came to me, mostly because he said the El'aras were converging upon the city."

Anna had come.

"You need to get word to Anna," Gavin said. Or could he do so himself? "I'll try to talk to her too, but let her know that Gaspar and I are trapped someplace. We're trying to get out, but we aren't sure we'll be able to in time. The El'aras can defend against the Sul'toral attack, and you can stay safe."

"When do you think you can return?" Wrenlow asked.

"I don't know. I don't know what it's going to take for us to get back. We've been searching—"

"You said you have been there for two days?"

Gavin tried to explain, but he worried that they didn't have time, and he had no idea how long the enchantment would hold. Thankfully, it seemed as if very little time had actually passed.

"Time is strange here," he said. "Find Anna. Let her know what I said. We are dealing with Sul'toral."

He almost mentioned something about the Ashara, but he decided against it. If he revealed that, he suspected that Anna might react in an unpredictable way.

"I will try," Wrenlow said. "I don't know if the El'aras are going to welcome me in."

"They will. Anna knows you, and she knows of your connection to me. We are still going to look for a way out. I don't know what it's going to take or if it's going to work."

"Gavin? I couldn't hear you there. You started to cut out."

"Wrenlow?"

The enchantment faded even more. Gavin pulled it from his ear and studied it. The mark that Jayna had made on it had started to shift, and the power within the enchantment was gone.

"Why didn't it hold longer than that?" he asked her.

Jayna shrugged. "We've said that things are different here. Less permanent. So even this enchantment isn't going to be permanent enough. I tried to place enough power into it to help, but... I'm sorry."

Gavin looked over to Gaspar. "We need to keep going."

Gaspar frowned at him. "How do you propose we do this? I know you have to have something in mind, but what do you think you can do that we can't?"

"We're in a second realm, right?" Gavin glanced at

Jayna, who also looked doubtful. "We need to get to the Ashara realm. We've seen evidence of smoke, and we know that the rock monsters have some way of connecting to that place. Why can't we use whatever they do to travel between realms?"

"Then you want us to follow these rock monsters," Gaspar said.

"Do you have a better idea?"

Gaspar shook his head. "Not particularly, but I do think I'm going to want more enchantments." He glanced between them. "I don't know if either of you can create some for me?"

"It might not be a bad idea," Jayna said. "If we have to scare off the stone monsters, or perhaps even use those enchantments to track them, we might need some defenses. I had not considered making them for myself before, since I generally don't make many enchantments, but given how weakened our magic is, maybe we need to create all the help we can."

"And Gaspar can help us gather supplies," Gavin said.

It would take time that he wasn't sure they had, but at least time worked differently here.

If they could still return before the Sul'toral started their attack, maybe they could intervene and help. Maybe they could stop them. Gavin wouldn't be able to do it alone, but if he could convince Jayna—and Eva, assuming they found her—to come with them, they might actually have a chance.

That thought stayed with Gavin as he made his way around the plains, collecting rocks, setting them in a pile, and looking for anything else that could be enchanted. Gaspar was quiet as they gathered items. At one point, Jayna muttered that the substrate might be too poor to be effective, but Gavin didn't concern himself with that. He had no idea what she meant by substrate, but he didn't care either. Gavin had seen that the enchantments would work. He had seen that he could get them to be effective.

By the time they sat down, it was late, and the sky had started to shift. Gavin wasn't sure if they should return to the water. He was starting to feel thirsty, though not nearly as thirsty as he thought he should be. But he decided to stay where he was, and he began to place enchantments onto the items.

He knew only destructive magic, but after dealing with what they had seen in this place and anticipating what they were probably going to have to do, destructive magic felt right. Each time he created an enchantment, fatigue washed through him. But he also liked that he had a plan. It wasn't a good one—it was the kind of plan that Gaspar would make fun of him for, but it was still something. That, more than anything else, helped him work harder.

His friends, and his people, needed him to.

CHAPTER EIGHTEEN

Gavin paused in the midst of making a steady circle around a small pile of stones. He traced his finger along the El'aras ring and tried to feel for the power within it, but he kept failing. The energy of the ring might be there, but he could feel how muted it was. Ever since he'd connected to the bralinath trees, there had been an improvement in his ability to reach for that power, but it still didn't flow within him the way he knew that it could and should.

"What's got you troubled, boy?" Gaspar asked. He sat on top of one of the boulders, holding a knife in hand and spinning it slowly, as if seeing if there would be some answers from it.

Gavin breathed out heavily. "All of this, probably, but I think the biggest piece is what's going on and whether it's connected to anything else. Look around us, Gaspar. We were forced here."

"To get us out of the way, or to torment us. Well, to get *you* out of the way."

Gavin stopped twisting his ring and instead grabbed for his El'aras sword, though he still didn't feel anything within it that might help him. He had hoped the blade would offer him any additional connection to his El'aras abilities, but it had not.

"I don't even know if it's about me," he said. "I keep coming back to what we had heard before we left."

"About the gods?" Gaspar said.

Gavin looked back. Jayna had been making a small circuit, though she had given them space. For the most part, she had elected to leave them alone, as if afraid of getting in the middle of whatever they might be discussing, but she would occasionally pause and glance in their direction. She would weave her hands in some pattern that left Gavin thinking that she was probably drawing on the power of one of her spells to listen to them, were it not for the fact that such spells likely didn't work nearly as well here as they would otherwise. Then she would turn her attention back to what she was doing.

"The gods? Can that really be what this is about?" Gavin said.

Gaspar snorted. "You know, if you would've asked me that question a couple years ago, I would've laughed in your face. But ever since getting to know you and dealing with some of the things the two of us have faced, I can no longer rule out the possibility that we might be dealing with something that has to do with the gods. Maybe not even gods we've heard about. But I suppose the better question is: What are the gods?"

Gavin glanced over and frowned. "Supernatural beings that control the magical fate of the world, I suppose."

"Or are they just supremely powerful beings?" Gaspar shrugged. "Think about what you might have thought of someone like Anna before you came to understand your own ability. Would you have thought of her as some sort of god?"

Gavin scratched his chin. "I don't think so, but only because I had experience with the El'aras before meeting her."

Then again, his encounters with the El'aras had never been anything like what he had experienced since he had spent time in Yoran. He understood where Gaspar was going with the line of questioning, though. The old thief wanted Gavin to think about the possibility that there might exist a power that seemed godlike to him. And he could easily fathom something like that.

When they had dealt with the Fates, that kind of power had seemed far and beyond him. But even that had been something he could handle. The Sul'toral had been difficult, but they had also managed to defeat that. But could there be something beyond a Sul'toral? Something that would be even more powerful, and therefore even more difficult for him to deal with? Enough that he would feel inconsequential next to it?

Gavin wasn't sure.

"I don't even know what would qualify as a god any longer," he said.

"Then you are better than most," Gaspar said. "I suppose I shouldn't be terribly surprised. Most people look for some higher power to attribute the fate of the world to. I shouldn't be shocked that you, of all people, would not be as compelled."

Gavin shot him an amused expression. "I don't know if that's a compliment or not."

"I don't either."

"I can't help but think that a place like this, though, is designed for a power like that," Gavin said. "If it can hold me—"

"Look who suddenly got confident in their abilities."

Gavin kicked one of the boulders. "It's less about gaining sudden confidence than it is about coming to understand that the kind of power I'm connected to is vast. If this place can hold me so easily, then who's to say that it couldn't do the same to something that others would consider a god?"

"And there's the point I've been trying to get you to see," Gaspar said.

Gavin chuckled. "I'm not your student."

"If you were, you wouldn't be a very good one."

Gavin laughed harder, but Jayna quickly cut them both off.

"I hear something," she said.

Her head was tipped to the side, and a hint of a breeze tugged at her hair. She held her hand outstretched in front of her, and the bloodstone on her ring glowed with a soft red light, reflecting some of the daylight, but not so brightly that it would draw attention to it. Gavin couldn't help but wonder what kind of power that ring possessed, and whether it was as similar to his El'aras ring as he had first believed. He no longer knew if that was the case.

"What is it?" Gavin whispered.

"I thought it was a rumbling sound at first, but now I'm not sure. If it was, then maybe it's another of those stone creatures."

Gavin reached for his sword and prepared himself. If it was one of those things, he would have to be ready to fight far more aggressively than he had. They had to stop running, and they were going to have to deal with the danger head-on. The only problem was that Gavin wasn't sure what he could do to deal with that danger, especially if whatever it was happened to be unlike anything he had faced in his world. But if it was an enchantment, then enchantments could be overpowered and overwhelmed.

"There's something else," Jayna said, her voice soft. "A slithering sound."

Gaspar jumped to his feet, grabbed for his knives, and looked all around him with eyes wide.

"She didn't say that she saw a spider," Gavin said.

Gaspar wrinkled his nose. "I don't like snakes."

Gavin let out a laugh. "You don't like snakes? I've seen you deal with all sorts of ridiculous magic, and the idea that a snake might be here—"

"*Is* there a snake?" Gaspar asked.

"Not that I see," Gavin said, striding over to him and scratching at the ground with his sword. "And if there is, I'm quite sure you could deal with it."

Gaspar seemed to gather himself, and he looked over

to Gavin, irritation flashing in his eyes. "Are you so certain of that? We're talking about a place that has creatures unlike anything you have ever seen before, ones that can keep us from using our power, to the point where we are essentially helpless. Is that what you think we can deal with?"

"Well, I think we can if it's a snake. I have a sword and you have your knives, and Jayna has…"

Gavin turned, and Jayna had her hands pressed out from her, forming a strange glowing blade out of her ring. The way she used it was intriguing to him, and he couldn't help but feel as if there was some other aspect to what she did that he wanted to know about. Could he do something similar? What if he could use his ring the same way? He had his own connection to the El'aras sword, but what would happen if he lost the weapon? Could he manufacture a blade the same way Jayna had, and use only his magic to fight?

Maybe he wouldn't need to. Tristan had taught him all sorts of fighting styles that did not involve a sword. But what would happen if Gavin used some aspect of the fighting styles and what he could draw through the ring, then created a weapon? What might he be able to do? It seemed like that might be useful.

"I hear it again," Jayna said. She elongated her blade.

"I'm not hearing anything," Gavin said, but as soon as he did, he realized there was something. At first, it came slowly and steadily, but then he noticed a stirring sensation, as if some part of the ground itself were rippling.

The stone started to slither.

He shoved Gaspar out of the way.

"What the—"

Gavin darted forward, driving his blade down, slamming it into the stone.

It wasn't like fighting the rock monster. There was a give to it, and he recognized that this wasn't stone at all. It was camouflaged in some way, probably through magic, concealed to blend in and look as if it were the stone itself.

Gavin drew back his blade, which was covered in some dark, inky substance that had to be blood, but it was blood unlike anything he'd ever seen before.

"Over here," he said, motioning to Jayna.

She sprinted toward them but tripped. She tumbled and sprawled on the ground, and she cried out as she pushed something that was above her. It was long and cylindrical but irregularly shaped. Grass and stone seemed to have blended together into some sort of disturbing snakelike creature that writhed in her hands as she held it out.

She tried to twist her hand and get her glowing blade into position, but she didn't seem to be able to do so.

Gavin looked over to Gaspar. "You doing okay?"

"Are you kidding me?" He motioned toward the creature slithering near him. Its inky blood spilled across the stone, but the thing didn't seem to be slowing, somehow.

Gavin shifted his sword and glanced over to Jayna, then back to Gaspar, before making a decision.

"You got this, Gaspar. Use your enchantments—as much as you can—and push it away. I've got to help her."

"If you let this thing kill me, boy…"

"It's not going to kill you," Gavin said, and then he jumped.

He was able to draw on some of his core reserves, but not nearly as much as he was accustomed to doing. He managed to clear the distance between him and Jayna, coming to land on a small rocky section near her.

At least, Gavin thought it was a small rocky section. When his foot rolled, he realized that he had landed on the same serpent. Somehow.

Jayna was still struggling with this thing, and Gavin hurriedly lunged forward, jabbing with his blade and slicing through the creature. The dark blood spilled out, splashing all over the stone and splattering Jayna. She spat, then flashed an irritated look in his direction.

He kicked, and the snake went slithering away.

Jayna held out the blade she had formed with her magic. "I could have done without that," she said.

"I'm sure you could have, but you also needed help. Just think of what would have happened had I not helped."

She scowled at him. "I would have been fine. You needed to give me more time."

Gavin shook his head. "I'm not sure you had more time. Now get up. There are more of these things here."

She scrambled to her feet and kicked, sending one of the serpents sliding across the ground. Gavin jumped toward it and drove his blade down into it. Its blood spurted out.

"I can't believe we didn't notice these before," he said.

"They blend into everything," she said. "But you're

right. I can't believe I've been here as long as I have and haven't seen anything like them."

Gaspar grunted. "I have." He was crouched on one of the boulders, fresh blood dripping from his blade. It looked as if he had carved through one or more serpents. "Outside of the city. Well, outside of Yoran. It was a long time ago. Never thought I would see them again."

"Is that why you are so afraid of them?"

Gaspar glowered at Gavin. "I'm not afraid. You see my knives, don't you?"

Gavin glanced over to Jayna, flashing a wide grin. "Now look at him. So confident. Well, I do think there are a couple more near us that you could take care of, if you'd like. We could wait."

Jayna smiled. "I can trade places with you," she told Gaspar. "That stone does look like it has a nice viewing angle for these things. From that vantage, I suspect that we should be able to see where they are moving to."

Gaspar looked like he wanted to murder both of them. "Just deal with them," he said.

"You don't want to help?" Gavin said.

"When I dealt with these, they nearly took off my arm. They took down one of the people I traveled with," he said, his voice becoming soft. "So, no. If I don't have to deal with anything like this, I'm not going to. And besides, considering how much power you both brag about having, I think it's more than fitting that the two of you have every opportunity to demonstrate what you can do. Now get on with it. Go to your carving."

Gavin shared a look with Jayna. "Any ideas on how we can figure out where they all are?"

"It's strange that there would be so many here now," she said.

"There's a nest," Gaspar said. "Or didn't you guess that? We must have fallen into it or stopped near one. And then when we started walking around, the sound drew them up. Some people used to call them sand worms, but that's not what they are. Sand worms are benign and can be useful. There is nothing useful about these."

Gavin had dealt with quite a few different creatures over the years, and many of them were dangerous. None had been what he would have considered a dark creature until he had encountered Jayna. Now, in this land, everything he came across seemed to be some sort of dark creature, the kind of thing he would destroy immediately if given the chance.

"I suppose I can create a tracking spell," Jayna said, frowning. "I think if we use enough of a connection, I should be able to push it through, but it's going to be tricky."

"I can do with tricky. Why don't you see what you can discover, and I'll clean up whatever we find."

She nodded. "Wish me luck."

She released her glowing blade and gripped her hands in front of her, though the glow didn't stop. Instead, it almost seemed to intensify. She started to murmur to herself, her lips moving but not making any sound, and her hand began to move as well. The longer she worked, the more Gavin noticed that there seemed to be a pattern to what she was doing. He could even follow it, though he wondered if that was necessary. Given the kind of connection she had to her Sul'toral, Jayna probably didn't need to use true sorcery, though she seemed to blend sorcery and her Toral magic together often.

A wave of energy washed outward from her in a pale pink glow, and then it faded.

Gavin didn't need to be told what to do as he prepared himself for the writhing mass of serpents all around. He darted forward and sliced with his El'aras sword, jumping, then twisting the blade in a flurry of frenzied movement. He carved through them until the tangle of creatures finally stopped moving.

Gavin looked over to Jayna. "You know, I'm starting to think that these things are trapped here the same way we are."

"Or they were drawn," Gaspar said, standing atop the stone.

"Drawn here for what purpose?" Jayna asked.

"To serve whoever is here."

Gavin frowned at Gaspar's statement. Whoever? Or maybe *whatever*. Maybe there was some other power here and that was what they needed to be careful of. Maybe a god *was* here. And if a god was restricting their magic and attracting these creatures, then they needed to be anywhere but here.

But as he watched Jayna, he suspected that it would not matter to her. If it meant finding Eva, Jayna would track down a god and try to take them on. As Gavin thought about it, if it were one of his friends, would he do any less?

"We should keep moving," Gaspar said.

Gavin smiled. "You just want to get away from these creatures."

"I do. They stink. But we need to keep moving before something realizes they're dead—and sends something worse at us."

CHAPTER NINETEEN

Darkness had fallen in full. Gavin was tired, which surprised him given how little sleep he normally needed. He didn't know if his fatigue was from the time he was spending in this place and barely getting any rest, or whether it had to do with the *way* he was spending his time. If only he had some sh'rasn powder, he might be able to fortify himself and may not need the rest.

They hadn't found any more serpents, though they'd dealt with a few smaller creatures that posed a danger to them, as if those things had been sent to test and weaken them.

Gaspar scooted closer to Gavin, holding onto one of the enchantments Jayna had made. "She says these will cause a fireball."

"They probably will," Gavin said.

"These Ashara have some sort of smoke magic. You don't think they can handle a fireball?"

Gavin shrugged. "Maybe they can."

He felt weary and tired in a way he had not been for quite some time. He thought it was tied to using his muted connection to his core reserves, but maybe it was just this place. Maybe it was draining him. He still hadn't given up on the possibility that some part of this place was designed to drain him of power, which was the reason the Sul'toral had sent him and Gaspar here. If that were the case, then he had to find a different strength.

He continued working despite the fatigue, though.

"What kinds of enchantments are you making?" Gaspar asked him.

"Most of mine are explosive rock. I have no idea if it's going to work for us, but at least it can shred some of these monsters. Besides, they scare easily."

"What's your plan with the rock monsters?"

Gavin looked up. "I think we need to track them to wherever they passed through. There has to be some central location. And if there is, maybe we can use that to escape." He kept his voice low, watching Jayna as she stacked branches, grasses, and other items together in a pattern that she pushed power into. Her enchantments were much more complicated than what Gavin had made. His were simple and all placed onto stone.

"So you are using her," Gaspar said.

Gavin shook his head. "I'm not using her. I recognize that she might have a different agenda than us. She wants to save Eva, and I don't have a problem with that, but we have to get out of here." He traced a pattern and placed energy into one of the rocks. "I don't know how much time we really have. Thankfully, it seems like we still have some, and if things are moving more slowly here"—or was it there?—"then we might be able to escape in time to help our friends."

"Assuming they don't send us back," Gaspar said.

"Well, now that we know how things work, if we do get sent back here, I'm hopeful that we'll be able to figure a way out again."

"And you would just leave her here?"

Gaspar seemed more troubled by that than Gavin would've expected.

"I'd like her to get out," Gavin said. "I think we will need her help when we leave. But I still wonder if finding Eva is how we should be spending our time."

He stacked another enchantment next to him, for a total of about fifteen. Each was similar, but he'd started to add different elements to them, thinking that perhaps he could make them a little bit more complicated. As he worked, though, Gavin didn't seem to feel anything change within them. He wouldn't know for sure if the enchantments even worked until he needed to use them. That was why he wanted to make as many as he could.

"I don't like the idea of leaving her behind," Gaspar finally said, breaking the silence that had grown between them. "She's here for her friend. Seems to me that you know something about that."

"You want to pull her into our team?"

Gaspar looked up. "Gods, if only we had our team."

"You just want Imogen back," Gavin said.

"I do. I think her sword would be useful."

"It's more than just her sword. I think she uses a form of magic. At least, when she uses some of her Leier patterns."

Gavin hadn't shared that with Gaspar before. But whenever he attempted to use those patterns in his own techniques, he noticed how they seemed to carry a measure of power.

"I know," Gaspar said. "When I first met you, I wanted nothing more than to see her spar with you. Never told her that, mostly because I suspected she wanted the same thing. She's always wanted to test herself against those she considered better than her. But then I learned just how you work. How everything you experienced was like a catalog you added to your fighting styles. Then I realized she didn't really have much of a chance."

"She had a chance," Gavin said.

"Not when you can incorporate her style into everything you use. Say what you want about your mentor, but he trained you well."

"There's something moving," Jayna called.

Gavin grabbed some of the enchantments and tucked them into his pockets. His cloak remained damp from where he had rinsed it in the water to try to clean it. There had been no further influence from that creature's saliva.

He got to his feet and looked off into the distance.

"Can you see what it is?" Gaspar asked as he picked up several of Gavin's enchantments. He arranged them in a way that looked like he was planning how he might use them, as if he needed to prepare to pull them out at any moment.

"I can't see," Gavin said. "It's moving toward us, though."

"If it's one of those giants..."

"We don't know," Jayna said.

Gavin followed her as she started forward into the darkness. As much as Gavin wanted to draw on enchantments to see more clearly, he also didn't want to waste them until it became necessary. He thought he might need to use the enchantments to face certain creatures, especially the stone monsters, but unless he came across some reason to use them, he was going to conserve them as long as possible.

None of them spoke as they moved.

A strange shriek echoed.

"Down!" he cried.

Gavin rolled and unsheathed his blade, and a dark shadow loomed over them. He prepared to throw one of his enchantments, but he realized he didn't need to.

Jayna looped her red power outward and seemed to snare the shadow. She pulled, constricting it, and Gavin jumped forward. He carved through the thing's head, decapitating it. The dark creature fell to the ground in a heap.

Jayna snorted. "That's one way to do it."

"I wasn't expecting that to work," Gavin said. "But then again, you held onto it in a way I didn't think we could do, either."

"We were lucky we heard it," she said. "When it comes to those things, most of the time we don't hear anything."

Gavin breathed out slowly, then turned his attention back to the darkness around them. "This is what we expected. We have to be careful, but we need to keep moving."

The others nodded, and they continued onward. Gavin flicked his gaze all around, focusing on the sky, not wanting to be surprised by another dark shadow. Those creatures' talons were sharp.

"Did you get any saliva on you this time?" Gaspar asked, and he chuckled.

"I should go back for its head and stick it on yours," Gavin muttered.

They moved forward until Gavin caught sight of one of the stone monsters in the darkness. It was not marching toward them but was lumbering away instead.

"What do you think?" Gavin asked, coming up next to Jayna. "Follow this one, and be prepared that there might be more?"

Jayna nodded slowly. She seemed unconcerned, which impressed him.

"Let's get moving," she said.

They chased her as she followed the stone monster, which moved quickly away from them. Its massive legs chewed up the ground faster than any of them could keep up with. Gavin tried to draw on more of the enchantment, wanting to use his core reserves, but even as he did, he could feel something starting to pull against him.

Jayna stopped and pointed in the distance. "I've never seen that before."

The stone monster headed toward a blackened shape, though Gavin couldn't tell anything else about it. "Have you come out here at night?"

"No. I try not to, mostly because you can't really tell whether something is coming at you. If I were to get caught by one of those renral, then I would get shredded."

"One of the what?"

"That's what the bird that attacked you is called. It's a renral."

"Look." He motioned, pointing to where the stone monster was disappearing. "It's going inside."

"That's where we need to go," she said.

They followed the monster and reached the darkened opening. As they did, Gavin realized that it was like some sort of portal into nothingness. On either side of it, the landscape appeared untouched, and as he circled around, he saw the opening from a new angle. It looked no different than anything else.

"That's where we have to go," Gavin said.

"And quickly," Gaspar said. "It's starting to close."

Gavin saw that Gaspar was right, and he looked over to Jayna. "Are you ready to take another leap? Maybe you can finally find Eva. I don't know if this takes us between different realms in this prison or not, but let's get through this... portal... and be ready for whatever we might find."

"I can go first," she said. "We're doing this because of Eva. She's my friend. I'll do it."

Before Gavin had a chance to argue, she jumped

forward, tossing one of her enchantments at the same time. It exploded in a burst of light. Somewhere distantly came the sound of a painful shriek from stone.

"She's a little bit like you," Gaspar said. "Jumped ahead without much of a plan."

"That's the problem," Gavin muttered, shaking his head. "I think she does have a plan. I just don't think she's sharing it with us."

Gavin followed Jayna into the portal, with Gaspar behind him.

In the distance, he caught sight of a faint glow. Jayna raced ahead, chasing the massive creature.

"That's not what we need to do!" Gavin shouted. "We aren't chasing the monsters. We're looking for your friend."

Jayna threw another enchantment, which exploded in a burst of bright white light, and then she turned to him. "What do you propose?"

Gavin looked back. The opening behind them was already starting to diminish. It would close soon. How long did those stay open? They might only be around in the nighttime. And given the strangeness of time here, what did that mean for them?

"We look for smoke," Gavin said. "We find one of the Ashara, and we use them to find Eva."

"I might be able to try something else," Jayna said, twisting her ring. "I can use the bloodstone to create a tracking spell. It might work, but I'm not entirely certain."

Gaspar nudged him, and Gavin looked up.

A pair of gigantic stone monsters were coming toward them.

"It looks like Gaspar and I are going to have to hold off these two while you do your tracking spell."

Jayna frowned. "I can help with them."

"No. Use your tracking spell. We will deal with this." He smiled at Gaspar. "Look big and scary?"

Gaspar sighed. "If this is their stronghold, I'm not so sure that looking big and scary is going to help us too much here."

"Maybe not. Let's give it a try anyway."

They started forward. Gavin threw one of his enchantments, triggering it as he did. He had no idea whether it was going to be effective here, and as the enchantment exploded, a rippling wave of power blasted, before constricting once again.

The stone monster shrieked.

Near Gavin, Gaspar used another one, and this one produced a flash of light. It blinded them for a moment, but Gavin had to hope that it would be even worse for the stone monsters.

They marched forward, Gavin holding his blade and ready to stab one of the creatures if it were to come at him. He was depleting his enchantments far faster than he'd expected. It had taken him such a long time to make them in the first place, and that process had drained so much out of him that using them this quickly felt like a waste. To give Jayna time to track Eva, though, they would have to use whatever it took.

"Come on!" Jayna yelled.

Gavin spun and yanked Gaspar out of the way as a massive hand swept toward him.

He swung his blade around. One of the stone monsters cried out and battered at him. Gavin deflected again, carving through the palm of the creature's hand. It was a panicked movement and not coordinated. He didn't know if it was attacking out of blindness, fury, or fear. The creature shrieked again, then backed away.

A burst of bright light exploded in front of them.

That wasn't one of Gavin's enchantments.

"I said, 'Come on!'" Jayna said.

Gaspar backed toward her, holding a pair of enchantments in hand. How many had he used? Gavin thought he'd only thrown one himself, and that was not counting the ones Gaspar had used. Had they burned through half of them already? He told himself that it didn't matter. At this point, the only thing that mattered was that they keep moving.

"I don't know how long this will hold," Jayna said. "Everything in this place is strange, and I don't know what measure of permanence this will have. Even enchantments don't hold indefinitely."

She moved forward, slipping through the darkness.

Every so often, Gavin heard a rumble near him, and Jayna would toss one of her enchantments. A blast of white light would explode, and shapes would scurry away. It didn't take long for Gavin to realize that the stone monsters weren't the only things around—there were other creatures here.

Gavin looked to Gaspar. "How many enchantments do you have left?"

"Three or four. How about you?"

"Maybe six." Not enough.

"Then give them to me," Gaspar said. "I don't have your abilities here."

Gavin smirked at him. "You don't have my abilities anywhere."

"Come on, boy. Hand them over."

Gavin gave Gaspar a pair of enchantments. He immediately tossed one into the darkness, which exploded. There was a strange shriek, a high-pitched yell that was different than what they had been hearing from the stone monsters.

"I wonder what's in here," Gaspar murmured. "It's not just those creatures."

"There are more than just those," Jayna said. "I can't tell what they are, but I feel something."

Gavin wondered if he might be able to empower his core reserves enough to cause the blade to glow. It might illuminate the chamber around them enough so that he could see what was here.

"Let me see one of those enchantments," Gavin said to Jayna.

"I wasn't able to make that many either," she said.

"Just let me see one."

She handed him one, and he squeezed it. It felt like it was made of wood and leaves, but there was a hint of something metallic within it. He hadn't seen any metal, so either she had used something she had brought here, or her act of enchanting had changed the material. It didn't work that way when he placed enchantments, but she was a sorcerer and a Toral, so her magic was different than his.

"Be ready," Gavin said. Then he hurled the enchantment, drawing upon as much power as he could.

As soon as it activated, the space they were in exploded with a bright light.

The light revealed hundreds upon hundreds of strange creatures.

There were stone monsters, as well as smaller things made of rock or some sort of leather. There were more of those snakes too. Everything seemed to move in the shadows. Gavin didn't have much more than a moment to see what was around him. He didn't know where they needed to go, but there had been no sign of smoke since the little bit he thought he had seen.

Which meant they were stuck here without a way to find Eva, and they had to deal with whatever nightmares were in this twisted, blackened realm.

"We need to find another doorway to escape," Gaspar said.

"What if we have to fight through all of that to escape?" Gavin asked, motioning to the creatures.

"Gods," Gaspar muttered. "We need more enchantments."

Jayna shook her head. "That's not going to be the way out. It wasn't the way in, so it won't be the way out."

They hurried forward. Anytime they felt something moving toward them, either Gavin or Gaspar tossed an enchantment, which would send a rolling wave of concussive power outward. Jayna threw her starlight enchant-ments, and they would explode, leaving streamers of light crackling for a moment before it faded. That, as much as anything, seemed to push back the dangers in front of them.

Finally, Jayna stopped. "I'm out of my enchantments."

"Same," Gaspar said.

Gavin reached into his pocket. He had one left.

"Well, other than the enchantments we came in with, I've only got one more that I made. Unless you think we can find anything in here that we can enchant—"

"We don't have time," Jayna said.

She focused on something behind Gavin, and he looked backward.

Shadows rippled. He couldn't make out much—not in this place, and not in the darkness—but he could see them. And he realized the danger within them.

"Run," Jayna said.

Gaspar ran after her.

Gavin hesitated and clutched his enchantment. If he timed it right, he might be able to buy them a little bit of time.

Jayna shouted something to him, but he ignored it.

The shadows moved toward him. He tossed the enchantment, and this time, he channeled as much of himself into the enchantment as he could. Gavin pushed through his core reserves and his connection to the ring, but he didn't know if it would work. Would he have to connect to the bralinath trees? Could he even do it? He had to find some way to draw on even more power.

And then the enchantment exploded. The blast was far more potent than the others had been, enough to throw him off his feet and send him flying backward.

Strange shrieks and howls, sounds that were unnatural and horrifying, echoed everywhere.

Gavin landed painfully. He rolled and scrambled to his feet as hands grabbed him. His first instinct was to fight, but he realized that those hands had to belong to Gaspar and Jayna.

"I see smoke," Gavin said once they pulled him to his feet.

Hopefully, that meant the Ashara. They had to find Eva, find the others, figure out a way to safety.

And then find a way out.

Jayna yanked him forward as they scrambled. Gavin's back hurt, and given the limitation of his abilities, he doubted he would heal quickly. He'd have to push that pain into the back of his mind, but he could feel some of it, and he started to lag.

Jayna shouted at him. Gaspar did as well, but their voices were muted.

Had he really gotten so far behind them?

He felt something move near him. He turned.

The others were too far ahead of him now. He was hurting, slow. And there were unseen monsters here.

Gavin held out his blade, prepared to fight and possibly die, so that Gaspar and Jayna could escape.

CHAPTER TWENTY

Gavin had prepared himself to die countless times before.

He had been trained to be willing to sacrifice himself for the mission. Tristan had warned him that there might be a time when he would have to fight and be prepared to die, when he would have to recognize that he had no choice but to take what was to come. His time in isolation and his training with Tristan had made it so that he accepted the possibility of that fate.

But his people needed him. If he were to die, what would happen to those he left behind?

It was reason enough to fight with a renewed fury.

He cried out. His voice was filled with rage, frustration, and weakness.

Gavin was not accustomed to the last feeling. He hated it.

Why did he have to be weak?

There was something here for him—his own core reserves, the connection to the bralinath trees, and perhaps something else. He started to focus on his core reserves, on the ring, and on his blade. He had to throw himself into this attack, using anything he had in order to create an opening for them to make their way through.

Gavin swung at the shadows moving near him, sweeping his blade to one side. He carved through something and kept going. He had no idea what it was, only that he could feel something close to him. Gavin spun, twisting his blade and slicing again. As he did, he heard a strange, whimpering cry. He swung and he stabbed, feeling some resistance against him, but he no longer cared about that resistance.

Gavin focused on his movements. He darted forward in the Bongan style, then shifted to Nor, before drifting into the Leier movements. Those seemed to be the most effective. His blade became a part of him. With the Leier patterns, everything was instinctive.

He slashed at the creatures, jumping and twisting and flowing through the movements. It amplified the power that blazed within him. He lost himself in the fighting. This was what he needed to do. By battling, Gavin cut down one creature after another. It might actually be enough.

Then a blow struck him.

Gavin staggered.

Another blow hit him, and something raked along his side. It felt like claws ripping through him. He ignored it, thankful that he still had some of the stone skin enchantment left, but those defenses would fade eventually. Gavin drew on his core reserves, pushing the energy through the El'aras ring, and tried to connect to the source of power from the bralinath trees.

Muted power came to him.

Gavin flew forward, then fell back into the familiar fighting styles again, twisting and kicking and stabbing. He defaulted to the Leier patterns, which were most effective with the sword. They amplified magic, after all.

He struck again and again. He cut down creatures that he could barely see, creatures that were little more than shadows against the darkness.

Then something hit him again.

He stumbled backward. He had to ignore the pain that bloomed in his arm, his leg, and continued to burn in his back. As Gavin spun, something grabbed him. He fought, but the pain seared through him.

Somehow, he managed to get free. Gavin tried to call on his core reserves, the magic within the ring, and even the nihilar energy, but none of it worked. There was too much power here.

And there was something else.

Warmth. Fire.

Ashara?

It wasn't harming him.

It was dragging him.

Something pulled him free, but it was strange. It might've been pressure, though it was unusual. As he was torn away from the fight, he noticed a soft glowing light behind him.

Gavin stopped resisting. As he reached the light, he passed through something. It felt like a barrier washed over his skin, hot and constricting. Then it was gone.

He still didn't have any access to his core reserves the way he should, nor did he have access to the power of the ring, but he no longer felt the pressure of the strange creatures assaulting him.

"There you are, boy. It seems like the Ashara have helped us," Gaspar said.

"Is this a portal?" Gavin asked.

"Not that I can tell. Though, to be honest, I *can't* tell. It's not like what we used to get here."

Gavin looked around, but he didn't understand what he was seeing. Light, warmth, a glowing sort of energy. But there was nothing else to it.

"He's safe," a familiar voice said.

Gavin glanced over, and he saw the pale-skinned, dark-haired woman he had always seen with Jayna. "Eva?"

When he had seen her before, she had been almost timid. She had seemed possessive of Jayna. The woman before him now was confident, practically commanding. Powerful, but something else as well. Regal?

"What are you doing here?" Eva demanded.

"How long have you been here?" Gavin asked, looking over to Gaspar.

Gaspar shook his head. "We tried going back for you, but we couldn't get there. The smoke started to build, and it prevented us from going anywhere. I think they were using it to hold you back."

"They have been moving," Eva said.

"What are they?" Gavin asked.

"They are the darkness."

Jayna watched Eva, saying nothing.

"We need to find some way to get out of here," Gavin said. "And we need to find some way to get back to my world."

"I'm not sure that's going to be possible," Eva said. "Not without getting to the ancient."

Jayna started toward Eva. "We've been trying to find you."

"I understand, but we are here for a reason."

It was only then that Gavin realized that there were two others with her.

One was a dark-haired man who looked something like Eva, but his eyes seemed to blaze, almost as if there was fire within them. He didn't have any weapons, but smoke trailed from him. It seemed familiar, and Gavin quickly realized that he had been the one who'd dragged him back here.

There appeared to be something wrong with the third Ashara. It took Gavin a moment to recognize that smoke streamed from her. He didn't know how their power worked, but he suspected that their magic came from their blood, as he had seen Eva bite her lip and squeeze something between her palms when he'd fought alongside her before. If that was the case, then the smoke pouring out from this woman meant that she was significantly injured.

"So we have to help the ancient?" Jayna said.

"The ancient is trapped here," Eva said. "What you have

seen are the guardians."

"I don't understand. When you left, you—"

"This was something I needed to do, not you," Eva said to her. "You should not have come for us."

"I came for my friend." Jayna sounded hurt.

"I traveled here for a reason, but you can't help with this. I need to free the ancient. That's why we are here."

"Why?" Gavin glanced from Eva to the other man, and then to the injured Ashara, before turning his attention to Jayna. "You have not really told us a lot about this place, only that it's some sort of world in between. From what I can tell, it's more like a prison. I thought it might be a place where the Sul'toral attempted to draw power from me so they could use it, but I don't think that's the case."

"They would not be able to use it," Eva said.

"Then why did they send us here?" Gaspar asked.

Eva frowned. "Perhaps they thought to trap you with the ancient. They may not have known the purpose of this place, and thought it nothing more than a prison. For them, it would serve as one. They wouldn't be able to escape. They would live without access to power."

"Not all of them," Gavin said. "They would have some way."

If they were connected to one of the ancients, such as they kept calling it, then they might be able to draw on power. It was the same way he could use his El'aras abilities, and how Jayna was able to call on her Toral power.

"It's possible, but they may not have understood it either," Eva said. "This is a trap that separates the ancients from our world. You can touch the power here, but only when you understand it."

"A trap?" Gaspar asked.

"One of the oldest of its kind," Eva said.

Jayna's brow furrowed. "How do you know this?"

Gavin understood the reason behind that, after Jayna had described Eva's memories as missing. How did she know? Could her memories have returned?

"It is the purpose of this place," Eva said.

"It's not a connection to Ashara power?" Gavin asked.

"It is meant to trap whatever power was believed to be a danger."

"And it can be used?"

Jayna looked at him. "What are you going on about?"

"The El'aras were attacked. I don't know exactly what happened, only that I heard something about a fire. An ancient threat." Gavin watched Eva and the other two, wondering if he might have said more than he should have. But he needed to know. When he got back to Yoran —not if, since he intended to return—and the El'aras, Gavin wanted to be certain that Eva and the other Ashara would not attack the city.

"We did not have anything to do with what happened to them," Eva said.

"Are you sure?" Gavin asked.

"We did not have anything to do with what happened to them," she repeated.

That should have reassured him, but he wasn't sure that it did. Not entirely.

"Let's just say that you need to free this ancient..."

Gavin said. And as he stood there and watched the Ashara, he wasn't sure if that was the right strategy or not. If this ancient power was tied to them…

Maybe it would be too powerful. And too dangerous.

"Why?" Gavin asked.

"Because they should never have managed to trap this power here," Eva replied.

How many ancients were trapped like this, though?

"Is that why there are so few of you?" Jayna asked.

Eva looked at the man with him. Jayna followed his gaze.

"None of us remember," the man said. "It's not just Eva who has struggled. When we change forms, we lose something."

"What are you talking about?" Gaspar asked. "Changing form?"

Jayna motioned toward the Ashara. "They can change form."

"What? Shapeshifters?"

"Nothing like some of the stories you probably heard when you were a child," Jayna said, "but they can take on different forms. None of them are their native forms, though. And they have been trying to understand why, but they can't stay in that native form." She looked over to Eva. "And it's because of this, isn't it?"

"It's tied to it," Eva said softly.

"What will you choose?"

Eva stared at her. "I don't know."

"But you have to choose, don't you?" Jayna said.

"Eventually."

Gavin frowned. He didn't think he had time to deal with this the way he suspected Jayna wanted to. He needed to get back. And increasingly, he wondered how much of what happened here was tied to what was happening beyond this world.

"We have power trapped here, maybe intentionally," he said. He suspected that it definitely was intentional, even if he didn't understand the reason behind it. "And we need to figure out some way of escaping, but from what Eva is saying, the only way we're going to escape is if we somehow free her Ashara."

"Only one of the ancients can free you from this place," Eva said.

Gavin doubted that was completely true. There had to be another way, given how they ended up here in the first place.

"You came here knowing that you wouldn't be able to get out unless you succeeded?" Jayna asked.

"It is my purpose," Eva said. Smoke swirled around her.

Gavin stepped to the side with Gaspar, moving away from the rest.

Gaspar rubbed his forehead. "What do you think about this? They make it sound like we won't be able to get out of here unless we somehow remove this other threat."

"It seems as if we were forced into a prison by those who knew what they were doing," Gavin said. "They may have known there wouldn't be any way for us to escape, and it's possible that they even knew the Ashara were here." He pursed his lips, looking from one person to the next.

"I don't like it," Gaspar said.

"I don't either. We are out of our depth. Then again, we've always been out of our depth. So we spring this ancient from prison, help our friends before the attack reaches Yoran, and then I guess we save the day." Gavin flashed a smile.

Gaspar scowled. "It's not going to be so simple."

"Oh, I'm well aware that it's not," Gavin said. He walked back to the group and interrupted the discussion Eva was having with Jayna. "So how do we get to the ancient?"

"You have seen what protects it," Eva said.

"All of those creatures."

"All of them were brought here with that purpose, and we have tried to disperse them."

Gavin thought that he at least understood why some of the creatures were outside of this portal and out in the rest of the strange realm.

"What if you disperse all of them out there?" he asked.

"They would not survive, and we would not be able to do it."

"What if we could draw them out?"

"It would not be possible," Eva said.

Gavin wasn't sure that was true, but he also didn't have any idea what else they were going to have to do.

"What were you thinking of doing, then?" He looked from Jayna to Eva, and then finally to Asaran, the Ashara man who seemed to be leading the three of them. "You obviously had some plan. What is it?"

"We intend to fight our way toward Ashara."

Gavin couldn't help but smile. "You intend to fight your way toward that?"

"It's the only way," Asaran said. "You've not been here nearly as long as the rest of us. We've tried drawing them out, and we've lost several." He nodded to the other Ashara woman. "Sharaaz is injured and no longer of much use, unfortunately. We have lured the creatures out, fought them, killed them, only to find that they return in greater numbers. It draws them here. The only way to get through this is to fight."

"Fight through what? What are you trying to do?"

"We are preparing," Asaran said.

Gavin glanced around. "Here?" Everything seemed pale and glowing, though he didn't feel the pressure from different dangers as he had in the other space. "I don't even understand what this place is."

"We have been here for what you would consider several months, testing and searching for a way through. We think we have a plan."

Eva nodded. "We do have a plan." She said it in a way that sounded fatalistic, and Gavin suspected what that plan would entail.

"You intend to sacrifice yourself to free this Ashara," Gavin said.

"If we must," Asaran said.

"We can help," Jayna urged.

Asaran turned to her. "You will be freed as soon as we do this."

"I'm not getting free just so you can sacrifice yourself," Jayna said to Eva.

Eva shook her head. "This is my fight."

Something passed between the two of them, though Gavin couldn't tell quite what it was. It was almost like they shared some understanding, but then it faded.

"How about the two of you get along so that we can do this. We get through this, we rescue Ashara—whatever Ashara is—and then we can get out of here. Once we do that," Gavin said, sweeping his gaze around everybody, "I'm going to need your help. My people have been attacked by the Sul'toral, and given that time is moving slowly out there, I think we'll have a chance to get back. But I won't be able to stop them on my own. It's going to involve whatever help you can offer." He arched a brow at Jayna and then turned to Eva. "If I do this, will you help?"

"If we survive, you will have our help," Eva replied.

It was good enough for Gavin.

"Now," he said, "if we're going to do this, I'll need something from you."

Gaspar looked over to him, frowning deeply. "What kind of foolish plan is this, boy?"

"Well, considering that most of my plans are quite foolish, I would say that it's about typical."

"But you want to take on some god?"

Gavin gestured to Eva, Asaran, and Jayna. "The way I see it, we're not taking on a god at all, are we? We're here to free one."

"Oh, so that makes it better?" Gaspar said.

"Not particularly."

"Have you forgotten something? How are you supposed to fight? You intend to stay here until you can make enough enchantments?" Gaspar looked around. "You took the better part of a night to make, what, fifteen? Maybe a little bit more. Even with those types of enchantments, it's not going to do that much."

Seeing what the Ashara could do had given Gavin an idea.

"No," Gavin said. "I don't think that my enchantments, muted as they are, will serve much of a purpose. I don't think Jayna's magic will either." He turned to Eva. "But you three have somehow managed to hold onto your power here. Why is that?"

"Because of the proximity to Ashara," Eva said. "We anticipated we'd be able to use it. It's why we came here."

"But Ashara can't use its power?"

"It is confined. The power in this place has subdued it, and it is asleep. We are here to awaken it. Once awake, Ashara will fight its way free."

That gave Gavin a little more optimism. If they didn't have to actually free a god and only had to awaken it, then maybe they had a chance.

"Then we need you to help us," he said. "Grant us a little bit of your ability and help us free ourselves from whatever is going to happen here, and then…"

Maybe with his El'aras abilities and with Jayna's Toral power and sorcery, they might swing the tide of the fight. He didn't know if it would make a difference, but he had to hope.

"There might be something we can try," Eva said.

CHAPTER TWENTY-ONE

Power filled Gavin.

The Ashara had some way of adding to enchantments, as if the proximity to their ancient had gifted them with even more power than before. It permitted Gavin and Jayna to form far better enchantments than they had been able to. He now could connect to his core reserves and, beyond that, to the bralinath trees that seemed to link him to some greater El'aras power, much better than he had in quite some time.

He felt almost normal.

Not quite, but it was nearly that. Having access to his magic once again was strangely relaxing. He had missed it in a way he had not expected.

Jayna seemed to feel restored as well. She was filled with magic, enough so that Gavin could practically see it radiating off her. Between the two of them, he thought that they could change the dynamics of the fight.

"What now?" Gaspar asked.

"Now we waken and rescue Ashara," Asaran said.

"We have two people here who are probably going to have a hard time fighting," Gavin said, looking to Sharaaz and Gaspar. "We need to protect them."

"I will do what I need so that I can free Ashara," Sharaaz said. Her voice was slightly hushed but harsh.

"You can't," Gavin said, taking a step toward her. "I can see your injury, even if you don't want to acknowledge it. Power is streaming out of you. Maybe you would be able to restore yourself if you were outside, but not here. Not the way that power is suppressed."

Gavin had no idea what ability she had, but he believed that there had to be some limits to even that. And with that being the case, she posed a challenge for them because of her injury.

"Keep an eye on her," Gavin said to Gaspar.

"I'm not staying behind," Sharaaz said.

Gavin regarded her for a moment. "You could—"

"She is not staying behind," Asaran said. "We will need all of us."

Gavin backed away and he looked at Gaspar. "You're going to need to help her."

"How do you think I can help her?"

Gavin had an idea, now that he could call on his core reserves, however strangely it might still be. "Hand me your enchantments."

"Which ones?" Gaspar asked.

"All of them."

Gaspar pulled them out of his pocket, and Gavin made

quick work of scratching symbols on them with his dagger and pushing power out from himself. When Gavin was done, Gaspar took them and slipped them on.

His eyes widened. "I feel that."

"Hopefully, they'll hold long enough in here," Gavin said. "I don't know. I tried to re-create the symbols on them, but…"

"But you don't know if it will work."

Gavin nodded, then turned to Eva. "Do you have a plan?"

"Something of one," she said, looking to Asaran. "We have been testing various pathways through here, but we do not know which one will be the easiest. We have an idea, but we run into danger whenever we fight."

"I guess it's time to put your theories to the test," Gavin said. "If we wait too much longer, then I don't know how long we have before the Sul'toral attack my city. So let's do this."

The El'aras might be able to help the people of Yoran, but that was only if they reached the city in time. And that was only if Anna recognized the need. Gavin had no idea if she would be willing to do it, and even if she did, he didn't know whether they would be able to defend themselves against three powerful Sul'toral. The El'aras were skilled and strong, but he didn't know what they had suffered prior to leaving their homeland. How many had fallen?

Eva turned to Asaran. "We have a plan. We did not expect outsiders to come and join us, but that doesn't take away from what we said we would do. If they help, it does increase the likelihood that we succeed."

"That was not the plan," Asaran said.

Gavin walked over to him and clasped him on the shoulder. "Listen. We don't know each other very well, but I can tell you that most of my plans don't work the way I want them to. But they almost always turn out the right way."

Asaran frowned. "Almost?"

"I'd like to say they always turn out the way I want them to, but unfortunately, that's just not the case." Gavin grinned. "We might as well get going. You aren't getting rid of me—or us—very easily."

Asaran regarded him for a long moment, and fire seemed to flicker in the back of his eyes. "We have to be the ones to awaken Ashara," he said. "Which means you must draw away the guardians."

"Not them," Gavin muttered.

"They are what surround Ashara. We must be the ones to reach our ancient. You will know when we do."

"Then what happens?"

"The prison will shatter," Asaran said.

"And us?"

"You will return."

Gavin peered around. "And what about the creatures forming the prison?"

"We don't know," Asaran said.

Gavin sighed. "So if we return, it's likely that they return too."

"Possible."

"Great," Gavin muttered. They might get out of here, but they might bring something worse into the rest of the world.

"We just have to kill as many as we can," Jayna said.

"Sounds good. Where is your Ashara?" Gavin asked Asaran.

"In the heart of the prison," he said.

"You intend to spread out around the periphery and then attack?"

Jayna looked over. "It sounds reasonable enough."

Strangely, Gavin found himself enjoying fighting alongside her. She needed about as much of a plan as he did.

"We stay together, or do we split up?" Gavin asked.

"Together," Gaspar said. "If we split up, we won't know if one of you falls. And we have a better chance of drawing their attention to us, especially if we slaughter most of these creatures."

Gavin snorted and shook his head. "Look at you getting confident now that you have access to enchantments."

Gaspar grunted. "I would say the same about you, boy."

Gavin pulled on his core reserves, focused on the energy within the El'aras ring, and then took a deep breath. "I'm ready."

"Then we begin," Eva said.

The light around them flickered and faded. As soon as it disappeared, they were cast in darkness.

"Now," Asaran said.

Gavin realized they were not going to use their abilities unless they had to.

"Jayna?" he said.

"How big of an explosion do you want?" she asked.

"Well, it seems we need to call them here, right?"

"Sounds about right to me," she said. As she did, a burst of white light exploded from her hands and shot up into the sky. It was followed by several streaks of what he would call bursting starlight. And then fire blasted outward.

"I hope you didn't waste all your power on that," Gavin said.

"Those are pretty easy spells," she said. "The challenging ones are coming soon."

Easy. Gavin was reminded of what she had said about sorcerers.

It wasn't always about power so much as it was about knowledge. She might be young, but she had power, and he suspected that she had knowledge as well.

Darkness streamed toward them. Gavin focused on his core reserves, the ring, and his El'aras sword. He added what he could detect of the nihilar within him. It seemed to have some hazy energy, almost as if there was a conduit to that power. He called it through him and let it flow out.

And it entered his sword.

The blade cast a gray light that spilled outward. He looked around in the darkness. They were in what seemed to be a chamber of nothingness, but beyond that, he saw dark shadows stalking toward them.

"It's happening," he said.

Soon Gavin fell into a pattern of fighting. What lumbered toward him first was something that looked like a massive wolf, and it reminded him of the stone golem he typically traveled with, though this was somehow larger and more ferocious. Its enormous fangs dripped something on the ground, and steam drifted up from where the saliva touched the stone. As that saliva burned away, Gavin was acutely aware that he didn't want that creature to bite him.

He danced back, calling on the power through his ring. He tried to channel as much of it as he could, then pushed it into the blade and into the creature.

A lance of gray light shot forward into the creature's side. It went tumbling away.

"That was new," Gaspar said.

Gavin nodded in appreciation. "It was. I have not tried it before. Seems like it works."

"You look like you're enjoying yourselves too much," Sharaaz said. Smoke swirled around her, and it looked as if it was creating some sort of a shell to protect her. Was she calling on too much of herself?

"Either we die, or we survive," Gavin said. "We might as well have fun with it." He frowned as another creature came toward him, and he forced power out of the end of his blade. It slammed into the creature, which went flying backward. "How injured are you, really?"

"I'll survive," Sharaaz said.

"Asaran and Eva aren't here. I need to know how much you're going to be able to protect yourself. Smoke is streaming from you, which I understand is tied to your blood power. And if you're failing—"

"I won't be able to offer much," Sharaaz said. "But if you get me through this, I will survive."

Gavin looked over to Gaspar, who took a position in front of Sharaaz. "Jayna and I will be the primary bait," he said. "I don't like it, but if anything gets past, then the two of you will have to deal with it. It's about to get worse."

A flood of dark creatures converged on them.

Something swooped over his head, and Gavin jumped. Thankfully, he had more strength, or perhaps it was the core reserves, and he could leap into the air. When he did, his blade carved into something. He pushed a burst of power out through his skin, thankful that he no longer had to invert the energy as he had before, then created a barrier around himself. If this creature was one of those strange birds that could poison him with its saliva, he wanted to protect himself as much as possible.

When he landed, three squat, gray-skinned creatures came toward him.

Gavin danced through movements, darting through Inril, Jasap, Jonal, then into the Leier movements that seemed to be so effective in this place. He stabbed one, carved off the arm of another, and came around, slicing through the head of the third.

Near him, Jayna battled using her sorcery. Power exploded from her, far different than what she had used when she had summoned the attack to them in the first place. He caught sight of a blast of light shooting into the sky, others that were firing toward the attackers, and still others that were indescribable. Whatever she used was immensely powerful. He had seen her using some of her sorcery and some of her Toral power in the time they had been traveling together through this strange realm, but now he felt the sheer magnitude of that power.

It was his turn.

Gavin rolled forward and slammed into the back of something that didn't give. What turned toward him looked like a miniature version of the stone monster.

When it brought its hand back, Gavin jumped, driving his blade into the palm of the creature. There was no shriek of pain. No cry as if the palm was sensitive like the other ones were. This one was also faster than its tall, lumbering counterparts, and it managed to grab his blade.

Gavin forced power through him, through the end of the blade, and poured it outward. With a burst, stone shattered, sending debris raining around him. He shredded the creature's hand and arm and was thrown free.

He became separated from the others.

Gavin moved in a circuit, darting in the Leier patterns and using the intrinsic power within them to create some space. It seemed to echo through him, carrying some of his own El'aras magical ability and augmenting the pattern itself, and it created a shield around him. It bought him time to find the others.

In the darkness, he could see Jayna fighting. She had created a ring of light all around her that was tinged with a hint of red energy from her bloodstone, and she sent streaks of it bursting outward. Gavin braced for explosions of power but felt nothing.

Creatures swarmed toward him. He would not let their group get split up. Gaspar and Sharaaz needed their protection. Gavin raged forward, spinning through a series of patterns that he modeled after what he had learned from Imogen, thankful for the power she had taught him to use. He barely had to add a little of his own El'aras magic in order to amplify these patterns.

In the distance, he noticed a faint surge of light, followed by a stream of smoke.

Eva and Asaran.

They weren't supposed to be drawing attention to themselves.

The creatures started to turn away from him.

"Jayna!" he shouted.

She glanced in his direction briefly, and white light glowed from her like a sword, which she used to carve through some of the creatures in front of her. The power split them in half. One of the things had the legs of a man and the head of a wolf, while another had a twisted body like a pig with something of a man's head. The third one she sliced through was a tall, spindly creature that looked to be made out of trees and stone.

All were massive, and all of them reminded him of enchantments he'd seen the Sul'toral use.

Something that Mekel had once said about his enchantments came back to Gavin. He had talked about creating enchantments in the shape of creatures he had seen in books, or that he had seen in real life, but some of the ones he had seen before seemed impossible to believe. But now that he was here, Gavin couldn't help but feel as if perhaps that was the case. Maybe those enchantment creatures were based on something real. Maybe they had been able to use something from real life to create these kinds of enchantments.

"Draw them here!" Gavin called out. "The Ashara had to use their power."

Jayna locked eyes with him for a moment, then turned away. He felt her power before he saw anything. It sent a surge of tingles along his skin, and the sheer magnitude of it left him close to trembling.

The creatures turned toward Jayna, and Gavin used that opportunity to begin his own assault.

He slammed into some of the spindly creatures made of wood, cutting through two of them before they had a chance to turn toward him. He rolled underneath the swinging arm of a miniature stone monster and blasted magic out through the end of his sword, causing it to explode. He kicked as a small weasel-like creature he had seen in the grasses snuck toward him, sending it tumbling away.

He dove forward.

But then he felt something coming from behind.

Gavin spun. The massive shape surging toward him was different than what they had faced before. The others had looked like real creatures, or at least tied to them in some way, but what came at them now was even larger than the stone monsters. It lumbered with a slow, dangerous, pace.

He focused on his power connecting him to the bralinath trees, and he pushed it out through the El'aras sword.

There were going to be limits to the energy he could draw on, but now seemed like the time to test those limits.

Shadows moved up ahead. He saw what was coming, and it looked like a nightmare.

The thing was nearly fifty feet tall, which was as tall as the stone monsters, but the sheer size of this creature was something else. It was larger than some houses Gavin had lived in, with an enormous head and short, stubby arms. Every part of its leathery skin looked like it was made of pitted marble and seemed to end in sharp razors, including spikes down its back. The creature stood on colossal hind legs, with a long, snakelike tail stretching behind it.

If the creature got close enough to him to attack, he wouldn't survive this, even with his abilities. He had a few enchantments remaining, and he called on the ones for stone skin, speed, and strength. He forced all sources of magic within him to react, and then he pressed power out of himself and into the blade, pouring it as hard as he could from him.

The magic shot out from the end of the blade and burst in a streak of light. When it struck the creature, nothing happened.

Gavin tried again, firing more power out of the sword.

Again, nothing happened.

Gods, what is this thing?

He backed away, hacking through some of the creatures that separated him from Jayna. By the time he reached her, he found the ground littered with some of the horrifying monsters, with others still trying to swarm toward them. Gaspar had taken to fighting, moving in a blur with daggers in hand. Even Sharaaz had been forced to fight, and the smoke swirling out from her created a layer of protection, though he could see even the faint color she had fading from her cheeks.

"This one is much bigger than anything we've faced before," Jayna said.

"What is it?" he asked.

He motioned, and she sent another burst of light streaking into the sky. When it exploded, the monster stopped moving and turned its eyes toward them.

"That's a Tistalt," Jayna whispered.

"At least you know what it is," Gavin said. "Seeing as how I've never seen or heard of them before, I'm not sure I can handle anything like that."

She shook her head. "I've heard of them, but I've never seen one. It's supposed to be mythical."

"Like dragons?"

She frowned at him.

The paper dragons that he kept with him were based on mythical creatures. Maybe this Tistalt was much like that. Or maybe dragons were real.

"Regardless, they shouldn't be here," Gavin said.

"Neither should we," she said.

Gaspar pointed in the distance. "There is more than one of them."

Gavin looked up and realized that two others lumbered toward them. "So... do you think those are the *true* guardians?"

"Gods, I hope so," Jayna said. "If we can hold them off,

we might be able to give Eva and Asaran a chance to do what we need, but…"

They wouldn't have enough time.

Gavin pushed as much energy through his blade as he could, but he didn't know if it was going to be enough.

He licked his lips. "Well, this one is more than what I can do anything with. Maybe your power will be better with it, but mine is nothing. See what you can do."

"I can try," Jayna said.

She held her hand out, and her power began to build. Faint red magic streamed away from her. As it did, Gavin darted forward, carving through a spindly stick creature, three wolves, and one short, squat goblin-like monster.

They all fell before him, and he was thankful for his renewed core reserves, but even that was starting to fade. He'd been drawing on considerable power.

As Jayna's spell exploded into the Tistalt, nothing happened.

"It seems to absorb it," Jayna said.

"It absorbs power?"

She nodded. "Unfortunately, it seems like it's taking in anything I throw in its direction. I can't do anything."

"Well, it sounds like it might be time for us to run."

"Run, but keep the creatures off of Asaran and Eva?" Jayna said.

"Right. We do that by running."

Gavin backed away. Gaspar trailed after him and remained close, and Sharaaz stayed alongside him.

He made a point of still pulling on his power, but each time he focused and shot power at one of the Tistalt, he knew it wasn't going to do much. It struck but did nothing else. He could feel power from those creatures and knew he had to try something different.

"Keep them off me," Gavin said to Gaspar.

Gaspar gestured to Sharaaz. "I thought I was supposed to protect her."

"Well, now you get to protect me and her."

Gavin continued focusing on his core reserves, on the El'aras ring, and even on the nihilar, and he sent all of it shooting outward. Each time he did, the creatures seemed to siphon that power off, as if they were absorbing it completely.

Jayna stayed with him, marching backward, and she continued shooting blasts of yellow and red light. Every time she struck a Tistalt, Gavin kept hoping that something would change and that the creature would back away, but it didn't. The magic seemed to flicker a moment, but then nothing changed.

Gavin had some of his power, but not enough for him to attack the way he would outside of this prison.

"How much longer do you think they need?" he asked Jayna.

"I don't know."

"What happens if the Tistalt catch them?"

"I don't know," she said.

The Tistalt moved toward them, forcing Gavin and Jayna and the others to continue retreating. Gavin did not care to retreat, but they didn't have much choice in the matter.

And then the first one was upon them.

Gavin shoved Gaspar away as the Tistalt loomed toward them, its breath hot.

There was a strange darkness about it, and an awful power emanated from the creature.

They weren't going to be able to get away.

All of this... to do what?

They had come to try to help Eva and Asaran, and then escape so that they had the help they needed to save Yoran, but now that wasn't going to work. He was about to fail.

They didn't all need to die here, though.

There was something he could do.

As the creature leaned forward, Gavin gripped his blade in hand, braced himself, and prepared to leap. He was the Chain Breaker. Regardless of what else happened, Gavin would take whatever steps he needed so that he could save his adoptive home. Yoran would be safe.

"If you get out of here, protect Yoran," Gavin said to Jayna.

"What are you—"

Gavin jumped.

Something grabbed him and squeezed. He hung suspended in the air for what seemed to last an impossibly long time. He was frozen.

But it wasn't only him that was frozen. The Tistalt seemed frozen as well.

Everything started to fold. Pressure around him, energy forcing down and crumpling him into a tight ball.

And then there was darkness.

In that brief moment before everything went black, Gavin feared that the Tistalt had crushed him, but then he realized that wasn't what it was.

This was a different kind of power. He had felt it once before.

He was returning.

CHAPTER TWENTY-TWO

S unlight shone down.

Gavin rolled over and immediately began reaching for his core reserves and the power of the El'aras ring, and he could feel it flowing within him. Thankfully, his power was there, and it was just as potent as it normally was. There was no need for the strange connection that he had noticed before, the hazy intersection between his El'aras power and whatever he'd encountered in the other realm.

He stood up and looked around. He was in a field of dark, broken stone. There was a sense of power and pressure and everything that filled him, but Gavin was free.

Gaspar stood up from lying on the ground. His face looked bruised, and there was a wound on one cheek that hadn't been there before, but he was alive. They both were.

"Where are we?" Gaspar said.

Gavin shook his head. "That's something we still need to find out, but it seems like we're out of that prison."

"Which means…"

"Which means they succeeded," Jayna said from behind them.

Sharaaz was with her. Smoke still streamed out from her. Gavin couldn't tell what injury she had, but whatever it was seemed significant enough that it still left her radiating smoke.

Jayna approached her and waved her hand, which caused Sharaaz to frown. Jayna placed her hands on Sharaaz, and the Ashara's eyes widened slightly. The smoke began to slow, finally coming to a stop altogether.

"I should have done that before," Jayna said. "I wasn't sure if it would work, and even if it did, I didn't know if it was going to hold."

Sharaaz nodded. "Thank you."

"We need to get back to Yoran," Gavin said. "I don't know how long it's been now or how far away we are, but—"

"We need Eva and Asaran," Jayna said.

"They could've come out anywhere. We don't know where they are or whether they were able to get out the same way we did."

"You're probably right." Jayna sounded irritated. She pulled something from her pocket and held it up to her mouth for a moment. An enchantment, Gavin suspected. She whispered into it, then placed it up to her ear, before finally shaking her head. "How do you intend to get us to your city?" she asked him.

"Well, I have something for just that purpose."

He took the paper dragon out of his pocket and set it down. As he pushed a bit of power into it and linked to the enchantment, it began to unfold and stretch out to an enormous size, though it didn't require quite as much power as he had expected. The paper became thicker as it expanded, giving the dragon something of a leathery appearance. It also took on almost a yellow quality, which was new. The spikes along its back looked sharper than usual, and the lines on its face were far less angular. The eyes seemed more knowing than they had in the past.

Some part of his power had changed. He was still tied to the trees.

Gavin turned to Jayna. "You still feel what you did there?"

"What do you mean?"

"It's just that I can still feel the effect of the bralinath trees. It's..." He closed his eyes, and he focused. "If anything, it's stronger."

Jayna frowned. She twisted the ring on her finger, and then her eyes went wide. "Gods," she muttered. "It's so painful."

"What is it?"

"That power is so much more. The Toral ring has always connected me to Sarenoth through Ceran, but now it's like I'm bound directly." She fiddled with her ring before looking up at Gavin. "Maybe that was a mistake."

"It saved us, so you did what you had to do."

She clenched her jaw. "This is going to make things more difficult."

"Or make it easier," Gavin said.

Jayna stared at her ring. "I doubt it will make it any easier." She looked at the paper dragon. "That can get us back?"

"It can. And quickly." Gavin glanced over to Sharaaz. "You don't have to come with us. I don't know where your homeland is or what you want to do, but you're injured."

"I made a promise," she said.

"Actually, Eva and Asaran were the ones who promised me, and I don't even know if they really intend to honor it. But we did get out of there, so I don't intend to hold you to it."

She shook her head. "We made a promise." She scrabbled onto the back of the dragon and took a seat, sitting up rigidly.

Gaspar nodded to her. "She's got a little fire to her, doesn't she?"

Gavin chuckled. "Ironic that you would describe an Ashara using fire."

He wondered what Anna would say about the Ashara. Showing up with them might be dangerous.

He ignored that thought and climbed onto the dragon's back. Gaspar followed him and took a seat next to Sharaaz. Jayna sat behind Gavin. Gavin leaned forward, and he tapped on the dragon, forming the connection between them. This time, he felt it take hold in a different way. And more than that, he felt it almost sink through him, and it bound him to something greater. He would have to think on that later.

The dragon took to the air.

"I need you to find your way to Yoran," Gavin said. "I have no idea where we are, but—"

The dragon streaked off, moving much faster than Gavin had anticipated. The ground blurred past them, so fast that he could scarcely see anything. Wind whipped at him, making his eyes water and taking his breath away. He had to focus on holding as tightly as he could so that he didn't fall.

Soon the landscape shifted. He saw the forest briefly, and then it was gone. The dragon started to descend, diving toward the ground. He heard a shout from someone behind him, either Jayna or Sharaaz, and the dragon quickly came to a stop.

Yoran stretched in the distance. From this vantage, everything seemed to gleam white, and there was an energy that emanated from the city. He saw familiar buildings, that of the constables' barracks, the remains of the Academy that had been here, and shops that Gavin had spent considerable time in. People filled the city, and as far as he could tell, everyone was unharmed.

Gavin climbed off the dragon and tapped it on the side. He pushed a little power through himself, and it folded back up. "Well, you've never flown quite like *that* before."

"What did you do?" Gaspar asked.

"Nothing different, but something about me has changed." He looked up at Yoran, having expected to find it in shambles, but thankful it was intact.

He started walking toward the city and froze.

Yoran wasn't fully intact like he had thought. Sections of it were being assaulted.

It seemed as if the ground itself had risen and had begun attacking the city. Creatures were storming toward the barrier, facing off with smaller stone golems, though they were quickly overrunning the protections. Before long, enchantments would overpower the barriers and protections within the city.

"You need to go and warn the others," Gavin said to Gaspar. "I'm going to go and deal with these Sul'toral."

"You remember what happened the last time," Gaspar said.

Gavin nodded. "I have something that I didn't have the last time, though."

And it wasn't just Jayna and the Ashara. They would help, but Gavin's own connection to magic had changed.

"Don't get cocky," Gaspar warned.

"Oh, I think it's too late for that." Gavin motioned him away. "Go. I will do what I can, but we need to make sure the city is prepared."

Gaspar started off.

Gavin sprinted forward with Jayna and Sharaaz alongside him.

"What do you expect here?" Jayna asked.

"Well, if we assume that we returned relatively close to the time we left..." He found it almost impossible to believe that was even likely, especially given that they were gone for the better part of three days. "We know there are three Sul'toral here. Given the enchantments storming the city, we need to figure out why they are here."

"They're attacking. What more do you need to understand?" Jayna said.

Gavin shook his head. "There has to be something more here. There has to be a reason they have been targeting Yoran. If it's all about Sarenoth, then you linking to the dragon stone in that prison—"

"I've been thinking about that," Jayna said, "and I don't really know. But let's assume that Ashara was imprisoned, much like we saw, and maybe they had some way of imprisoning Sarenoth."

"What if *all* of the ancients were imprisoned?"

"Maybe."

"And freeing them might have started a new war," Gavin said, realization dawning on him. He'd been trying to understand the ancients better and didn't know if he had a clear sense of them. Not yet. But what if this was nothing more than some attempt to try to create power?

Jayna cocked her head to the side. "I feel something. It's not far from here."

Gavin looked over, and he realized that she was heading toward the El'aras ruins.

"That was where we were attacked before," he said.

Gavin ran after her. Now that he was back here and had access to his core reserves, he felt as if he were able to move more fluidly and faster than he had in the past, and he kept up with Jayna. Sharaaz managed to keep pace as well. Between the three of them, they might actually be enough to stop the Sul'toral, figure out what happened, and then...

They reached the stones. There was a faint blur around them. It was subtle, and had he not seen it the other time, Gavin wasn't sure that he would've known what it was. But this time he recognized it.

He nodded to Jayna and Sharaaz. Jayna reacted immediately, her power beginning to build, and the red energy washed outward from her and her ring. It was brighter and more vibrant than it had been in the other space.

"Time to fight," Gavin said.

"What do you think I'm doing?"

"I don't know," he said. "I was just trying to be encouraging."

The blur shifted. The sorcerer that stepped forward was one of the three he had seen outside Yoran. He was tall and thin, and he had long, flowing black hair. If what Jayna had said about the Sul'toral was true, then he was one of the original members of the Society. And powerful. Of course he would be.

The Sul'toral frowned.

Gavin smirked at him and immediately called on his El'aras ability, then started to trace a pattern of the explosion he had used. He didn't need an enchantment to use that power. He drew on the energy in the ring and let power blast outward, where it collapsed down on the man.

Gavin had half expected that it would crush the sorcerer, but when that energy cleared, the man still stood there, a sneer on his face.

"You escaped. Interesting."

"You didn't think I would?" Gavin said.

"It is not meant for escape. Not for one such as yourself."

"Well, what about one such as her?"

Gavin stepped to the side, and Jayna blasted her power at the sorcerer.

The man merely held his hand out and absorbed it. "Do you really think someone like her can overpower me?"

"He's a Sul'toral," Jayna said to Gavin. "I'm not sure how easy it's going to be. Even with the bloodstone, I struggle against them. I've stopped them before, but I was better prepared then."

"Work with Sharaaz," Gavin said. "The two of you can deal with this one. I'm going to take on the others. Do whatever you did when we were in that prison."

The sorcerer tried to loop bands of magic around him, but Gavin flexed outward with the increased connection he had formed with the bralinath trees and burst through it. He sent another wild explosion out from him.

"When you tapped into the dragon stone and connected to Sarenoth, it made you stronger. It has to be no different than what the Sul'toral is doing," he said to Jayna.

A dark smile curled her lips, and she looked to Sharaaz. "I might need you to add some of your smoke to stabilize me. That's what Eva does. If I start to get a little out of control, add more smoke. I will handle this as quickly as I can so that we don't injure you further."

Sharaaz nodded.

Jayna began to form patterns, her hands flicking and tracing out spells that Gavin could scarcely keep up with. When the next explosion burst from her, it was even more powerful than the last. It rocketed toward the Sul'toral.

He tried to deflect it, but Jayna had used a different technique. Not only that, but there was the power Sharaaz used that mixed with what Jayna was doing. The two powers blended as they struck the Sul'toral.

Jayna glanced back at Gavin. "Go. Find the others."

He searched for the other Sul'toral. There had to be at least two more. Now he had to find them and overpower them.

But he wasn't sure how.

Enormous stone golems rose in front of him. They reminded him of the stone monsters in the prison realm, but they weren't quite like that. They didn't have the same overwhelming energy he had felt, though he had to think that they were filled with a similar magic. Still, he could tell they were powerful.

They lumbered toward Gavin, and he braced himself.

Gavin jumped.

He landed on top of one of the stone creatures, and he searched for the enchantment that would be engraved on it. He found it on the back of the thing's neck, hurriedly scratched with his sword to place his own mark on it, and pushed power out from him. When he was done linking to it, he jumped to the next, doing the same thing on the other one.

Now he had two stone golems under his control, and

the connection felt stronger than when he had done this before.

As he focused on them, he had a distant awareness of them in the back of his mind, and he sent them marching toward Yoran to defend it.

In the meantime, Gavin would find the other Sul'toral.

Somewhere nearby, he felt Jayna and the Sul'toral battling. The power that exploded from them was overwhelming. It was a clash of sorcery unlike anything he had ever felt. Smoke swirled, suggesting that Sharaaz was adding to the fight, but Gavin wondered if even that was going to be enough.

As he reached a small opening in the ground that had rocks around it, he felt a surge of power. Gavin sighed, then brought his arms up and braced himself, blocking the blast he knew was coming toward him. When it struck, it threw him back, but he twisted in the air and landed behind the stones that formed a barricade.

A sorcerer strode toward him.

Then another.

They weren't shrouded in shadows, and magic crackled from them. One of them had dark hair and eyes that were almost black, and he was dressed in a robe of blue so dark that it nearly looked like the night. The woman next to him had flaming red hair that made her look almost like she could be Jayna's mother or sister. He hadn't seen either of them before.

They both regarded him.

"Sul'toral, I presume?" Gavin asked. "Because if you're Toral, I'm going to make quick work of you."

The woman laughed. "You will not made quick work of anything."

"I can handle Toral."

"Then your first instinct was correct," the man said. His voice was accented and harsh, and there was an anger that seemed to burn within it.

Gavin smiled. "Good. Because I've got this." He held up his ring, and they flicked their gaze to it before turning to look at him.

"Do you believe I fear your pale form of power?"

"I think the other one of you did." Gavin cocked his head to where Jayna and the third Sul'toral were fighting, but he kept his focus on the two of them. "Though he's kind of preoccupied right now. You three thought you might hold us in that prison realm, but little did you know that you only made me stronger. And angrier."

"I am most curious how you escaped," the woman said.

"Why? Is somebody there that you want to find?"

She glowered at him.

"I see," Gavin said. He was prepared for a blast, but one didn't come.

Instead, he noticed smoke in the distance.

The woman followed his gaze and spun. "I will take care of them," she said, and she rushed away.

"Oh, don't leave!" Gavin called.

If he was right, then the smoke meant that Eva and Asaran were coming. Gods, he hoped he was right. The remaining Sul'toral stood before him, power building. The energy shot out like a whip and wrapped around Gavin faster than he could react.

But he had felt something like this in the past, and he was prepared.

When it began to squeeze, he exploded power out from him. He released far more energy than he had attempted before. It poured free of him and slammed into the man. The bands around Gavin shredded.

Gavin snorted. "See? I guess I *am* more powerful now." He took a step toward the man, already beginning to call on more power.

"You know nothing."

"Don't I? I understand you want the power of Sarenoth."

"As I said, you know nothing."

Gavin readied himself and let as much energy blast outward as he was able to. It was an uncontrolled use of his El'aras abilities, but it wasn't confined to just what he possessed, nor to what the ring and sword gave him. It was more than that—the bralinath trees.

The Sul'toral sent another whip crack at Gavin, and then another. The bands wrapped around his body, working in opposite directions to snake around him. The tight constriction was more than Gavin had felt from him before.

He could feel himself starting to fold.

He's trying to send me back to the prison?

Gavin had no idea if the prison was even intact, especially given that they had been thrown free, or maybe he was being sent to another prison. Or perhaps the Sul'toral was just trying to crush him.

Though Gavin attempted to call on the power within

332 | D.K. HOLMBERG

him, he knew it wasn't going to be enough. This Sul'toral was squeezing him too much. Even as he drew on his core reserves and the El'aras ring, even as he formed the connection to the other realm that bound him to the bralinath trees, it wasn't enough. He was constricted. The magic was going to overwhelm him. This man was far more powerful than Gavin.

The sorcerer took a step toward him. "I have faced many El'aras over the years. Do you think you're the first Champion I've killed?"

Gavin's heart hammered. The constrictions were tightening.

No. He wasn't going to just crush Gavin. This was an attempt to kill him.

"Did you do all of this to free Sarenoth?" he managed to get out.

The Sul'toral took another step forward.

Gavin needed time. He was being suffocated, and he didn't know how to withstand it. He tried to push, tried to resist, but even his Chain Breaker techniques were not enough. They had always worked before, up until the point where he had been sent into that strange prison realm. Now, as the power squeezed down on him, he knew that it wasn't going to be effective.

As the man neared, Gavin tried one more time to push outward. He had to succeed.

If he failed, Yoran would fall.

That was the thought that stayed with him more than anything else. If he failed here, the Sul'toral would attack the city. If he failed here, he wouldn't be able to help his friends.

Gavin strained to get free, resorting to the Leier fighting style. But when that failed, he flipped to others Tristan had taught him, thinking that one of them had to work.

The man was now close enough that if Gavin could break his arms free, he could stab him. Pressure continued to build, more than he thought he could withstand.

Another step.

The Sul'toral sneered. "You will be just one more in the line of all the others we have defeated." He flicked his gaze to Gavin's ring.

"That's what this is about?" Gavin glanced down at the El'aras ring. "I thought you didn't fear the Champion."

"It has always been about unification," the Sul'toral said.

Gavin couldn't move. He couldn't breathe.

With every step the man took, the bands around Gavin squeezed even more. He was being compressed down into a tighter and tighter form.

Through all of this, an idea came to him. It was dangerous, out of desperation, but what other choice did he have?

He didn't need to draw on his power this way, did he? It was the only way he knew *here*, but in that prison, he had channeled it in both directions. What if he pulled it the opposite way?

Gavin had learned to invert that power. He had no

idea how he could do that or whether he even could, but trying to flex free was not working.

So he pulled himself down.

As he did, he felt himself shifting.

A face appeared off to the side. Darkness swirled around him.

Chauvan is here?

Gavin hesitated, and the bands that the Sul'toral had wrapped around him continued to constrict.

Gavin sunk down into that power. He was pulled into an ever-narrowing trace of energy, but he pulled himself through it and let himself sink all the way down, until it was gone.

And then there was nothingness.

He floated like that for a moment.

He was aware, though.

It seemed like an eternity stretched, but he didn't know if it was real or not.

Somewhere in the back of his mind, there was a thought. He had shrunk, and now it was time to expand.

He started to press outward, flexing with his power much like he had when he had been the Chain Breaker. He started to reverse the effect of his power, and as he did, he felt the energy begin to flow away from him.

Then he exploded outward, light surrounding him.

Gavin stood out in the open. He was free of the bands.

The Sul'toral was in front of him, but the man's back was to him.

Gavin lunged with his blade, stabbing it into the Sul'-toral's back. As he did, he pressed outward again, forcing the power of his El'aras abilities into the blade, into the sorcerer.

It exploded.

The Sul'toral crumpled.

Gavin didn't wait, and he spun around immediately.

Shadows swirled around him.

Nihilar.

Gavin recognized it was nihilar, and he had to try something to stop Chauvan and his attack, but he didn't see the man. There were just shadows.

When they lifted, Gavin was alone.

The body of the fallen Sul'toral was still there, and Gavin nudged him over. The man was dead. The necklace he had been wearing—one that Gavin suspected was an enchantment that tied him to Sarenoth—was missing.

And he suspected he knew what had happened.

Chauvan had taken it.

CHAPTER TWENTY-THREE

Gavin focused on the power within himself, breathing heavily while searching for someone else he might have to fight. There had been another Sul'-toral, but Gavin didn't see her now. The air hung with a faint haze, and he strode toward where he expected Eva and Asaran to be fighting, if he was right.

As he penetrated the haze, he saw them, wrapping power around the Sul'toral and constricting her with it. The woman collapsed as their power continued to squeeze. Even as they did, Gavin recognized that she was using the folding technique. When the smoke cleared, he knew what he would find.

A hint of smoke drifted around Eva as she approached, her dark hair moving in the wind or perhaps the smoke she controlled. Her eyes flared with a sense of her power. "Where did she go?" Eva asked.

Gavin shook his head. "She's escaped. I killed one of them."

"Are you sure? It's easy to believe that. They have ways of disappearing."

"I'm quite sure," Gavin said.

He could still remember how he'd been crushed and the pain that had traveled through him, and he wondered if he could re-create what he'd done to escape. It would be one more thing for him to test, especially now that he was out of the prison world.

"We must claim the marker," Jayna said, striding up behind him.

Sharaaz followed her, smoke swirling from her. The injury she had sustained before must've opened back up during the fighting. There had to be a limit to how long she could survive like that, but perhaps the Ashara were stronger than he realized.

"It would look like this," Jayna said, holding up a white ring that looked like a spiral. Gavin could feel the power coming from the ring, the darkness woven within it, even if he couldn't do anything with it.

"Someone else took it," Gavin said.

Jayna frowned. She hurried away from him and went over to the man's body, then came back. "Someone has it."

"His name is Chauvan," Gavin explained. "He was trained like me. He was supposed to *be* me, but I don't know if he failed or succeeded." He shook his head. "I don't really know."

"So now he has a Sul'toral marker," she said.

"It seems like that."

Worse, Chauvan might know how to use it. Gavin's training wasn't enough for him to use a marker like that, but somebody like Chauvan…

It would make him powerful. Incredibly powerful. Essentially, he could become like one of the Sul'toral, but he would know how to use the nihilar as well. More than one power would be at his disposal.

"The Sul'toral mentioned something about unifying," Gavin said.

"That must be why they trapped Ashara," Eva said. She shared a look with Jayna.

Gavin looked back at the city. "I need to go and make sure everyone else there is unharmed. What are you going to do?"

Jayna frowned. "We've defeated two Sul'toral today. I think we will return to our home and regroup. Then we can plan for what comes next."

"What if we shouldn't have?" Gavin asked.

Jayna furrowed her brow. "Why would you say that? You've seen what they will do."

Gavin hadn't worked through everything just yet, but worry had started to creep in. "What if they aren't just drawing upon Sarenoth, but holding him?"

"I don't know. I've always assumed they were trying to free Sarenoth, but learning that there is a balance to the kind of power I can draw leaves me wondering if that's the case." She let out a frustrated sigh.

There was too much here that Gavin didn't understand.

"I'd like some way of reaching you," he said.

Jayna shrugged. "I suppose I could make an enchantment like that." She reached into her pocket, pulled out a
copper coin, and traced a quick pattern onto it. When she
was done, she handed it to him. "If you need me."

Gavin chuckled. He pulled one of the bands off his
wrist and traced his own marker on it, then squeezed
power out from him and into it. "And for you. I don't have
a coin, but maybe I'm more familiar with this anyway."

She glanced down at it. "Thanks for your help, Gavin. I
don't know if we could have done it without you."

"And I don't know if we could have stopped these Sul'-
toral without your help. Thank you," he said, looking to
the Ashara.

They all nodded, and then smoke swirled as it built
from Eva, Asaran, and Sharaaz. It worked its way around
Jayna, and all four of them disappeared.

It didn't take long for Gavin to reach the outskirts of
Yoran, and he realized that the battle had already died
down. He stepped through the barrier and found a collection of familiar faces.

Gaspar stood with Davel, who led dozens of constables
and enchanters, with El'aras interspersed between them.
Gavin nodded to Mekel and Zella as they tried to look as
if they weren't uncomfortable by the presence of the
El'aras.

Anna stepped toward Gavin. "You survived. I thought I
should go and help, but Gaspar claimed you did not
need it."

"It's probably better that you stayed," he said. He could
only imagine her reaction had she found him fighting

alongside the Ashara. "They are gone," Gavin said, looking to Gaspar.

"You took care of all of them?"

"Unfortunately, only two of them. There was a woman who got away." He frowned as he turned to Anna. "When you were attacked, when the fire came, was it the Ashara, or somebody else who used power like that?"

Anna regarded him for a moment. "How did you know it was them?"

"What you said. Great threat. Fire."

"We have not spoken about the Ashara."

"Well, I have a little experience with them myself," he said.

Anna's jaw clenched and her fists tightened as she took a step toward him.

Gavin shook his head. "No. They helped. They defeated a Sul'toral. They aren't your enemies."

"You don't understand them like we do," she said.

"Sort of like how I don't understand sorcerers like you do? I get that the El'aras have ancient enemies, but given the fact that you've fought with people your entire lifetime, don't you think everybody has become something of an enemy? Maybe it's time that ends."

Anna pressed her lips together into a tight frown. "You don't understand."

"What I understand is this," Gavin said. He had been trying to work through everything that had happened so far, and he wasn't entirely sure he had all of the details right, but increasingly, he thought he had some understanding. "All of us access the power of some ancient." He tapped on his ring. "This helps tie me to the El'aras. The Sul'toral and Toral reach for Sarenoth. The Ashara reach for... well, Ashara. I don't know about the nihilar, but I suspect there are others we don't even know about. 'Ancients' is what you call them, but they are gods. And they didn't always get along. Much like the servants of those who follow that power don't always get along."

Anna regarded him but said nothing.

"So there was a war," Gavin continued. "We were part of it, but do we get to choose which side?"

"We are meant to be a part of it," Anna said.

"And I have to be the Champion?"

"You still don't understand."

Gavin smiled tightly. "I think I do. When I was trapped in a prison that held Ashara, I connected to the bralinath trees." He watched her, curious about her reaction to that news. He didn't know if there would be more of a reaction to him commenting on being in a place that had imprisoned Ashara or to connecting to the bralinath trees. Regardless, her expression remained neutral. "I can still feel them."

Anna said nothing for a long moment. "You feel the trees?"

"I do. I'm not exactly sure what that means, but..." He twisted the ring, and he realized he could move it now. It was almost as if he could take it off, whereas before, it was tight and constricting. Maybe he had damaged some aspect of his connection to the El'aras power.

If so, then did that mean he was no longer the Champion?

Gavin didn't know how he felt about that. He had not wanted to be the Champion, but he also didn't want someone else to take that mantle and use that power in a way he knew it should not be used.

"The trees are the oldest," Anna said.

"The oldest what?"

"The oldest of the El'aras. If you connected to them, you have done something that very few El'aras have ever done. You reached the power of the elders." She said nothing for another few moments. "Perhaps you truly are the Champion."

"For a long time, you made it sound like I was," he said.

"I believed, but others doubted." The way she said it left Gavin wondering if she truly had believed. "Some thought Tristan had trained you to be a pretender. But reaching the trees and the elders and..." She glanced behind her. "I must speak to the others. We are permitted to remain here?"

"I told you they would let you," Gavin said.

"Very well. Thank you, Gavin Lorren."

As she left, he stared at her retreating form for a moment. "That's strange," he said. "Have I misunderstood something?"

Gaspar clasped him on the shoulder. "She's always been strange. I suppose it is no different now."

Gavin twisted the ring. This time, it came off easily.

"I don't feel like I reached any elders," he said.

"What kind of power can you draw upon without the ring?" Gaspar asked.

Gavin looked at it. That was a good question. The Champion wouldn't need a ring, would he?

He began to reach for his core reserves. That power was there, but there was something else. Something more. He felt the power he had attributed to the ring, still present within him.

It was tied to him now, not to the ring.

"Oh," Gavin said.

Gaspar arched a brow. "What is it?"

"Maybe she was telling the truth."

"Jayna connected to her power differently, didn't she?"

"Directly to Sarenoth," Gavin said.

"As did you. What about those who reached for Ashara?" Gaspar asked.

"I suspect they're tied to it more now as well."

Gaspar glanced over to where the El'aras had departed. "I don't like any of this, Gavin. We're caught up in some greater battle than I think we understand."

"What do you think it means?" Gavin said.

"I don't know…"

Gavin waited for Gaspar to say something more, but instead, he turned his attention to the distance. He pulled something from his pocket, squeezing it tightly in his fist, before opening his palm and looking down at what looked like an enchantment.

"Gaspar?" Gavin said. "What is it?"

Gaspar glanced in his direction briefly before looking toward the northeast again. "It's Imogen. She's coming back."

The Chain Breaker continues with: Faith of the Fallen

And please check out a new series in the world of The Chain Breaker, The Dragon Rogues!

An impossible heist only the thief known as the Dragon could pull off.

Fresh out of prison, Jonathan Aguelon wants one big score before he leaves the city for good. The job will be more complicated than any that he's ever attempted, but this time he can steal more than money, he can get revenge—but only if he follows a mysterious benefactor's plan.

With the right team, Jonathan can succeed, but much in the city has changed during his time away, and the Dragon doesn't have the draw he once did. The team of outcasts he assembles needs time to prepare, but time is the one luxury they don't have.

As his benefactor pushes him into action, Jonathan refuses to be used by anyone, but can he refuse when his team might be all that stands before a coming war—if they can find a way to work together first?

SERIES BY D.K. HOLMBERG

The Chain Breaker Series

The Chain Breaker

The Dark Sorcerer

First of the Blade

The Executioner's Song Series

The Executioner's Song

The Dragonwalkers Series

The Dragonwalker

The Dragon Misfits

Elemental Warrior Series:

Elemental Academy

The Elemental Warrior

The Cloud Warrior Saga

The Endless War

The Dark Ability Series

The Shadow Accords

The Collector Chronicles

The Dark Ability

The Sighted Assassin

The Elder Stones Saga

The Lost Prophecy Series

The Teralin Sword

The Lost Prophecy

The Volatar Saga Series

The Volatar Saga

The Book of Maladies Series

The Book of Maladies

The Lost Garden Series

The Lost Garden